Chasing Nightmares

I.V. Everts

Printed in the United States of America
A 2 Z Press LLC
PO Box 582
Deleon Springs, FL 32130
bestlittleonlinebookstore.com
sizemore3630@aol.com
440-241-3126
ISBN: 978-1-946908-64-3

DEDICATION:

For her support and encouragement,
I dedicate this book to my publisher,
Lee Sizemore

Contents

Prologue

1. Ten Years Later 1
2. The Party 7
3. Eric and Steve 15
4. Dr. Patterson's Office 23
5. After the Break-up 33
6. The Pills..39
7. The Hospital...47
8. Home Again...55
9. Dinner...61
10. Seeing Eric...67
11. The Summer House 75
12. Settling In 85
13. The Cabin 93
14. The Photo 103
15. Years Earlier 111
16. The Search 119
17. The Mystery Continues 125
18. The Coffee House...131
19. Eva's Nightmare 139
20. A Possible Connection...145
21. Ms. Gimble 153
22. In Love Again..161
23. Liz and Monica 167
24. Confessing and Hair-Do's 173
25. Another Party..179
26. Defending Eva 185
27. Mrs. Austin..191
28. What Next?...199
29. How It All Began 203
30. More Investigating..211

Contents Continued

31. After the Incident 217
32. The Explosion 225
33. Tempers Flaring 233
34. Staying with Liz 239
35. Burgled 247
36. Planning Another Visit 255
37. Café des Arts 261
38. The Gas 267
39. Mrs. Austin in Danger 277
40. Saving Mrs. Austin 285
41. Discovered 289
42. Sisters 299
43. How it All Worked Out 313

Epilogue

Prologue

Twice, the screeching bell at the orphanage rang, summoning its forty resident girls for lunch. The overwhelming noise of the girls at the Mercy Home Orphanage entering the gloomy dining room was deafening. Even the smallest spoon hitting the floor echoed loudly in the high ceiling.

The building was constructed in the 17th century and had served as a residence for Baron Middleton. After his passing, several aristocrats lived there until they no longer had the funds to keep the property and left. The house lay dilapidated for many years until the council restored the large residence and turned it into an orphanage.

Mercy home was set in the delightful countryside. The outside of the house still had the understated grandeur and elegance typical of the Georgian era. The home was in dire need of renovation. It had leaky faucet washers, the plumbing traps needed cleaning, and the rain gutters needed replaced. The janitor was able to do most of the repairs, although others were best left to experts. Also, an unfortunate incident with water infiltration resulted in soft, rotted wood that became an invitation for termites and other wood-damaging insects.

Everyone worked hard to keep the orphanage open. At least the children had fresh air and were able to enjoy playing in the fantastic gardens and woods. No one wanted to think of where they would be moved to if Mercy Home closed.

As the girls entered the dining hall, several long dark brown tables and benches, each seating eight girls, were the room's only furniture. The dining hall was dark and uninviting because only cheap wall lights were hung and, even on a bright summer day when it stayed light until at least nine in the evening, these made precious little difference. Colourful prints were placed on the walls to brighten the room, but now they were discoloured and had just the opposite effect.

At the far end, a high oriel window held the promise of light, but a large oak tree obscured that light from coming in. The management at the orphanage asked the council for permission to cut the tree. This request set off a whirlwind of opposition and the initiation of a petition by those in the surrounding villages who believed the tree should stay untrimmed. Management had to take only a cursory glance to gather the list of influential names on the petition to know that it was a lost battle.

Today, dinner was served without incident, but a noise of discontent arose as the girls received their lunches. The head matron clapped her hands abruptly to silence the girls. In the past, children were sent to their rooms without food if they did not obey. Serving the girls inexpensive and bland food was not done on purpose; it was what the budget allowed. Now and then, the orphanage organised a collection in the nearby villages for money, clothes, and books. Often, after a collection, the management served cake and a fruit salad after dinner. The girls always considered this an enormous treat.

While the girls reluctantly ate their food, several caretakers and volunteers walked around the room. One volunteer, Jane Gimble, spotted Christine playing with her food. Christine showed no intention of eating her meal. Jane walked over and said, 'Christine, why aren't you eating?'

'I'm not hungry, Miss.'

Eva, Christine's best friend, wasn't eating either. She didn't wait for Jane Gimble's inquiry as to why she wasn't eating, she merely stated, 'The food is disgusting.'

The six other girls at the table let out muffled giggles. Jane ignored them as she stared at Eva. 'You should both eat something.'

'Thank you, Miss Gimble. We'll try to eat,' Christine replied for both girls. Christine looked at Jane, who gave her a quick wink when she walked away.

'Don't be so rude, Eva,' Christine said coarsely.

'Why? What are they going to do? Send me away so I miss this wonderful meal?'

Christine ignored the snappy reply. 'Miss Gimble is right, though. We should eat something,' she said.

'You eat!' Eva shoved her plate away. 'I can't wait to get out of here.'

At the other end of the hall, Jane Gimble remarked, 'Just look at Christine and Eva,' to one of the primary staff caretakers.

'I know. They look exhausted.'

'How is it possible they have the same nightmare?' Jane Gimble asked.

'Not sure,' the caretaker replied. Jane wondered if the caretaker took sufficient interest in the girls. Jane continued watching Christine and Eva. She promised herself to visit them before she left for the day.

Christine and Eva suffered horrific nightmares and hardly slept. The nightmares started a month ago. Christine's nightmare started first, and then Eva inexplicably had the same nightmare a week later.

During the night, their screams distressed the other girls so much that the management decided to give Christine and Eva their 'own' room together. The small room had a bunk bed, a wardrobe, and a small desk with one chair.

Christine and Eva's tiny room had a window overlooking the Mercy Home entrance. Christine would stand by the window for hours and fantasize that *a private detective in a fancy car entered the driveway, hired by her wealthy parents to find her,* but the car and the detective never came.

Jane Gimble knocked on the girls' door, 'May I come in?'

'Ms. Gimble, of course.' Christine jumped off her bed and stood before Jane as though she was an army soldier ready for a room inspection.

'I just wanted to hear how you are coping with your nightmares,' Ms. Gimble said and then continued, 'Relax Christine, I'm here as a friend, not to interrogate you.' Christine smiled. 'How are you sleeping?' she asked

'Not well. We - Eva and I - have nightmares every night. Dr. Patterson visited this morning and has decided to give each of us mild sleep medication. We'll take it tonight.'

'That's great. Hopefully, you will both sleep well,' Jane Gimble said and nodded her head with approval.

Christine also nodded and wiped the nervous sweat from her hands onto her skirt. Jane wondered how two such completely different girls got on so well.

'Promise me you'll tell me if you have any problems, Christine,' Ms. Gamble said sincerely.

'I will. Thank you, Miss Gimble.'

Jane Gimble wished she could do more to help the girls. Deep inside, she felt prescribing medication for fifteen-year-old girls was irresponsible. However, she also knew the girls were desperate for sleep.

1

Ten Years Later

Christine woke up screaming. Her body was frozen by the terror she felt. It took several minutes for her to get her bearings. She looked down at her uncovered body and realized she had kicked off all her covers. She turned on the light, looked at the clock on her nightstand, and discovered it was only 4:30 am.

'Chris, what on earth happened? Are you okay?' Eva said as she ran to Christine, who appeared completely confused.

Christine's large T-shirt, with a faded print of the Scooby-Doo team, and her thick, massively curly hair pointing in all directions, made her look like a medusa. 'It…it happened again,' Christine said in an exasperated tone.

'What happened again? Chris, calm down.' Eva sat next to her on the bed.

'Eva, I had the nightmare. This can't be happening, not after so many years. I'm taking my sleep aid.' Christine pleaded as if Eva could magically make the nightmare disappear.

Eva stared at Christine in disbelief. 'Are you sure? Was it as before, with the blue light?' Eva probed.

Christine nodded; with tears running down her cheeks and panic in her eyes. She pushed herself up against the pillow. Her thick, curly brown hair hung in wet strands around her face. She clumsily tried to push the tangles of hair away without success.

Eva continued staring. She was worried and scared. Suddenly, she snapped out of it. 'Chris, why don't you freshen up? I'll get you a glass of milk.' Eva was happy she could do something even if she had no real idea how to comfort Christine. She recalled the nightmares all too well.

While Eva sprang into the kitchen, Christine went to the bathroom to freshen-up and change into a clean nightie. When she walked back into her bedroom, Eva was sitting on the edge of the bed, holding a glass of milk for her.

'Will you stay with me until I fall asleep?' Christine begged.

'Of course, I will,' Eva assured her.

After leaving the orphanage, Eva and Christine decided to share an apartment. They always felt like sisters and no one else understood their nightmares. They felt safe together and shared a common bond.

Eva stroked Christine's hair over and over to calm her down. When she was sure Christine was asleep, she got up and went back to her own bedroom. There, she sat awake in bed, worrying about Christine and what might be ahead for her. She tossed and turned the rest of the night.

The next morning, Christine was up early. She knew she'd have to see Dr. Patterson and discuss the nightmare. Dr. Patterson remained their doctor after they left the orphanage. They were convinced they would never have been able to see a private doctor.

As Eva walked into the kitchen, Christine picked up her handbag to leave for work. Eva looked somewhat surprised. She and Christine always had a coffee together in the morning.

'Are you okay? Did you get some sleep?' Eva asked.

'I did. I want to make an appointment with Dr. Patterson

for some stronger medication,' Christine mumbled in a rush.

'Are you sure that's the right thing to do?' Eva was concerned.

'What else can I do?'

'Why don't you wait for a while and see what happens. The nightmares may not come back,' Eva suggested.

'Maybe,' Christine said in disbelief of that happening. 'I have to run now, or I'll be late.' Christine rushed out the door, leaving a perplexed Eva standing by the coffee maker. It was obvious Christine did not want to discuss the nightmare.

***

Around seven-thirty that evening, Christine walked into the apartment and heard the shower. As she passed, she shouted a quick 'hello' to Eva.

'I'll be out in a minute, Chris,' Eva said.

'Take your time, I don't need the bathroom, I just wanted to say 'hello' to you.' Christine changed into a pair of comfortable slacks and a t-shirt. She walked into the living room and turned on the television.

'How was your day?' Eva asked as she walked into the room, still drying her thick, curly brown hair with a large towel.

'Nothing special. You?' Christine asked.

Eva shrugged her shoulders. 'I'm going out with some of my colleagues this evening. Do you want to tag along?'

'No, thanks. I'm planning to watch a film and go to bed early.' The real reason Christine didn't want to go was her insecurities. Eva's colleagues intimidated her. Eva worked for a modelling agency and her colleagues were all beautiful and always fabulously dressed. They gave Christine the feeling they were judging her. She never felt as beautiful or fashionably clad as they were.

'Fancy a game of Chaser Blazer before you go?'

'Sure, why not?'

Both walked to the kitchen, where Christine picked up a stack of magazines.

'Ready, go!' Eva shouted.

They invented this game when they lived in the orphanage. Nobody else understood the game and, since the girls were unwilling to explain, it remained their game.

'Have you decided if you want to ask for stronger medication?' Eva asked.

'No. I'm nervous to take more medication but, if the nightmares return as before, I feel I have little choice,' Christine replied.

After a moment's thought, Eva agreed with Christine; without sleep, no one can function. She also knew that Christine was downplaying the problem. Eva knew Christine would be up for most of the night and probably try to drink a little wine to feel drowsy and allow her to sleep.

Eva walked down the street to meet her colleagues who truly were a group of 'stuck-up' people, but they always knew the nicest restaurants to catch an appetizer or light meal since they were always on a perpetual diet. In addition, Eva looked forward to an evening out.

As she walked into the restaurant, she noticed the approving stares. Beautiful, but not arrogant. She felt it was her right to enjoy the 'gift' God had given her. He blessed some people with a fantastic brain; others are excellent painters or designers. They used their gifts, why shouldn't she? Thus, this is how she justified the pride she felt in her physical appearance.

Her favourite colleague, Tony, was here. She looked at him with questioning eyes and tilted her head towards a group of starved-looking girls. Beside the agency staff, a group of models was present.

'I didn't know some models were coming.' Eva stated her question.

Tony threw his arms in the air. 'They heard we were going out and invited themselves.'

While she took off her coat, Eva surveyed the models' skinny knees and shoulders and wondered if this starving madness would ever stop. TSC (The Starvation Chic) she called them. They paid the rent, so who was she to complain.

Tony, who noticed her noticing the models, said, 'I prefer a voluptuous look like yours. At least you have wonderful body parts.' Tony always made her smile.

As she walked over to the models, Eva laughed at Tony's remark. As usual, the models' conversation was about diets, castings, and who would land the next big job. Eva stared at her empty glass and debated going home to Christine.

'Ladies, compliments from the gentleman at the bar,' the waiter said as he put a flask filled with virgin daiquiris on the table. She decided to have a glass. It was her motto in life to never turn down anything free. She raised her glass.

***

The next morning, Eva woke refreshed; *it was the miracle sleeping pills* she thought as she looked in the bathroom mirror. After her shower, she put a towel around her hair and walked into the kitchen. 'Good morning. Did you sleep well?' she asked Christine.

'Sure,' Christine replied.

Filling a cup with freshly brewed coffee, she ignored Christine's bad mood. They had their breakfast in silence; each of them caught up in their own thoughts. Eva looked at Christine.

'What?' Christine was annoyed.

Eva was unaware she had been staring. 'You know *what!*' Eva snapped back.

Christine got up and put her plate and cup in the sink.

'Leave it alone,' she said while she passed Eva on her way out.

Eva knew Christine had a nightmare. She was impossible without an eight-hour sleep.

2

The Party

'Have you seen my black top? It has glitters on the sleeves,' Christine shouted over to Eva's room.

'No,' Eva yelled back.

What am I going to wear this evening? she asked herself. *I feel like cancelling.* Christine felt she was losing her cool. She didn't recognize herself lately. Ever since her nightmare returned, she had become more irritable. She thought the nightmare was gone forever. Now that it was back, she felt like the hopeless fifteen-year-old girl she was at Mercy Home.

'Don't be so dramatic. Why don't you wear your red dress? You know you look great in that,' Eva said as she peeked into Christine's room on her way to the bathroom. The red dress was perfect. It was a Boho, off-the-shoulder dress with a tight body and a dip hem that made her look like a catwalk model.

'I suppose I'll have to. Otherwise, I'll have to go in my underwear,' Christine said with a smirk.

'I'm sure Marlene would appreciate that, but not as much as Dr. Patterson,' Eva remarked.

'Oh, shut up,' Christine said before realized Eva was smiling.

The Patterson's invited both girls to an annual party at their home. Once a year, Marlene Patterson, Dr. Patterson's wife, asked them to what she referred to as her 'special party.' She always called Christine to invite them, never Eva. Christine revelled in the Patterson's attention. She was convinced they considered her a daughter.

These get-togethers, however, embarrassed Eva. She felt they were being paraded in front of Dr. Patterson's friends. Every year it was the same group, mostly fellow doctors. How Christine and Eva fit into this select group was always a mystery to Eva.

When they were children, the 'party' was always in the afternoon. There were never any presents, which upset Eva. To her, a party spelled presents. 'Presents are for birthdays and Christmas,' Christine tried to convince Eva. This didn't deter Eva from bringing it up for the next five years.

That evening, the taxi, organized by the Patterson's, pulled up to the front of the elegant house on Fairmont Street, Knightsbridge, just before eight. Eva was the flamboyant one and wore her spirally curled hair loose. Christine wore her wavy long brown hair in a ponytail.

'How do I look?' Eva asked as she posed like a 'model' outside the manor. Ignoring Eva, Christine walked up to the front door.

'Calm down, Chris. I'm sure your boyfriend 'Doc' won't mind that you're a tad late,' Eva said sarcastically.

'You are so juvenile,' Christine snapped back and rang the doorbell. A maid dressed in a pristine traditional black-and-white uniform answered.

'Good evening. May I take your coats?' the maid asked with a heavy accent which neither Christine nor Eva were able to place.

As the girls took off their coats, Marlene Patterson emerged with a forged smile on her pumped-up lips. She was impeccably dressed in an embellished gown with a deep V-neck and stone-embellished cuffs by Donna Karan. Marlene was chic. No matter what she wore, she looked miraculous.

'Girls, how marvellous to see you,' she said as she air kissed them. 'Come in. All the guests are in the library.' Marlene led the way.

'Did she have more surgery?' Eva whispered to Christine.

'Stop it,' Christine said tersely, and, with a hand signal, Christine stopped Eva from speaking.

A group of men in their mid to late sixties stood in the far-left corner. Their wives were seated across the room on two large sofas near the window.

'Please, everyone, say 'hello' to Christine and Eva,' Marlene said.

With awkward smiles on their faces, Christine didn't know whether to laugh or cry. Being the centre of attention always made Christine uncomfortable. Then, she felt Eva squeeze her hand and collected herself. 'Good evening. It's very pleasant to see you all again,' she said.

The men smiled at the girls. *A cattle market*, Eva thought and managed a smile. 'Hello, everyone,' she said.

Well-mannered, but insincere, smiles came from the ladies who turned away quickly to talk amongst themselves after acknowledging the introduction. None of the ladies seemed interested in Christine or Eva.

'What can I get you to drink?' Marlene asked.

'A gin and tonic please,' Christine stated.

'A dry Martini for me,' Eva said.

Marlene snapped her fingers at the waiter and Eva hastily asked for a double. This caused a round of laughs from the men's corner.

'An easy crowd,' Eva remarked.

Dr. Patterson walked toward Eva and Christine and remarked, 'Every time I see you, I could swear you are more alluring.'

Although they were in the house many times, this was the first time they were ever in the library. 'Your library is a most impressive room, Dr. Patterson,' Christine said.

'Thank you. I'm very fond of it myself.' His chest inflated as he spoke.

'Exquisite,' Christine said as she walked past the rows and rows of books. Christine was most impressed by the acquired books most considered difficult to find. She loved the written word.

While Christine and Eva talked with Dr. Patterson, Marlene left the girls and her husband and returned to 'her' ladies. After a brief conversation, Mr. Patterson returned to his colleagues, leaving Christine and Eva to their own devices. They stayed in the library, sipping their drinks. Eva's face lit up when she spotted Steve Patterson, the youngest son of the Patterson's.

'Good evening, everyone,' he said as he gave the men a nod and bowed to the ladies. He inherited his bright blue eyes from Mrs. Patterson and, along with a mischievous smile and thick black hair, it was impossible not to be charmed by him.

'Steven, darling, I didn't know you were coming this evening,' Marlene said as she nearly tripped when she loped towards her son.

'I knew you were expecting exceptional guests, mother. I just couldn't resist greeting them myself,' he replied. Marlene ignored his remark; the remark she knew was for Eva. A member of his mother's staff gave him the beer he requested on his way into the room.

'Beer is so ordinary. We had a delivery of an exceptional Chianti from Italy just yesterday,' Marlene said in a loud voice, so everyone was sure to hear her.

'No, thank you, mother. I'm thirsty and I need a beer.' He took his first mouthful and winked at Eva and Christine.

The two girls smiled like teenagers.

'Why don't you accompany me to greet the ladies?' Marlene ushered the girls to the other side of the room.

'Thank you, Marlene,' Christine answered, as if being

invited to join Marlene's acquaintances was an honour. The welcome by the ladies was distant. They were not inclined to entertain girls with whom they had nothing in common. Christine and Eva were of very little importance to these high-class ladies.

'How are you girls doing? It has been ages since I last saw you,' Marlene said to Christine and Eva. If she wanted to keep them close to the ladies and away from Steven, she would have to entertain them herself.

'Very well, thank you,' Christine answered. Eva just smirked.

'How is work at the National Art Library? How long have you worked there?' It came as a surprise to Christine that Marlene remembered where she worked. It was an even greater surprise that she sounded sincerely interested.

'Four years now,' Christine said.

'Hmm?' Marlene mused.

'It was fortuitous to find a position straight after college,' Christine continued the conversation, unaware of Marlene's lack of true interest.

'Are you still in the modelling industry, Eva?' Marlene continued.

'Yes. I'm still a booker,' Eva responded.

'How glamorous,' Marlene said enthusiastically.

'No. Not really. But I do enjoy working with the agency people,' Eva stated matter-of-factly. And, managing a polite smile, Marlene ignored everything Eva said.

Eva looked at her empty glass. She finished her double Martini in record time and, as Eva ignored the disapproving glares of Marlene and her lady friends, she awkwardly excused herself and walked over to the bar.

'How are you these days?' Steven sneaked up on her.

'Peachy, as I told your mother,' Eva said with a crooked smile.

Steven laughed out loud. 'A good-looking girl like you

need not complain.'

'What about you? How is your design business doing?' she asked, determined to distract the attention away from her. She had a crush on him since she was fifteen years old.

'Well,' he said, 'mother and father are horrified that I left medical school, but my business is doing well.'

'Why did you leave medical school again? You were almost finished.' Eva remarked as she stirred her Martini with the olive skewer.

'All blood and long hours. Daulton is pursuing the dream for both of us. In the medical world, he is fast becoming famous,' Steven said.

'A man's got to do what a man's got to do,' Eva said as she tried a John Wayne impression that failed miserably.

Feeling ignored, Christine decided that enough was enough and walked up to the bar and ordered another gin and tonic before joining Eva and Steven.

'Hello, Christine. How are you? Any wedding bells?' Steven asked.

'We're thinking about it. Eric is in line for a huge promotion and works ridiculously hard. After his promotion, he can decrease his working hours and we can plan the wedding.'

Although Eric had never proposed, it seemed naturally implied for the two to marry after his promotion.

'Excellent! Congratulations!' he exclaimed and gave Christine a kiss on the cheek. 'What about you Eva? Any boyfriends?' Steven probed.

Taken aback by Steve's directness, Eva felt uncharacteristically self-conscious. Eva and Steve had always flirted at the parties but there were never any direct advances made.

'Still looking,' she said as a quick come back.

'Your father needs to speak with you, Steven,' Marlene interrupted.

'He'll come and find me, mother,' Steven responded firmly.

'*Now*, Steven,' Marlene said as she tilted her head back slightly and squinted her piercing blue eyes. A sign she meant: *Better do as you are told.*

'Excuse me, ladies. My father wants my company. I hope we can catch up later,' Steven said with a slight head nod and walked away to join Dr. Patterson and his colleagues.

The evening progressed slowly. Eva was bored, so she excused herself to a vast marble guest bathroom and stared at her reflection in a large Yorkshire gold bevelled mirror. She wondered what she was doing at this party. She washed her hands and picked up an Irish linen hand towel. 'Here we go, brave face,' she said to her reflection.

As she returned to the party, she noticed Christine talking with Dr. Patterson. *It must be about her nightmare*, she thought. She waited for them to finish. After five minutes, Dr. Patterson and Christine re-joined the group. As she came closer, she heard one doctor say, 'Most amazing. It's astonishing.'

'Are you talking about me?' Eva asked inquisitively.

Dr. Patterson opened his arms in a welcoming manner and said, 'We were. You and Christine are a sight for sore eyes.'

'Are you in therapy too?' Dr. Abrahams, one of the regulars, asked.

'Well, sometimes I am and sometimes I'm not,' Eva retorted.

'Eva, please,' Christine whispered.

Eva saw Steven talking to the ladies who were hanging on his every word. She lost interest in the whole party and seeing Steven and whispered in Christine's ear, 'I want to go home now.'

Christine looked at her. She could tell Eva was uncomfortable.

'Okay, let's say goodbye to everyone, and we'll leave,' Christine said gently to her friend.

As they left the mansion, Eva let out a sigh of relief. 'I'm glad that's over for another year.'

A taxi was waiting for them in the street.

'Why do we attend this party once a year?' Eva asked.

'Because they enjoy seeing us. They want to know how we are,' Christine said, trying to convince herself this was true.

'Every year they invite us and the moment we walk in they can't wait for us to leave,' Eva said as if Christine was not already painfully aware of the same observation.

'Get in the car, Eva, please,' said Christine.

During the taxi ride home, Eva started complaining, mostly about Marlene, Dr. Patterson, and the other guests. She complained about everyone except Steven, actually. Each year it was the same scene. Eva's frustration mounted as she spent time with all of them and she expressed herself loudly in the taxi.

Christine just nodded at everything Eva said. She learned long ago that Eva wasn't interested in her opinion and, if she said something, Eva became even more enraged. She would then start calling them names. So, the two of them drove home in the taxi and finally, Eva calmed down as they arrived at their apartment.

3

Eric and Steve

'Not again, Eric,' Christine said dejectedly to her fiancé. 'You've worked so much the past two weekends. I was looking forward to spending a little time together.'

'It's important. It's my career, Christine. I have to be in the office to show them I'm the best man for the job,' Eric replied.

'How much time do they need?' Christine pleaded.

'As long as it takes. Don't give me a guilt trip, Chris. I need to focus on my career now,' Eric stated firmly.

'Excuse me. What does that mean?' Chris asked. She felt a pain in her stomach. 'Have you even considered my feelings?'

'That's not what I meant, and you know it,' Eric responded in a slightly softer tone.

'If I'm not mistaken, you just said it,' Christine said, determined to keep the argument going. A long silence followed.

Finally, Eric spoke, 'Let's have a good talk soon, Chris.'

'Whenever your job allows it,' Christine said and put down the phone.

She felt angry as she sat on the sofa. Why was he such a workaholic! There was a time she considered ambition a positive quality, but not so much now that she and Eric started spending less time together. All he seemed focused on was the promotion at Meditech. She often wondered if there was somebody else. Another woman? As soon as that thought crossed her mind, she dismissed it. Eric was too occupied with his career to juggle two women. Thoughts of other women was what Eva would think. The last thing she needed was Eva's opinion. A battle with Eric was enough. There had always been bad blood between Eric and Eva. Christine grew weary defending him. Why is there bad blood?

Christine convinced herself that providing for her and their future family was his aim. Growing up, Eric's father never did this. He wanted a better life for her, but Eva disagreed.

'Another weekend without Eric?' Eva asked as she walked into the room.

'Grow up, Eva. Life isn't just partying or looks,' Christine snapped.

'Sorry, jeez,' Eva said as she walked away.

Christine didn't answer. Eric was slipping away and there was nothing she could do.

***

Christine first met Eric at a local restaurant near the library where she worked. They shared an after-work tradition of appetizers and listening to music on Friday nights. Originally, the group was just the people she worked with, but somehow Eric became part of the mix. She was flabbergasted when he sat next to her for a chat and offered to buy her a drink.

Men as handsome as Eric never approached her. He was tall with blond hair, blue eyes, and a fabulous physique. Eric could be a model. Christine was too shy to speak to him but, with much insistence from him, she finally opened-up, and they chatted for hours. She was so engrossed in their conversation that it seemed like just minutes.

They discussed everything from future dreams, family plans, ambition, and financial independence. Christine was won over. All she had ever wanted to do when she turned eighteen was to be married and have a family. To make it all even more fabulous, she and Eric set a time for a date for the next weekend. This made Christine more than happy; she was elated. When she arrived home, she woke Eva to tell her everything that happened that evening.

Now, it seemed everything was different. Eric, once giddy to talk about a future, just wanted to work and not spend the time Christine needed to feel close in the relationship.

***

Having ordered herself to stick to window shopping only, as she could not afford to buy any more clothes and shoes, she knew all too well that she would buy something, no matter how small, whenever she entered a shop.

Her cell phone rang. She rummaged around in her large, full handbag to find it. 'Hello?'

'Eva? It's Steve Patterson.'

'Steve, uh, hi. How are you?' Eva was pleased that she never pushed the 'video' button on her phone.

'Not too bad. Yourself?'

'Very good,' she said. For a moment, she thought he could see her blush or hear her increased heartbeat over the phone.

'It was great seeing you again the other night,' Steve continued.

'It was.' She couldn't think of anything else to say and waved her arm in the air making a *what* pose.

'Am I catching you at a bad time?'

'No, no. It's fine.' Just then, a woman passing Eva told

her to move. She looked around herself and realized she was standing right in the middle of the sidewalk. She leaped to the side.

'I was wondering if you would enjoy having a drink one evening.'

'Okay,' she answered. Eva felt foolish because she didn't seem able to string more than two words together right now.

'What are you doing tomorrow evening?'

'No plans. I could meet you somewhere in town.' Eva knew she was making herself far too available and gave herself an imaginary slap on her head.

Steve suggested a wine bar in Soho around eight o'clock. She didn't know that bar but decided she would look it up rather than ask him. After they said 'goodbye,' Eva couldn't get off the phone fast enough. She pressed the end call button several times to make sure he couldn't hear her anymore.

She leaned against an office building. Despite what she considered harmless flirting, she never expected that someone like Steve might find her interesting enough to ask on a date. He was handsome, a successful designer with his own company, and he came from an influential family. Any girl would date him. Assuming he would fall for someone from his own circle, she knew that Marlene would have a fit if she knew that one of her boys paid attention to either her or Christine.

***

'Christine, are you home?' Eva yelled as she rushed into the flat.

'I'm in the kitchen,' Christine replied.

'Steve Patterson phoned and asked me on a date.'

'Whoa! I can't say I am surprised. The two of you have always had a thing,' Christine said and, not looking up, continued preparing dinner.

'What do you mean?' Eva asked. All she wanted to do was talk about Steve.

'It's always been obvious he likes you. He's always at his parents when we're there. I'm sure it's not for the other company the Patterson's invite,' Christine said.

Eva could feel her heart skip a beat. She couldn't stop making improvised pirouettes.

'Only a blind person couldn't see it,' Christine continued. 'Why do you think Marlene always gets in the middle when Steve pays any attention to you?'

Eva clapped her hands together. 'What should I wear?'

'Are you asking me for my opinion?'

'Yes. I like Steve and I want to look super-great!' Eva was shaking her hips like an Arabic dancer.

'Maybe you should wear something less obvious, keep him guessing a bit.'

After Eva thought for a while, she said, 'You are so right, Chris. I still have so many things to do before tomorrow evening. I have to shave my legs, do my eyebrows, my nails, and try to get this curly mess I have on my head, under control.'

'Well, you'd better get started then.' Christine smiled and returned to preparing dinner. Eva skipped out of the kitchen.

The next day as Christine was sitting in the kitchen looking at all the advertising material that arrived despite the 'no advertising' note on their post-box when Eva walked into the kitchen.

'What do you think of this?' she asked, posing with a hand on one hip. She was wearing a pair of tight dark blue jeans with a simple white t-shirt and a fitted black leather jacket.

'That looks great.' Christine looked at Eva and, for a moment, wished she had her confidence.

'Are you sure?'

'You look fantastic.'

Eva had been to the hairdresser that afternoon and her untamed, spiralled hair now cascaded down across her shoulders as shiny curls. 'Thanks. What about the make-up?'

'It's perfect, Eva. You look wonderful. Go and have fun.'

Eva kissed Christine on the cheek and giggled as she left the apartment.

When she entered the wine bar and spotted Steve sitting at the bar, she felt her heart jump. He was wearing a dark grey t-shirt and jeans. Eva smiled. 'Hi Steve,' she said.

'Eva, hi.' While he kissed her on the cheek, she caught the scent of his aftershave and the faint masculine smell of his rough leather jacket. 'What can I get you to drink, a dry Martini?'

'You remembered.'

He smiled and ordered. Eva didn't know how to start the conversation, so she asked about his parents. She couldn't care less how Dr. Patterson and Marlene were, but it had been some time since a man made her nervous.

'They are doing well, I think. You know them, not the most talkative people. And when they speak, you wish you had a pair of earplugs in your pocket.' Steve handed her the Martini, and she took a large sip. 'You look fantastic,' he said.

Eva felt her cheeks getting warm. She smiled, cursing herself for behaving so infantile. 'I'm pleased I mustered up the courage to ask you for a drink,' Steve said.

'You?' She didn't quite know how to respond. She only hoped Steve was sincere. Eva took another sip from her Martini to calm herself down. She looked at Steve and felt an overwhelming desire to kiss him. She glanced away; scared he may be able to read her mind.

'How's business?'

'Can't complain.'

'Your mother must be proud of you. Your business is doing well, and you did it all by yourself. I think any parent would be proud.'

'Ahh, correction,' Steve said, pointing his index finger at her. 'Normal parents would be proud. In case you hadn't noticed, my parents are anything but normal.' He took a large sip from his beer and continued, 'They had big plans for me. They had my life planned before they even conceived me.' As Steven joked about his parents, Eva could see how he struggled with their disapproval. 'Have you eaten?' he asked.

'No.'

'We can have dinner next door. I heard it's the best Italian restaurant in town.' Eva nodded and finished her drink. 'There's just one thing I have to do before we go.'

Eva picked up her jacket. She thought Steve had to make a telephone call but instead, as she put her jacket on, he kissed her. Eva was speechless. When she collected her thoughts, she looked up at him and without hesitation, she kissed him back.

'We'd better go to the restaurant before...' Eva said in his ear. He put his arm around her waist and gave her a soft squeeze. This small gesture made Eva feel wanted. She looked up at Steve with a tender smile.

4

Dr. Patterson's Office

Christine woke at 6:30am the next day and had her breakfast. Dr. Patterson's practice opened at 9am. She decided to call from the library to make an appointment. Christine had been taking the same sleeping medication for years and was aware of the long-term effects and addiction.

Eva walked into the kitchen with a goofy smile still plastered on her face. 'So, you and Steve Patterson,' Christine said in a parental tone of voice.

Eva just continued to smile. She felt incredible. She had never felt this kind of happiness before.

'Are you going to see him again?'

'I am. Steve is incredible,' Eva said. 'All I want to do is see him again. Now I understand why you get so upset when you don't see Eric.'

Christine smiled. She didn't want to talk about Eric. If she opened the discussion that she was not sure about Eric, Eva would never put it to sleep. 'That is fantastic. Steve is an exceptional guy.'

'I know. Isn't he just the best man ever?'

'He sure is handsome. I'm planning to see Dr. Patterson today about the nightmares,' Christine said, changing the conversation.

'Do you want me to come with you?' Eva asked.

'Don't worry. I'll be in and out in ten minutes.'

***

Christine waited in the reception area of Dr. Patterson's practice. As she sat on a large, dark brown, Chesterfield sofa and stared at *The Lady With a Green Hat* by Jozef Israëls hanging on the wall in front of her, she thought, *the place reeks of money*. To pass the time, she flicked through one of the medical magazines as she waited for Rebecca to let her know Dr. Patterson was ready for her.

Christine always thought that Rebecca looked like she would be more at home at a fashion shoot than working in a doctor's office. It amazed Christine that a girl like Rebecca was not working for a prestigious fashion or cosmetic company. She was a beautiful woman in her early thirties and looked flawless with her blond hair tied in a bun. Her make-up, even though it seemed a tiny bit over-done, looked professional. Today, she was wearing a tailored trouser suit with a blue pinstripe that impeccably complimented her figure. Suddenly, the intercom on the reception desk rang and Rebecca looked up.

'Dr. Patterson will see you now,' she announced.

Christine jumped up and smiled, but Rebecca did not acknowledge her. When Christine entered Dr. Patterson's office, she was surprised to see he was not alone. Dr. Bernard, who was at the party, was sitting next to Dr. Patterson.

'Good morning, Christine,' Dr. Patterson smiled as he greeted her. 'I hope you don't mind if my colleague, Dr. Bernard, joins us.'

Christine smiled, but she felt trapped. She could hardly say, '*no*.' After all, Dr. Bernard was already here. She only wanted to see Dr. Patterson.

'Dr. Bernard was at our yearly party. He is a world-renowned doctor and has done a great deal of research in the areas of dreams and sleep deprivation. I thought it might be a good idea to hear his opinion.'

He was not expecting any objections from Christine. She felt calmer thinking of how Dr. Patterson had gone to all the trouble to have his colleague join them for a second opinion. Dr. Bernard got up, walked to Christine, and shook her hand. 'It's nice to see you again, Christine,' he said.

Dr. Patterson asked Christine to take a seat in a large deep cream leather sofa on the other side of the office. Dr. Patterson and Dr. Bernard sat facing her on two cream-coloured wing chairs.

'Did Rebecca offer you a refreshment while you were waiting? Would you like coffee or tea?' Dr. Patterson asked politely.

His kind manner also helped put her at ease. 'Nothing for me, thank you,' Christine said.

Dr. Patterson walked back to his desk and asked Rebecca to bring in two black coffees and a bottle of sparkling water.

'Dr. Patterson has been filling me in. He tells me you have not been sleeping well,' Dr. Bernard said.

Christine told Dr. Bernard how she has been having the nightmare since she was fifteen. 'I have slept well for ten years with the medication, but now the nightmare is back.'

Speaking with Dr. Bernard made her feel awkward. The truth was that talking to Dr. Patterson was uncomfortable enough. Now, two doctors were probing and asking her questions.

Dr. Bernard asked, 'Is there anything in particular you can tell me about these nightmares?' Christine looked at Dr. Patterson for support. She wondered why he had discussed her nightmare with Dr. Bernard.

'Are you able to tell me anything? For example, what happens in your nightmare and are there people in it you recognize?'

'No. It's always the same. There is a dreadful earthquake and people are trying to escape but cannot. I see people around me being crushed by buildings and falling into cracks that the earthquake creates. When everything appears to be quieting down, there is a blue light in the distance that flashes into my eyes. I know I can't escape it. I stand there terrified as the blue light is in the distance and it begins to come towards me. I know I cannot escape it. I stand there, panicked until the blue light overtakes everything. Then, I wake up.'

'Are there any people you recognize in the nightmare?'

'No. No one looks familiar. They're just people.' Talking about the nightmare was almost as bad as experiencing it. Christine felt drained.

The door opened and Rebecca came in with the coffees. 'Is there anything else you need, Dr. Patterson?' she asked.

'No, thank you, Rebecca. That's all.' Dr. Patterson watched Christine as he picked up his coffee.

'Obviously, you need some help. I'm incredibly pleased you came.' Dr. Patterson nodded in agreement. Christine didn't reply.

While Dr. Patterson and Dr. Bernard sipped their coffees, Dr. Patterson mentioned that Dr. Bernard wanted to hypnotize her. Christine tensed and dug her nails into the chair. The endless stirring of his coffee was all she heard. It drove her mad. Her first instinct was to kick the coffee cup out of his hands.

Then, after taking a small sip, he told Christine that through hypnosis they would be able to understand the root of the problem.

'Hypnotize me? I'm not hiding anything. I have always told the truth,' Christine said. Why did Dr. Patterson put her on the spot?

'We don't think you're hiding anything. It may be something you have hidden and do not remember or do not realise you have hidden deeply in your memory.' Dr. Bernard continued, 'Research has come a long way. These days, we can better understand the reasons people suffer with nightmares or sleep disorders. There is an array of possibilities to help people deal with nightmares and other interrupted sleep patterns. Some benefit from psychotherapy – something like cognitive behavioural therapy, to be more specific. This can help change negative thought patterns.'

'I'm not sure. I wouldn't enjoy being hypnotised,' Christine whispered. She had only ever spoken a few words with Dr. Bernard at Dr. Patterson's house. She knew nothing about him.

Dr. Patterson gave her a cold stare. 'Dr. Bernard is doing us a great favour by joining us today. I hope you understand this, Christine.'

She fought back her tears as she listened to Dr. Patterson's condescending words. Why was he acting like this? There had been so many times she spoke with him about her nightmares and asked why they were so horrific. Why couldn't he show her sympathy now? Why was he was trying so aggressively to convince her to undergo hypnosis? This was not a manner she was accustomed to. All she wanted to do was to run out of the room. Instead, she whispered, 'I will think about it. I do appreciate your help, Dr. Patterson, and I'm sorry if I seem ungrateful.' Christine had nothing more to say and just stared at Dr. Patterson and Dr. Bernard.

'Well, that's all for today,' Dr. Patterson said and got up and walked to his desk. 'I'll prescribe additional medication. When you decide to undergo hypnosis treatment, feel free to call me.' He wrote a prescription and left it on his desk for Christine.

She collected the prescription and, as she walked towards the door, Dr. Patterson called her back. 'I mean no harm to you. I am strongly convinced that this is something that will benefit both you and Eva; whose nightmares may return as well. Christine, you know you can trust me.'

That was it. It suddenly dawned on Christine that she did not trust Dr. Matthew Patterson. Nor did she trust Dr. Ronald Bernard. 'I do trust you, Dr. Patterson.' She thanked Dr. Patterson and Dr. Bernard for their time and left the office as quickly as she could.

On the bus ride home, she thought about what Dr. Patterson had said. At first, she was angry. Now Dr. Patterson thought she had psychological problems. He knew her for most of her life and should know her psyche is fine. He never mentioned it before.

But then she thought, *maybe he was right*. Maybe he had excellent reasons for wanting her to undergo hypnosis. Perhaps it really could solve everything. She told herself that Dr. Patterson knew what he was doing. Heck, he even invited Dr. Bernard, who was an expert in this field, to see her. Her previously suspicious instinct was wearing off. This was always Christine's problem – self-doubt.

'It appears she is not very keen, Matthew.' Ronald Bernard closed his briefcase.

'No problem, Ronald. Somehow, I will convince Christine that this is the right thing to do. She has always trusted me.'

'Okay.' Dr. Bernard picked up his briefcase and coat and walked to the door. 'We must get all the research done. They are getting older.'

***

Christine left work early that day. The library wasn't busy, and her supervisor told her she could take advantage of the quiet period. As she walked into her apartment, her phone rang.

'Christine, it's Matthew Patterson.' Whenever Dr. Patterson announced himself by his first and last name, it meant he was in an excellent mood.

'Hello, Dr. Patterson.' It seemed odd to receive a phone call from him after their meeting at his practice. She was not expecting to hear from him and felt nervous.

'I'm phoning to apologise about this morning. I must have seemed impatient, but I always have your best interest at heart. Please believe that.'

'Dr. Patterson, as I told you, I trust you and your opinion.'

'Excellent! Because I need to dig deeper to understand why you girls suffer the same nightmare. I promise no harm will come to you, Christine. I love you like a daughter.' He paused for a moment. 'This morning, I was feeling unwell with a headache. I asked Dr. Bernard to come to my office to meet you. I felt somewhat embarrassed because I felt he made his precious time available for nothing. If I have hurt your feelings, please accept my apologies.'

'Thank you, Dr. Patterson. You are right. I apologise for doubting your opinion. I'll consider the hypnosis test.'

'That's my girl,' Dr. Patterson said. She closed her cell phone, but was not feeling relieved. She needed a caring shoulder and phoned Eric.

'Hi, Eric. Can you come over this evening? I'd like to see you.'

'Sure. I need to talk to you, too,' he said. Christine felt a stone in her stomach. His words had an ominous tone. Their relationship had become a one-way street with her making plans and him cancelling. 'I'll be at your house at 8 o'clock.' Before she could say *goodbye*, he put the phone down. She felt very fragile. The nightmare was back, and Dr. Patterson had given her such a time about the hypnosis. She needed Eric's support.

Christine watched the clock; it was already seven. She rushed to take a shower. She wanted to be sure she looked ravishingly. While she showered, she thought about her day.

She asked herself again, *Why did Dr. Patterson wish to do*

these tests? And why did he seem overly keen for her to see Dr. Bernard? He had never referred her or Eva to another doctor.

She wanted to shower her depressing thoughts away and started soaping her body. After she dressed, she walked into the living room; she still had twenty minutes. She got up several times to check herself in the mirror. At precisely eight o'clock, the doorbell rang. Eric was always punctual. Christine rushed to open the door.

'Hi Eric,' she said. 'I'm so thrilled you're here. I've missed you.' She took Eric's hand and walked him to the living room. 'Can I get you something to drink?'

Eric didn't say anything. Christine began feeling nervous and when she was nervous, her hands perspired. Eric took a seat in the Napoleon III-inspired chair. He didn't sit with her on the sofa.

'Is everything okay? Did something happen in the office?'

'No. Not the office…' he started to say. Christine sat forward on the sofa, trying to get closer. She tried to touch his hand, but he pulled it away. 'I know I've been working a great deal and we haven't spent much time together lately. I've been thinking about our relationship and concluded that, while I have been working long hours, I don't miss you.'

Christine could feel her stomach turn. 'What do you mean?'

'It's not fair that we continue seeing each other. You deserve someone who can spend more time with you.'

Christine couldn't hold back her tears. 'What about your work schedule? I understand you can't to see me due to your work.' She was desperately trying to not fall apart. This could not be happening.

'No. It's more than that. Chris, I'm sorry, but I don't love you anymore.'

'Please, Eric. Don't leave me. You know I'll do anything for you. I can wait. We can take some time apart and see how things are in a few months.' She grabbed his arm and tried to stop him. 'Please, Eric. Stay with me. Tell me what you want me to do and I'll do it.' She felt desperate and helpless.

'Christine, I've made my decision.'

'But I love you, Eric. What am I going to do without you?'

'Christine, please. Christine, I'm sure you'll be fine and get over me.' With that, he pulled his arm away. Christine looked into his eyes. He didn't feel sorry for her. His eyes were cold. He walked to the door and, without saying *goodbye*, he left.

The front door slammed. Christine stared at the door in disbelief. She felt herself getting nauseous and ran to the bathroom. She sat on the floor crying and asking herself, *What just happened? We have been together for three years. How could he break up like that?* She walked into the bedroom and flopped on her bed. Staring at the bottle of her new sleeping pills, she decided to take one. *No pain*, she thought.

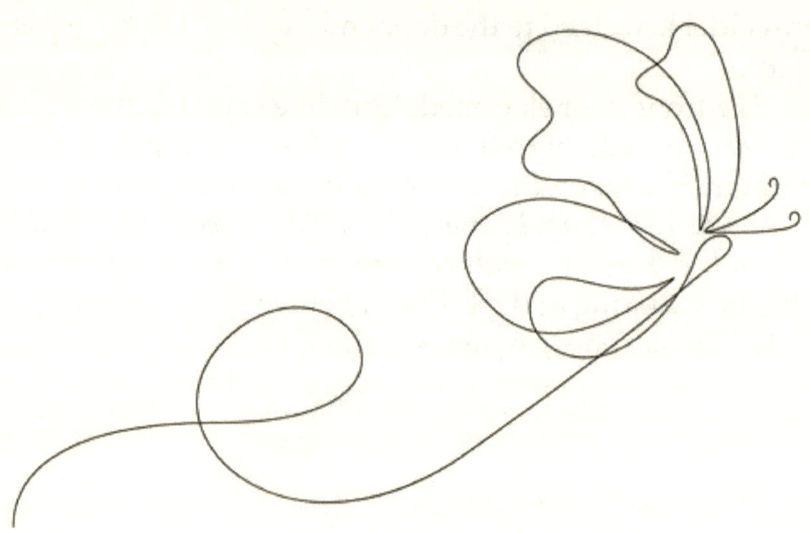

5

After the Break-up

Christine woke from a restless sleep early the next morning. She put on a warm cardigan and walked to the kitchen. Eva was already having breakfast. Christine was in no mood to talk. She didn't want any, *I told you so's,* from Eva; who never liked Eric. Christine hesitated for several moments outside the kitchen but realized she would have to face Eva eventually.

'What happened to you? You look like awful,' Eva said, looking up from her bowl of cereal.

'Thank you.' Christine opened the fridge, poured herself a glass of orange juice and sat down at the table.

'Well, what happened? Nobody looks like a ghost for no reason.'

'Eric broke off our engagement,' Christine said. Eva sat up straight and stared at Christine without saying a word. 'He came over last night, told me he didn't love me, and five minutes later he was out of the door. After three years, you'd think he could dedicate more time to breaking my heart.'

'That guy never treated you well. It wouldn't surprise me if he already has another girlfriend.' Eva was getting angry, oblivious to the fact that Christine didn't need to hear these remarks right now.

'I love him,' Christine said, her eyes sparkled with tears.

'I thought we were getting married after his promotion.'

'I know you did,' Eva said. 'I'm so sorry. You don't deserve this. It's a shame you ever met him.'

Christine felt like she had the life sucked out of her. All that remained was a sad, weak little girl. 'Do you mind phoning the library for me to tell them I won't be in? I'm going back to bed.' Christine left without waiting for a response.

'Sure.' Eva wanted to help. Many thoughts went through her mind. Why had she been so untactful to Christine this morning? She wished she was more like Christine, who was always understanding and never judgemental. She was glad Eric was gone. Now, she could find someone who really loves her. Eric never deserved Christine.

***

As Eva left the apartment, her mobile rang. She saw Steve's number on display. 'Morning, gorgeous,' he greeted her.

'Good morning to you.'

'Are you free this evening? I'd like to see you!'

'Well...,' Eva said. 'Eric broke up with Christine last night. I would love to see you, but I think I need to stay home and look after her.' She paused for a moment. 'How about tomorrow night?'

'Tomorrow night is perfect. Shall I pick you up around seven?'

'Great. Sorry about this evening.'

'I understand. I must miss you another day. Please give my love to Christine.'

Eva felt torn. On the one hand, she was falling in love but, on the other, Christine's pain was too much to ignore. Eva had never been in love with anyone like Christine loved Eric. They were so different. Christine wanted a husband and children. Getting close to anyone was one of Eva's problems.

Steve was different, though. She was convinced things would work out for them. She felt it.

***

When Eva returned from work, she walked straight into Christine's bedroom. Christine was asleep. Eva saw the bottle of sleeping pills next to her bed.

'Christine...,' she whispered. No response. Eva assumed that the sleeping pills would keep her asleep for the rest of the evening. She checked her watch. It was only 6:30pm.

Christine woke around 7:30pm that evening. Thanks to her new sleeping pills, she had slept the whole day. Her head felt heavy as she stumbled out of bed and used the wall for support as she walked to the bathroom. It was as if her head was a fraction of a second behind her movements. She knew she took too many sleeping pills but, at the moment, she couldn't care less. Each time she thought of Eric, she was filled with feelings of desperation. She felt sick; especially when she remembered his cold eyes.

She stood looking at the shower for a moment and then decided it would take too much energy; so she walked to the kitchen instead. She opened a bottle of wine that was on top of the fridge. Then, she picked a tall glass from the cupboard and poured wine into it to the brim. She started crying again the moment she sat on the sofa. *What happened? Why had he changed his mind?*

Eva, who had been listening to her music in bed, walked into the living room. She sat next to Christine on the sofa and put her arm around her. 'How are you doing?' she asked.

'How do you think I am doing? I have been ditched by a man I hardly know.'

'What do you mean?'

'I don't know.' Christine shrugged her shoulders. 'He was so cold last night I didn't recognize him. It's almost as if

35

he switched a button and I didn't exist any longer.' Christine stopped and wiped her nose. 'Just like that.' She snapped her fingers. 'Within five minutes; no explanation and not the slightest consideration for my feelings.' Christine started to cry so hard that her shoulders and chest shook. She hurt to the very core of her being.

'I am so sorry, Chris. I am.'

'He said that when he was working all hours, he didn't miss me. What does that mean?' Christine tried to speak through her tears.

Eva watched her with a heavy heart.

'It was his decision to work all those hours and not spend time together - not mine.'

'It's not your fault, Chris. None of this is your fault.'

'Maybe I should have nagged him less, or maybe I wasn't supportive enough.'

'Stop it, Chris. You are the most devoted person I know. If he can't see that, then that's his loss.'

'I thought he was the one.'

'You will find someone else. Someone who'll appreciate you and see what a wonderful person you are,' Eva said. She felt ridiculous. It seemed like such a cliché, but it really was the truth. Christine could do so much better.

'I want to go back to bed now.'

'I'll cook something and call you when it's ready.' Eva cooked rice with curry chicken while Christine stayed in bed, unwilling or unable to eat. When Eva walked into the bedroom to check on Christine, she sat on the edge of the bed. Christine hadn't told Eva she'd already taken several sleeping pills and took another two. She fell asleep quickly.

'It'll get easier, sweetheart. You'll see. You'll find someone who absolutely loves you,' Eva whispered. She made sure Christine was fast asleep and switched off the light. She decided to phone Steve and walked into the living room.

While sitting on the sofa, she thought about all the little fights she had with Eric over the years. She and Eric butted heads the moment they laid eyes on each other. Eva never liked him. She thought he was an arrogant and narcissistic man who would never love anyone but himself. She was sure Christine would see this one day even if she was not able to today.

'Hello,' Steve answered the phone.

'Hi, it's me. I just wanted to hear your voice.'

'How's Christine?' Steve asked

'She's in bed sleeping now, but she's not doing so well. I suppose that after three years you don't expect someone to break off an engagement in five minutes saying that he doesn't miss you that much when he doesn't see you.' The more she thought about it, the angrier she became. 'I think that's what bothers Christine the most. She just doesn't understand why Eric changed his mind overnight.'

'Is that what he said?'

'Yes. Isn't it sickening?'

'It is. However, there's never a good or painless way of breaking off a relationship, especially after so many years,' Steve said.

'That's ridiculous. After three years, you'd expect to get a bit more than, *I don't miss you that much*. And all of that in five minutes. The guy's a total schmuck,' Eva said. She was annoyed that Steve seemed to be justifying Eric's behaviour.

'I suppose you're right.'

'I've never been in a relationship that long, have you?' The moment she asked the question, she felt silly. Was she being too direct?

'My longest relationship was two-and-a-half years. We were both young. We met when we were nineteen. By the time we were twenty-two, we knew it wasn't going anywhere and mutually agreed it was best if we went our separate ways. What about you?'

'I think it might have been eight months. I liked spending time with him, but I was never really in love. I thought it would be better to call it off rather than hang on in the hope things would change.'

'Well, I am pleased you dumped him,' Steve said.

Eva laughed. 'You are evil, Steve Patterson, but I like that about you.' She really wanted to be with him right now. She wanted to feel his arms around her. 'Christine is fast asleep. I know it's late, but I would really like to come over.'

'My door is always open for you,' Steve replied.

'Give me an hour and I'll be there.' Eva put the phone down and ran to her bedroom to pack a bag.

6

The Pills

Matthew Patterson was working in his study as he always did when he returned from his practice. Although his study was smaller than the other rooms in the house, it was a beautiful space. The walls were painted deep green. A stately mahogany desk took up most of the room. One wall was an inset bookshelf and was covered from top to bottom with medical books and publications. The opposite wall displayed a collection of valuable paintings. Matthew Patterson was checking bills when he heard a knock on his door.

'Yes,' he answered in his usual short way. Marlene Patterson walked in. 'Yes, Marlene. What do you want?' He didn't look up from his paperwork as he spoke to his wife.

'We need to talk.'

'Can't it wait till tomorrow? I'm busy.'

'No. I need to speak with you now and would appreciate it if you could pay attention.' Marlene sat down on the small leather sofa facing the desk. 'I wouldn't be here if I thought it wasn't important.'

Marlene was accustomed to Matthew's manners, or the lack of manners. She wasn't upset by this. He gave her the life she had always wanted. She had the respect and admiration that came with being the wife of one of the country's foremost doctors. The truth was that she had never needed the love of a man and was content. Matthew didn't take up any of her time and she wouldn't have it any other way. She helped Matthew to get where he was now and felt she deserved everything he gave her. 'Rita Thompson phoned me this morning. She told me she saw Steve in town with Eva Williams.'

Marlene always referred to both Eva and Christine by their first and last names. Matthew dropped his pen immediately and looked at his wife. 'With our Eva?' he asked.

'That's what I said Matthew. Eva Williams.'

Matthew Patterson knew his wife's feelings towards the girls. She only allowed them in her home because her husband asked her to. 'Was this the only time they were seen together?' he asked angrily.

'How should I know? Stop asking me ridiculous questions. This is why I'm here speaking to you now.' She knew her husband was a genius, but sometimes he would ask questions only a simpleton would ask. 'We can't tell Steven he isn't allowed to see her anymore. You know what he's like. He'll continue dating her to spite us. That boy has always been trouble. We should have sent him to military school.'

'I can't believe it!' Matthew shouted as he slammed his fist on the table.

'Don't get so angry, Matthew,' Marlene said primly. Marlene, however, secretly enjoyed seeing Matthew angry. She loved seeing him pushed to his limits. It made her feel in control.

'Don't get angry?' He was furious. 'You come into my office and tell me my son is going out with one of the girls, and you tell me to not get angry!' His face was red with anger. 'Do you know what this means?' Matthew was screaming now.

'I know very well what it means, and I am sure we can do something to stop it.' Marlene spoke calmly to her husband.

'Like what?'

'Matthew, please. You must calm down. You're not resolving anything with this attitude.' Matthew leaned back in his chair and looked at his wife.

'Rita also told me that Annabel Malmesbury is back in town from her travels,' Marlene said with a conniving smile on her face. 'You remember the Malmesbury's?' she asked without expecting a response. 'They are a well-respected and influential family. Annabel is a beautiful young woman, who, according to Rita, is looking to settle down. I will organize a dinner where she can meet Steven. I will, of course, have a word with Annabel about Steven's availability, and will let nature take its course.'

Marlene had the entire plan worked out in her head. She would love for Steve to become engaged to someone who came from such an influential family. This would also enhance her status.

'You'd better be right, Marlene. If not, we might have a huge problem on our hands.' Matthew had calmed down but was still very agitated.

'There is absolutely no way he will find out anything. Leave it to me, Matthew Patterson. Have I ever let you down?' Marlene got up from her seat and walked to the door.

'Hum,' Matthew was no longer paying attention to his wife. He was staring at his desk, chewing over what his wife had just told him.

***

Eva arrived at Steve's late that evening. His apartment was on Ainger Road, Primrose hill; even though not in the centre, it remained a wealthy area. His apartment was open and plain, but very spacious. There were two levels with two bedrooms upstairs; each with their own bathroom. There was a stunning terrace that overlooked the canal. She was

41

impressed by the apartment, but really preferred the more traditional houses.

Eva sat quietly in the living room for a while and finally looked up at Steve, 'I can't believe that Eric managed to hurt Christine so much.'

Steve sat next to her and took her in his arms. Eva remembered his smell and could feel that special feeling of attraction coming over her. She pulled back, looked at Steve, and then kissed him passionately.

After kissing for a while, Steve said, 'There is a more comfortable place in the house.' Eva looked deeply into his eyes and saw his passion. And they continued their evening.…

***

Eva woke the following day, screaming. She was trembling. It was her turn now. The nightmare was back. She didn't respond to Steven. She was still shaking and unable to find her voice.

'I'm going to the kitchen to get something to drink,' she said after a few seconds.

'No worries. I'll get it for you. You stay in bed,' Steve offered.

'No, no. It's okay. I need to get up; otherwise I'll never fall back asleep.' She grabbed her shirt from the chair next to the bed and walked into the kitchen. She opened the fridge to get some milk. As she poured the milk in a glass, she realized that this was the first time she had a nightmare while taking her sleeping pills. She could feel her breathing getting shallower and her shoulders tense up. What was she going to do now? She had assumed Christine had other problems and felt terrible for not supporting her more. Eva never expected her nightmare would come back too. The more she thought about it, the more worried she became. She decided she also needed to see Dr. Patterson for something stronger. She knew that the pills she was taking now were already heavy. Anything more substantial would probably affect her daily life considerably.

'Everything okay?' Steve asked as he walked into the kitchen.

'I did have a nightmare.'

Steve sat next to her and took her in her arms. 'I'll look after you and make sure nothing will happen to you. That nightmare really scared you, didn't it?' He kept a close eye on her.

'It did,' she whispered, trying to avoid eye contact.

'Nightmares are nothing to be embarrassed about.' Steve kept looking at her while he poured water into a glass. 'Mostly, they are a reflection of something going on in your life. You're probably dealing with a problem or something that has upset you.'

'Maybe,' she said and gave him her most confident smile. 'You should go back to bed. I'll be there in a couple of minutes.' She wanted Steve and his probing eyes away from her. 'Really. I'm fine. It happens. I just got spooked when I didn't recognize where I was.'

'Are you sure?'

'Steve, I don't want to talk about it now. I think it's best you go back to sleep. We both have to get up early,' she snapped at him.

He nodded and walked back to the bedroom. 'Well done, Eva, now you've pushed him away,' she whispered to herself. She placed her glass in the sink and followed him back to the bedroom.

Steve looked at her when she walked in. 'You can tell me anything, Eva,' he said and kissed her neck.

'Maybe some other time.' She crawled on his chest. She lay awake for a long time. She could hear Steve's regular breathing. He was already asleep.

Matthew Patterson woke early and sat on the edge of his enormous bed. He shuffled his feet along the floor, looking for his slippers. After he showered and had a glass of orange juice, he left the house. 'We'll be making another stop before going to the office,' he said to his driver. The driver gave a short nod.

He rarely went to see the girls in their apartment, but this time he felt it was a necessity. He had to find out what was going on and somehow convince Eva to stop seeing Steven. There was no way he could allow him to date her. They drove onto Burrows Road in Kensal Green. It was an ordinary road with regular houses, most of which had been converted into apartments. He remembered how he used to live on a street pretty much like this and how he hated it.

The driver stopped in front of the apartment and opened the car door. Dr. Patterson walked up and rang the doorbell. He looked at his watch. It was almost 7 o'clock. After he rang the bell several times more, there was still no answer. He took out his cell phone and rang Christine's number.

'Hello…,' a sleepy voice answered.

'Christine. Good morning. This is Dr. Patterson. I hope I'm not waking you.'

'Dr. Patterson?' Christine's voice was very faint.

'Are you okay, Christine…? I'm outside your door. I wanted to see how you are. Can I come in?'

Christine didn't reply. He could only hear her heavy breathing and realized something was wrong. He took out his gold key chain, which had about twelve keys attached to it. He struggled to find the key to the apartment. After several tries, he finally found it and opened the door. He ran into the apartment, looking for Christine.

She was on her bed with the telephone receiver on the pillow next to her. She was almost unconscious. Dr. Patterson picked up the bottle of sleeping pills from the bedside table and understood immediately that Christine had taken too many pills. He picked her up and rushed her to the bathroom. He laid Christine in the tub and opened the cold-water tap.

Christine was slowly getting her senses back. 'Cold....' she mumbled.

'I know, Christine. But you need to stay awake. How many pills did you take?' Dr. Patterson was shaking her by the shoulders.

'Don't know,' she whispered

'Christine......,' Dr. Patterson tried again. '*How many?*' He was shaking her violently and Christine accidentally hit her head on the tiled back wall.

'Don't know.....maybe six.'

Dr. Patterson shook his head and kept Christine under the cold running water. He picked up his cell phone and called for an ambulance. When he heard the siren in the street, he walked to the front door, leaving Christine under the cold water.

'This way,' he said to the paramedics and introduced himself. 'She's in the bathroom. She has taken too many sleeping pills. She's conscious, but only *just*. I need you to take her to Hampstead Hospital and have her stomach pumped.'

The paramedics rushed into the bathroom. They pulled Christine out of the tub, put her on their stretcher, and wheeled her to the ambulance.

'Dr. Patterson, where is Dr. Patterson?' Christine mumbled.

Dr. Patterson was leaning against the doorpost. He was ignoring her cries and his eyes were stone cold. When the paramedics were out of sight, Dr. Patterson walked back inside.

He opened all the doors and called for Eva. When he realized Eva was not in the apartment, he walked back to his car, picked up his phone, and called his son, Daulton.

'Daulton, it's your father,' he said. And, without waiting for a response from his son, continued, 'Christine Rhodes is on her way to Hampstead Hospital. She has taken an overdose of *Zolpidem*. I need you to look after her before I get there. Do you hear me? Do not let any other doctor near her!'

'I'm rather busy with my patients, father,' Daulton replied. 'Isn't Middlesex Hospital closer to her home?'

'Daulton, I'm not going to discuss this with you now. You see to that girl *immediately*!' Dr. Patterson slammed the phone down.

7

The Hospital

Eva stretched her long legs to the other side of the bed. She realized Steve was already up. 'Steve?' she called out. 'Where are you?'

'I'm in the living room,' he yelled back. She could hear him walking towards the bedroom.

'Come and be by me.' She patted on the bed next to her.

Steve smiled, laid down, and took her into his arms. They laid there for several minutes with their arms tightly around each other. 'How are you this morning? Did you manage to fall back asleep?' he asked, stroking her back gently.

'Yeah,' she said and snuggled closer. She loved the security of Steve's chest. She felt like a little girl, protected and safe. This was the first time in her life that she experienced this feeling. She felt as if nothing could touch her. Steve would look after her, no matter what.

'Shall I make you some coffee?' Steve asked.

Eva nodded. She looked at the clock and sighed. She had to get ready; otherwise, she would be late for work. She looked at Steve, crawled back on his chest, and started to stroke him. 'Maybe we should phone in sick, and stay in bed all day?'

'I think that is the best plan you've ever had.' He tickled

her. She jumped and giggled. She fell on her back, laughing, and begged him to stop. He looked into her eyes and kissed her passionately.

'Before we continue,' she said and held up her hand, 'let's make those phone calls.'

Eva grabbed her handbag from the chair next to the bed and switched her cell phone on.

'You can use my phone,' Steve said.

'No. It's better if I use mine. My office has caller ID.' She gave him a crafty look. 'I am just too cunning for my own good.' Immediately, when she switched her mobile phone on, she saw a text message. 'Oh my, I have a message from your father.' She looked around as if Dr. Patterson was in the room and quickly covered herself. While she read the message, her face went pale.

'Eva, what's the matter?' Steve asked.

'I have to go to Hampstead Hospital. Christine has taken an overdose.'

'I'll drive you there.' Steve jumped up immediately and grabbed his keys.

'I should have stayed with her,' Eva said as they ran to Steve's Land Rover. 'I should have never left her. I knew she was extremely fragile. I should have been there for her.'

'It's not your fault,' Steve said, trying to calm her down.

'*Yes, I know*, but I could have prevented it.' Eva looked out of the window. The city was already awake, and the traffic was starting to get heavy. She thought about Christine and how selfish she had been to leave her alone. A few minutes passed. 'I'm sorry, Steve. I didn't mean to snap at you, but Christine is all I have. She's like a sister to me.'

'I understand,' he said and kept his eyes on the road. He put his hand on her leg.

As they drove up to the hospital, Eva asked Steve to drop her off at the entrance. She didn't have the patience to look for a parking space with him. She needed to see

Christine. Steve pulled over and let Eva out of the car. She ran inside, desperately looking for the information desk.

'My sister was admitted this morning. Christine Rhodes….' Eva knew that they would never allow her to see Christine if she told them she was just a roommate.

The receptionist looked at her computer. 'She's in room 503, wing F5.'

Without responding, Eva ran to the elevator. While pressing the call button, she felt herself getting so worried it made her nauseous. 'Christine, what did you do?' she asked herself out loud. Eva saw Dr. Patterson and his son Daulton standing in the corridor when she got off the lift.

'Dr. Patterson!' she called. Both men turned around. 'Where's Christine? Is she okay?'

Matthew Patterson took Eva by the arm and walked her to the grey plastic mounted wall seats. 'She's still recovering from having her stomach pumped, but she's doing very well.'

'What happened?' Eva was crying.

'She took too many of her new sleeping pills. She didn't realize how strong they are.' Dr. Patterson was very calm. 'I did tell her. I went to see her this morning and found her asleep on her bed.' He had no other choice but to tell Eva the truth. She would eventually find out it was him who called the ambulance.

'Thank God you were there.' Eva wiped tears from her eyes. 'When can I see her?'

'I think she'll be ready for a brief visit in about half an hour,' Daulton told her.

'Thank you, Daulton. Thank you for looking after her,' Eva said. She looked up at Daulton towering in front of her with his arms crossed.

'You're welcome.'

While Eva was speaking to Daulton, Steve arrived and walked towards them. 'Steven?' Matthew Patterson look surprised. 'What are you doing here?'

Steve walked up to his father and brother and greeted them. Both of them gave him a silent nod. 'I drove Eva to the hospital. She was too upset to drive herself,' Steve answered his father calmly.

'How on earth did your paths cross this early in the morning?' Matthew Patterson asked, his eyes squinted.

Steve didn't answer. He looked at Eva. 'You alright?' he asked and hugged her.

Eva smiled at him lovingly. Dr. Patterson felt his jaw clench as he saw them together. Something needed to be done, and soon. His wife's information was correct. The relationship between Steven and Eva was much more advanced than previously feared.

'Dr. Patterson,' Daulton looked up when he recognized the voice of one of his nurses. 'Miss Rhodes is ready for her check-up.'

Daulton Patterson walked into Christine's room. Eva paced up and down in the hospital corridor, chewing her fingernails.

'Steven, before I forget, your mother wants you to have dinner with us Thursday evening,' Dr. Patterson said.

'I'm not sure if I'm free.'

Matthew put his hand on his son's shoulder. 'You know your mother, Steven. You better not disappoint her.'

'I'll try,' Steven replied absent-mindedly.

Daulton came out of the room. 'She can see you now,' he said to Eva. 'But only for five minutes. She's still very weak.'

Eva ran into the room. She started crying when she saw Christine in the hospital bed. Her wavy brown hair was pulled back and her eyes were swollen and red. She looked so fragile and weak. 'Christine, what have you done?' Eva asked.

A tear fell down Christine's face. 'The pain didn't stop. I only wanted to sleep and forget.'

'Those things take time, Chris. You dated Eric for three

years. The pain won't go away overnight,' Eva said, holding Christine's hand tightly.

'All I want is to start a family and have a place where I belong. Is that too much to ask for in life? Am I asking for the impossible?'

'Chris, I'm your family,' Eva said. 'You are all I have… I can't lose you. What would I do without you, Chris?' Eva became more emotional with every word. Christine started to sob uncontrollably. Eva hugged her and slowly rocked her back and forth. 'We'll always have each other, Chris; no matter what.'

Christine calmed down and looked at Eva with big childlike eyes. 'I'm scared, Eva. I don't know why, but I am. Everything is going wrong.'

'It'll be fine. I promise. Together we will overcome everything.' They looked at each other and, for the first time in their lives, realized they were not alone. They had each other.

***

Daulton Patterson walked into the room. 'Eva, Christine needs to rest now. You can come and see her again this evening.'

'When can she come home?'

'We're running some tests. If everything is in order, she can go home tomorrow morning.'

'I'll come and see you this evening, Chris. And tomorrow, when you come home, I'll make such a fuss and serve you hand on foot.'

'You might regret you said that,' Christine said managing a little smile.

Eva leaned over and kissed Christine on the cheek. 'See you later.'

Christine grabbed her hand, 'Thank you….'

Eva walked out of the room into the hospital corridor. Matthew Patterson was still there and walked up to her as soon as he saw her. 'I am so sorry, Eva. Are you okay?' He asked and gave her a quick, uncomfortable hug.

'I'm fine, Dr. Patterson,' she responded. 'I'm just incredibly pleased she is recovering well.'

'So am I,' Dr. Patterson replied, 'You go home and get some rest. I'll write you a sick note for your office.'

Eva waited for Dr. Patterson to give her the note and looked at Steve, who was standing by the window. She smiled at him. 'I'll drive you home,' he said and put his arm around her as they walked away.

Matthew Patterson watched them. 'Steven,' he called, 'don't forget that your mother wants to see you for dinner Thursday.' Steve didn't reply and kept walking.

'Daulton,' Matthew Patterson walked over to his son, 'make sure that no other doctor comes near Christine.'

'Why not?' his son asked, surprised.

'Just do as I ask,' Dr. Patterson ordered.

'I'll do my best, father.'

'No, Daulton,' Matthew grabbed his son by the arm, 'this is not a request; it is a *demand*.'

Daulton looked his father in the eyes. 'Of course, father. I understand.'

'Good boy.' Matthew gave his son a pat on the back and walked to the lifts.

Daulton stared at his father as he walked away. He wanted to shout after him that he was a successful doctor himself and that he deserved some respect. Daulton had never been able to stand up to his parents. He spent his life doing what they wanted and worked hard to gain their approval. He attended the schools they chose, had the friends they picked, joined the appropriate country clubs, and had specialized in his parents' preferred specialty.

Daulton understood that no matter what he did, he

would never receive the approval he so desperately wanted. As his father barked his demands at him, he felt he was losing patience. He knew that sooner rather than later he would have to confront his parents.

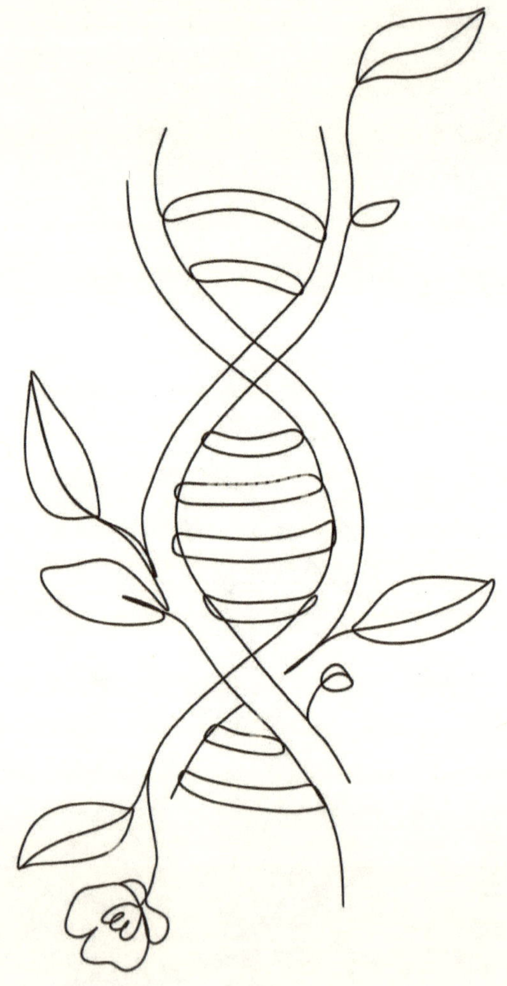

8

Home Again

Eva was in the kitchen, preparing sandwiches. Steve watched her. She felt his stares and turned around.

'You do have a strange family.'

'What an earth do you mean?' Steve said with fake surprise on his face.

'Could Daulton be any colder and more impersonal?'

'He's not that bad. Daulton is like my father. They are both devoted to their work. He's rapidly becoming a well-known doctor and, like my father, he lives for his work. The thing is, Daulton genuinely loves helping other people, but he has problems connecting with them.'

'Yeah, about that. Isn't it strange?' Eva said with a puzzled face. 'Daulton looking after Christine. Isn't he specialized in gynaecology? Also, why Hampstead Hospital? Middlesex Hospital is so much closer.'

'My father probably made the request. You girls have always had his full interest.'

'I know. Why do you think that is?' Eva was asking herself more than Steve.

'I think he sees both of you almost like daughters.'

'I don't think so. Christine, maybe. But not me. To be honest, I don't even think he even likes me,' Eva replied.

Steve started to laugh. 'Welcome to the amazing

parenting world of the Patterson's.'

Eva put a cup of coffee and a tuna fish sandwich on the table for Steve. 'How do you feel?' he asked. 'You didn't exactly get a perfect night sleep last night.'

'I'm fine,' Eva said. 'I suffered quite a bit from nightmares as a child. Now they're back. So, if you intend to hang around, you'd better get used to it. Maybe it was just a one-off.' They ate without speaking.

'Maybe you should see a specialist. Someone who specializes in that field.'

'I'm not sure,' Eva replied. 'I think it's just one of those things. It will pass.' She got up from her seat and put her cup and plate in the sink.

'I think you should speak to my father. He has many contacts, and he may be able to refer you to a specialist.'

'Maybe I'll do that.' Eva had no intention of asking Dr. Paterson for help. She didn't want to talk to Steve about her nightmares. She had to get to know him better before doing that. The thought of telling him about the nightmares was terrible enough, telling him about Chris was unthinkable right now. She didn't want to think about it anymore. She looked over at Steve. He seemed oblivious to her tension.

***

Eva put fresh flowers in Christine's bedroom and hung a sign, *Welcome Home*. She heard the phone ring and walked into the living room to answer it.

'Eva, it's me. Daulton told me I can come home. I'll take a taxi and should be there in about twenty minutes.'

'I can come and pick you up.'

'No worries. The traffic is bad. I'll take the taxi.'

'Okay, see you soon.'

When Eva heard a car pull up outside the building, she rushed to the window. She saw the taxi driver help Christine out of the car. Eva ran to the door and before Christine could ring the bell, she had already opened the door. Christine walked in and hugged Eva.

'I'll walk you to your room. You can relax and I'll look after you. I've taken the rest of the week off, so I'm all yours,' Eva said and kissed Christine on the cheek.

'Whoa! You didn't have to do all this,' she said as she looked up at the sign and saw the flowers.

'Impressive, no? I'll make you something to drink. What would you like?'

'Some tea. But first, I want to take a shower in my own bathroom. I want to get this hospital smell off me. Give me ten minutes.' Christine walked into the bathroom.

The bathroom, like the rest of the house, was in desperate need of refurbishment. She stepped into the large tub and closed the white shower curtain. The bathroom may be old, she thought, but the water pressure was terrific; a real plus in London.

She stood for minutes, just letting the hot water run over her body. She forced herself to close the tab. She could stay under the hot running water for hours. Although she still felt weak, the shower had done her good. She walked into her bedroom, smelled the flowers Eva put on the table, and then laid on her bed. Eva walked in with the tea and biscuits and sat next to her.

'I didn't try to commit suicide,' Christine said

'Oh...?' was all Eva managed to say.

'Don't be nervous. It's important I tell you. I got carried away with the sleeping pills. I just wanted to sleep, and that was all. Every time I woke up, I felt myself getting nauseous with pain.' Christine took a sip from the steaming hot raspberry tea. 'I just wanted to numb the pain. I really shouldn't keep those sleeping pills next to my bed. They are too accessible.' Christine looked at the small bottle on her bed stand. 'I was very hurt by what Eric did, but not enough to kill myself. I feel better already. I did so much crying when we were together. The countless times he cancelled at the last minute, the cold treatment lately, and his selfishness had me in tears so many times. A part of me was expecting he would call off our engagement. It was just the way he did it,' Christine paused and hesitated. 'He was so cruel. He didn't show the slightest sympathy. I think that's what hurt me the most. It was as though I meant nothing to him as a person. He didn't care how much he hurt me. It was almost as if he cancelled a subscription over the telephone.'

'You're better off without him.'

'I wish I could believe that. I'll miss being in a relationship and the thought that I might have a family soon,' Christine said, finishing her tea.

'You will find someone far better to do that with.'

'Easy for you to say. You always have men chasing you,' Christine said

'Yeah, sure. All they have are poor intentions,' Eva responded and pulled a face. Christine giggled. 'You know what we should do?' Eva jumped up from the bed, spilling some of the tea over her shirt. She wiped it off without paying attention. 'We should go to a fancy hair salon and have our hair done. Chris, you should do something with your hair and not wear it in a ponytail all the time. I have enough points from the modelling agency we can use to go to an exclusive salon.'

'Uhmmm, not so sure. I like my hair in a ponytail. Unlike you, I'm not that keen on blow-drying.'

'But you have beautiful hair. You shouldn't hide it. Come on, Chris. Let's do it. It'll be fun.' Eva was getting excited.

'I'll let you know. My hair isn't high on my list of priorities,' Christine said while snuggling under the blankets. Eva made her smile and got on her nerves at the same time. What made her think about a haircut at a time like this? For

Eva, clothes and make-up were essential. They were the cure for almost anything. It was a good thing she also had a heart of gold.

'I'll let you rest for a while. If there's anything you need, just yell,' Eva said while fluffing Christine's pillows. As she walked out of the room, she blew Christine a kiss.

9

Dinner

Steve stood in front of his parent's house, dreading the evening ahead. He looked up and saw that the lights were on all over the house. His mother sure did enjoy wasting money. Fairmont Street, Knightsbridge was exceptional; about five steps were surrounded by immaculately kept ornamental conifers leading up to the imposing oak door. He should have been thrilled to grow up on this magnificent property, but the house gave him the shivers. He rang the doorbell, and the door was answered by one of his mother's maids.

'Good evening, Mr. Patterson. May I take your coat?' she asked without making eye contact.

'Thank you, Maria.' He stood in the entrance hall for a moment and took a deep breath. He looked at the imposing chandelier over his head and wished himself good luck.

'Please follow me,' the maid said and showed him to the reception room, as though he didn't know where it was.

As he walked into the reception room, he saw his mother had invited other guests. Marlene got up from her seat, looking frightfully skinny in her soft pink Channel suit. 'Everyone, this is my youngest son, Steven. Come, Steven. Let me introduce you.' She took him by the hand and walked him towards the other guests. 'Mr. and Mrs. Malmesbury and their charming daughter, Annabel.' Steve shook their hands.

'Over here are Dr. and Mrs. Thompson, Mr. and Mrs. Devonshire, and last, but by no means least, your brother Daulton.' Everyone in the room let out a polite laugh.

'Good evening, everyone,' Steve said, feeling uneasy. He had no idea why his mother had invited other people for dinner. If he'd known, he would have cancelled for sure.

'Steven, what would you like to drink?' his father asked. Steve glanced around and saw everyone was drinking wine.

'I'll have a glass of wine.'

His father walked over to the drinks' cabinet, poured the wine, and handed him the glass. 'Tonight, we're drinking a *Château Rayas*. It is listed as one of the 12 red wines one simply *must* drink before one dies. I am not one to talk about money but, my son, this is not cheap.'

Steve was becoming more and more suspicious. It was not like his parents to be this jolly and it had been years since he had seen his father pour a drink for someone other than himself.

The atmosphere in the room was as pompous as the room itself. Steve never understood why someone wanted to live in a room that looked like a museum. The furniture was mostly antique in a Louis XV Rococo style. The large ornate French dresser displayed a series of Italian crystal vases. As a child, Steve always hated this room and remembered one specific episode:

> *'Steven, you silly child, what have you done?'* Steve stood frozen on the spot and looked up at his mother's angry face.
>
> *'Have you got any idea what I paid for that antique plate?'*
>
> *'No,'* Steve said, almost inaudible.
>
> *'Speak up. I can't hear you when you mumble.'*
>
> *'I'm sorry mother. It was an accident.'*
>
> *'That is the problem with you. Everything is an accident. You are the clumsiest child ever.'*

'I am so sorry, mother. Please don't be angry,' he said, tears running down his face.
'Go away, Steven. I can't stand to look at you.'

She didn't speak to him for two weeks after the unfortunate episode. Although he did appreciate the beautiful antiques in the room, he never felt comfortable in the room again after that incident. He also made sure he only bought furniture or dishes he would not care if they broke.

***

'We were just discussing the enchanted travels of Annabel, Steven.' Steven snapped out of his thoughts when he heard his name. 'She has just returned from a year-long journey around the world,' his mother continued pretentiously.

'Steven loves to travel. He was particularly taken by Rome. Did you spend any time in Rome?' Dr. Patterson asked Annabel.

'I did,' she said. 'It is a most wonderful city; a bit manic for my liking but the museums, art galleries, and charming little back streets more than make up for that. I stayed for about six weeks, but I'm sure I still have not seen half of its treasures.' Annabel spoke with a very proper, almost aristocratic, accent. 'How long did you stay in Rome?' she asked Steve.

'For about three weeks; when I was twenty-two.'

'How wonderful,' Annabel shrieked. 'Were did you stay?'

'I stayed with a friend in Trastevere.'

'How quaint. I adore Trastevere.'

Steve smiled. *What an appalling woman,* he thought; *so phony. No wonder his mother thought she was great.*

'You should introduce Annabel to some of your friends.

She has been away for so long that some new friends might be in order,' Marlene interrupted. 'Maybe you can show her some of the wonderful new restaurants that have opened in town.'

The penny finally dropped. His mother was trying to set him up with this woman. *How was he going to get out of this one?* His mind was racing. His mother was not about to give up and kept looking at him, waiting for a response. Steve knew he was cornered. 'Yes. I would love to show Annabel some new, exciting places to eat. However, I'm not very well informed.' He looked to Daulton. 'Daulton, you should show Annabel some trendy fresh places. You are far more aware of what's going on.' Steven saw his mother fume with anger.

As soon as she realized people were looking at her, she changed her expression and continued, 'Well, Annabel, I'm sure that one of my sons, if not both, will take you under their wing.' Annabel smiled politely. As arrogant as she was, she was oblivious to the fact that Steve had turned her down.

The rest of the evening was torture for Steve. His mother had worked her charm and placed him next to Annabel at the dinner table. She bored Steve with her travel stories, which were no more than consecutive stays at 5-star hotels and visits to exclusive restaurants. She had not experienced anything real in any of the countries she visited.

She should have stayed home, Steve thought, as she talked about the delights of Paris. All she had to do was buy a slide show of all the famous sites and she would have the same information.

'I'm sorry everyone, but I have a very early start tomorrow,' Steve said and got up. His mother accompanied him to the door and, while one of the staff retrieved his coat, she expressed her frustration.

'Steven, Annabel is a fantastic girl. Her family is very well respected. I went through all this trouble to organize a meeting so you two could meet and you act ungrateful.'

Steve looked at his mother, surprised. 'Mother, I have not asked you to organize anything. Also, I'm quite capable of finding own dates.'

'Are you really? I have never seen any proof of that.'

Steve kissed his mother on the cheek and decided not to argue with her. He learned early on in life that arguing with his mother was useless. He understood that she made it her mission to find him a suitable partner. He was surprised; however, she wasn't more focused on Daulton. Daulton was so much more 'sellable' than he was.

As Steve stepped out of the house into the fresh air, he let out a deep sigh. He knew this wasn't the end. Marlene was not a woman who gave up easily. Steve knew he would meet Annabel several times more.

10

Seeing Eric

Marlene Patterson was having breakfast. She waited patiently for Matthew to join her. She needed to speak with him. The breakfast room was at the back of the house. The enormous French doors overlooked the well-maintained back garden. The room was never used for guests. Whenever they accommodated visitors overnight, which was rarely, they served breakfast in the impressively large dining room.

'Bring me another pot of coffee,' Marlene ordered the new maid she hired two weeks ago.

'Certainly, madam. Immediately.'

Marlene liked all her maids. They were submissive and never argued about living conditions or money. She had gone through a string of maids in the past who would argue for increased wages or larger accommodations. Some of them even tried to argue about how she should run her household. Marlene would not tolerate a maid with an opinion. She released them on the spot. This new maid brought her a pot of coffee, avoiding eye contact with Marlene.

Matthew finally came to breakfast and took a seat without greeting his wife. Marlene followed her husband closely with her eyes. She allowed him a sip of juice first before speaking with him. As they both sat in silence, the maid brought Matthew's breakfast. Obsessed with health and his diet, he only ate fresh fruit in the morning. Like Marlene, Matthew didn't acknowledge the maid and started eating.

'Matthew, we need to do something about Steven. It's obvious he has no immediate interest in Annabel, which I am sure has to do with that dreadful Eva Williams.'

'What do you suggest we do?' Matthew asked, annoyed.

'I was hoping you could come up with some suggestions. He's your son too. I think there's more at stake for you than for me.' Marlene replied calmly, but her voice was threatening. Matthew looked up at his wife and sighed heavily. 'You can't expect me to take care of this all by myself.' Marlene gave Matthew a cold smile. 'Besides, if it wasn't for me, you wouldn't even know he was seeing that common girl.'

'I see. What can I do? Maybe I can send him to the country home with the excuse that work there needs overseeing. At least he would be gone for a few weeks, and maybe forget about her,' Matthew suggested.

'Whatever you can do to stop this relationship at once.' Marlene poured herself another black coffee, which was probably all she would have that day. 'We have worked too hard and have sacrificed too much to let her spoil things for us,' she said.

That, Matthew agreed on. He looked at his wife. No matter how much he wanted to live without her, he also realized that without her, he would have never achieved the fame and fortune he had.

'Apropos,' Marlene said. 'I'm meeting with Eric this afternoon.'

Matthew gave Marlene his warmest possible smile and stood up. 'I will speak with Steven today. Give my regards to Eric.'

Marlene nodded as her husband left the room. She sat back and looked around. She thought back to the days when she competed in beauty contests. The day Marlene realized she was beautiful; she made it her mission to snag a rich husband, or at least a husband with great potential. Marlene worked hard to get to where she was now. There was no way she would let Eva Williams destroy it. Eva Williams would be stopped no matter what.

***

Christine was feeling better. Several weeks had passed since Eric so brutally dumped her. She even began eating again. During the first weeks after the break-up, she wasn't able to eat and lost fourteen pounds. Her clothes were far too big, and she thought it was time for some new outfits.

Christine wanted to shop after work. She liked to shop alone, that way she didn't end up buying something she didn't feel comfortable in or follow others into shops she didn't like. She thought that one of the large department stores would be an excellent place to start.

The National Art Library where she worked was near Knightsbridge, a short stroll to the shops. As she stepped outside the large, modern building, the sun was out. It was a beautiful spring day and she looked forward to her walk. As she passed an ice cream van, she decided to treat herself.

'I'll have a cone with chocolate, please.'

'You can add another flavour,' the ice cream man said, uninterested

'No, thank you. I don't like to mix anything with chocolate. It's perfect on its own.'

'Whatever,' the ice cream man replied. He didn't care about her preferences and handed her the cone. As she walked to the shops, she realized she was humming a song she had heard on the radio earlier that day. For the first time in weeks, she felt good.

She purchased several skirts, tops, and trousers and decided she needed new shoes to go with all these beautiful outfits. She walked out of the department store and made her way to a small shoe shop that was hidden in one of the narrow side streets.

As she entered the shop, she was pleasantly overwhelmed with the aroma of new leather. The shop was cosy but didn't feel cramped. There were many shoes and boots displayed on large dark solid wooden tables that were partially covered with luxurious coloured fabrics.

Immediately, Christine's eyes were drawn to a pair of red leather boots. The red was a warm cherry, and the leather had a slight motif of leaves. She just knew those lovely red boots were calling her as she walked up to them in a trance.

'Hello, my beauties,' she said and picked up one of the boots. The leather was soft and supple. She looked under the boots and saw it was her size. She almost skipped over to the luxurious dark purple sofa to try them on. As she slipped in, she could barely feel the boots on her feet. They fit like a glove – so to speak. It was as though they were made for her. Before looking in the mirror, she already knew she had to buy them, no matter the price. A sales assistant, who noticed her eager face, walked over to her.

'Aren't they wonderful? They arrived only yesterday.'

'They are dreamy,' Christine replied without taking her eyes off the boots. 'Not my usual style, but I love them.'

'They make a statement,' the sales assistant replied.

'I'll take them,' she said with a big smile. 'I would also like to have a look at the other shoes.'

The sales assistant treated her like a princess. He was already counting his commission. Christine bought two more pairs of shoes, ones less obvious and more her style. One was a pair of elegant black leather open-toed shoes with a patent finish and the other, a brown leather shoe with wedge heels.

'Goodbye, Ms. Rhodes.' The sales assistant read her name on her credit card. 'Hope to see you again soon.' She felt like a Hollywood socialite when she left the store draped with bags filled with clothes and shoes.

She walked to the Knightsbridge underground. As she walked around the corner onto the main road, her heart stopped. Eric was standing on the other side of the road. It was obvious he was waiting for someone, as he kept checking his watch and hopped impatiently from one leg to the other.

He must have spotted the person he was about to meet, as his face lit up. Christine followed the direction of his eyes and was shocked to see Marlene Patterson walk towards him. Eric kissed Marlene on both cheeks and haled a taxi. They were speaking like old friends. She saw Marlene laugh at something Eric said. A taxi pulled over. Eric opened the door and followed Marlene inside.

Christine stood cold, unable to move. It was difficult to see him for the first time after their break-up. It was as though the world around her didn't exist. She didn't hear any of the noises around her and was unaware of the people passing her. She snapped out of her trance when someone pushed into her. Christine walked to the side and rested against the wall.

'Are you alright?' a lady with large sunglasses and a bright orange trench coat asked. 'You look like you've seen a ghost.'

'Yes, thank you.' Christine smiled at the lady's choice of words. 'I'm fine. Just a bit light-headed.'

'If you say so.' The lady walked away and looked back once more to check on Christine.

Christine rested her head against the building for another couple of minutes to get her breathing under control. She knew she had to see him sooner or later. She just wished she could have been more prepared.

When she felt calmer, she picked up her shopping bags and walked into the park and headed toward the library. Once in the park, she found herself an empty bench and took a seat. She thought about what she had just seen. Eric and Marlene...?

***

'Well, well. Someone had a good day,' Eva said when she saw Christine coming through the living room door looking like a packing donkey. 'Let me help you with that.'

'Thanks, Eva. I never knew shopping could be so tiresome.'

'It's not the shopping,' Eva replied. 'It's getting the darn bags home.' Eva was standing with her hands in on her hips. She had to contain herself not to open all the bags. Christine saw the look on her face and took out her red boots. She was glowing with pride as she held them up.

'These are not just boots; these are my children.'

'Whoa! Those are something else! You have to let me borrow them one day.'

'Maybe you can babysit them when they are a bit older. For now, they have to stay with their mummy,' Christine said and hugged one of the boots. 'The funniest thing happened. I saw Eric in town today.'

'That's not funny. That's scary.'

Christine ignored her remark and continued telling Eva how she had seen him on the corner of Main Street waiting for someone.

'And..?'

'Turned out he was waiting for Marlene Patterson.'

'Marlene Patterson? Are you kidding?' Eva said with a doubtful face.

'I'm not. I'm 100% sure. The strange thing is, I don't remember ever introducing them. Eric never wanted to come along when we were invited at the Patterson's and he never mentioned he knew Marlene. Don't you think that's a bit odd?'

'Well, maybe they met after the break-up.'

'I don't think so. Marlene doesn't seem the type of person who would be all chummy with someone of Eric's social standing.'

'What do you mean, chummy?' Eva asked.

'When they met, they kissed each other on the cheek and Marlene laughed out loud at something Eric said. Marlene Patterson needs to know someone well to do that, or someone must be particularly important. I don't think that in two weeks, Marlene gets friendly with anyone. The woman has a busier schedule than the queen of England.'

They both sat in silence for several minutes. Eva thought about Marlene and Eric. She had to admit she never expected those two together. Surely, they must have met after Eric broke up with Christine. But no matter how she looked at it, it made absolutely no sense.

'I want to show you what else I bought,' Christine said enthusiastically.

'Great. Let me see what else I can borrow besides the boots!' Eva giggled…

After Christine showed Eva all her new purchases, she walked into her bedroom and started to hang up her new clothes. While she was unpacking, she thought about Eric. Somehow, he had always been too good to be true.

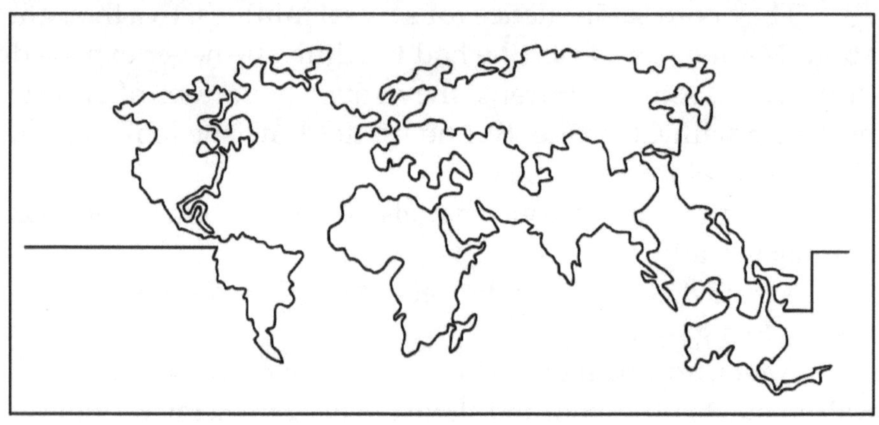

11

The Summer House

Steve was waiting for Eva in what had become their favourite Chinese restaurant. He admired her as she came through the door wearing a simple pair of cream trousers and a cream top. The large, dark-brown leather belt that was hanging around her hips matched her handbag. Her long, brown, abundantly curly hair framed her radiant face. She walked up to the table and kissed him on the mouth.

'Hello, beautiful,' he said and kissed her back.

She took a seat across the table and immediately picked up the menu. 'I'm not sure why I'm looking at the menu. We always order the same thing,' she said.

'Why ruin a good thing.'

'You're right.' She looked around and waved at one of the waiters. After they placed their order, Eva put her hand on Steve's. 'I'm so happy you invited me to have lunch out of the office. I was bored stiff. Some days I really like my job, and other days I feel like jumping out the window.' She took a large sip from the Chinese Tsingtao beer and licked her lips contently. 'How was dinner the other night at your parents?'

'*Bo*-ring,' he said. 'My mother tried to load the daughter of one of her friends on me.'

'Really?' Eva was all ears. 'Who is she?'

'Her name is Annabel Malmesbury. She has been

traveling the world. And when I say traveling, I mean going from one 5-star hotel to the next. My mother wants me to introduce her to my friends.'

'Maybe you should introduce her to me,' Eva said half-jokingly, half-seriously.

'Well, well, isn't this interesting, Ms. Williams. I didn't know you were the jealous type.'

'I am not jealous. I'm a friend, aren't I?'

'You are more than a friend, and you know it,' Steve said and squeezed her hand,

'Do I?' Eva looked in Steve's eyes, feeling herself getting all tingly. *My*, she thought, *I adore him*. She let go of his hand when the waitress placed the bamboo baskets filled with delicious dim-sum on their table.

'Saved by the bell,' she said with a big smile, showing off her perfect teeth.

They ate their lunch in silence. Both of them dug in as though they hadn't eaten anything in days. After several servings, Eva put her chopsticks down and placed her hands on her stomach. 'I'm never eating again.'

'I've heard that before. I'll finish the last pieces,' Steve said, already emptying all the baskets on his plate. 'It would be a shame to let it go to waste.'

As soon as Steve emptied the baskets, the waitress appeared and cleared all the baskets and Eva's plate.

'This is what I love about the Chinese,' Steve said, chewing. 'You pick up the last piece and before you can put it in your mouth, they clear dishes.'

When he finished, he picked up one of the steamed cloths. 'I need to leave town for a couple of weeks,' he said as he wiped his hands.

'Where are you going?'

'My parents need me to go to our country home. Some builders are coming to replace parts of the roof of the boat house.'

'Why do you need to go there? Don't they have staff for that?'

'Usually they do, but this time my father wants a member of our family to be there to oversee the work.' Steve threw the cloth back in the basket. 'Since I'm the only one who can work from home, I guess that family member is me. It will hopefully only be for a couple of weeks.'

'Your parents are odd. What on earth do you know about roofing? With all the staff they have, they need their son to leave his business to oversee work he doesn't know anything about?' Eva had a *what's-that-all-about* look on her face.

She didn't like what she was hearing. First, Steve was introduced to another girl, and now this. It was apparent that Marlene was behind this.

'Don't get mad. You can come and visit me for a couple of days,' Steve said. 'The weather is beautiful, and the house is big enough.'

'I could.... couldn't I?' she said, tilting her head to one side.

Steve picked up her hand and kissed it.

'That's settled then. I was dreading being there by myself all that time. The house is just too big for one person. There are six bedrooms and that's only in the main house.'

Eva's eyes got bigger. 'Can Chris come too? She would love it so. That way, when you need to supervise the builders, I won't get bored and Chris will have a well-deserved break.'

'I think that's a wonderful idea. I always dreamed of going on holiday with two women.'

'You calm down,' Eva said and slapped him on the head.

Eva walked into the apartment, shouting Christine's name.

'I'm in the bath,' Christine yelled back.

'Can I come in?'

'If you must.' Eva enjoyed the soothing scent of lavender that filled the room as she walked in. Christine was sitting in a sea of bubble bath. 'What is so important it couldn't wait for ten minutes?' she asked.

'Can you take some days off work next week?'

Christine couldn't help but smile when she saw Eva's happy, excited face. 'Maybe…depends what for?'

'Steve needs to go to the Patterson's country home to supervise the works there and we can go with him. We've seen a photo of it, remember? We can soak up the first spring rays of sun and take long walks in the forest.'

'Are you sure you want me to come along? I don't want to be a third wheel,' Christine said.

'Are you kidding me? Steve will be working, and we can pretend to be ladies of leisure. Please. Pretty, please,' Eva pleaded. 'We haven't left town for years.'

'Okay,' Christine said, 'But please check with Steve to make sure he is okay with it.'

'I already did,' Eva said smugly, 'and he loved the idea. He is organizing our travel passes as we speak.'

***

They put their suitcases in the back of their bright yellow rental car. All rentals were bright yellow. This made them recognizable. 'Country home, here we come!' Eva shouted out the window.

Christine brought one of her favourite tapes along. Their car only had an old cassette player. Neither of them felt the need to replace it. Sometimes the tapes stuck, and they had to force them out with a knife. They learned to treat the cassette player with great caution.

Christine took the tape out of her bag and pushed it carefully into the player. Tom Petty's, *Into the Great Wide Open,* blasted out of the speakers. They knew all the words to the song and sang along loudly. They hit the motorway out of town quickly and Christine sat relaxed behind the steering wheel. She felt good. And for the first time since Eric left her, she felt optimistic about the future.

Eva looked forward to seeing Steve again. He had left the week before and, although he phoned her every day, she couldn't wait to see him. She wanted to feel his warm kisses and feel his strong arms around her.

'Looking forward to seeing Steve?' Christine asked.

'Are you reading my mind? I was thinking about him.'

'You two make a wonderful couple.'

'I think so too,' Eva said. 'I've never met anyone like him. He treats me like a princess and I never have to pretend to be something I'm not. Even if I say or do something idiotic, he still loves me.'

'Love. Aaah,' Christine teased.

'Well, we haven't used the L-word yet but, for me, it is. Somehow it feels right.'

'I am pleased for you,' Christine replied. 'Love is a wonderful thing.'

'I'm sorry, Christine. This must be hard for you.'

'Sometimes it is…but I'm feeling better. And just because I was hurt, that doesn't mean you can't be happy.' Christine turned her head toward Eva and smiled.

'Thanks,' Eva said softly. She looked out the window at the beautiful countryside passing by. The rolling hills were lusciously green. Suddenly, she felt a sense of insecurity. Her life was perfect at the moment. She felt scared it would all be taken away from her. She tried to shake off this horrible feeling and changed the tape to *Saturday Night Fever*. A bit of disco always cheered her up. Christine smiled at her and, on queue, both girls started to make the up and down arm movements.

***

79

They arrived at the country home in the Cotswold's late that afternoon. There was a sign by the road saying 'Beatus Vista,' Latin for 'Beautiful View.'

They drove up just as the sun was going down. The sky was starting to turn a warm orange. The house was Georgian with spectacular views. There were extensive ranges of traditional stone barns around a courtyard.

They parked the car in front of the house and opened the trunk to get their luggage.

Steve came running from behind the house. 'Hi. Welcome,' he shouted from a distance.

Both Christine and Eva looked up and waved at him. 'Did you find the house okay?' he asked and walked over to kiss Eva. She was glowing with happiness.

'Hi Christine,' Steve said and kissed her on the cheek. 'I'm thrilled you're here. I'm sure you'll love it. This is the best time of the year to come here.' He picked up both suitcases. 'Beautiful days, cold evenings and, best of all, not a tourist in sight. Come,' he said, 'I'll give you a tour of the house.'

Christine and Eva stood for a minute, taking in the sight of the beautiful house and the surroundings. 'Dear, oh dear,' Christine said, 'this is amazing.'

They ran to catch up with Steve, who was opening the front door. As they walked in, they couldn't believe their eyes. The house looked traditional outside, but the inside had been totally refurbished. The home had three reception rooms, which were all tastefully decorated, and all had great views through large windows. All three rooms had fireplaces, which made them look very inviting. The open-plan kitchen had an enormous island and a comfortable breakfast room. The room had bi-fold doors opening onto a romantic terrace.

'Your parents must come here a lot,' Eva remarked to Steve.

'You would think so, but they hardly visit anymore. We used to come here when Daulton and I were boys. I think we came regularly up to the age of ten. After that, we visited only when the city became too hot for my mother.'

'What a pity,' Christine said. 'What a shame to leave this property unattended.'

'Well, there are Mr. and Mrs. Theakston. They have been the caretakers ever since I can remember. They live in one of the cottages further along.'

'Come,' Steve said, 'I'll show you the bedrooms. On the first floor, the master bedroom has an in-suite bathroom and dressing room. There are four more bedrooms on the first floor and three bathrooms. The second floor has a large attic room, which is where Daulton and I used to play when it rained.'

Eva squeezed Christine's hand as they walked to one of the two large wooden stairs into the hall leading to the bedrooms. Christine smiled and squeezed back.

'Here's your room, Christine. Mrs. Theakston prepared it today,' Steve said as he walked into a large, beautiful bedroom overlooking the hills and the stream at the end of the property.

'Whoa! This is amazing,' Christine said to Steve. There was a lovely birch and leather bed with an enormous headboard. The bed was large enough for at least three people to sleep comfortably. As she stepped on the carpet, her shoes sunk into it. She couldn't wait to take off her shoes. Beside the bed was a matching dresser with a large wooden mirror hanging over it. Two beautiful leather chairs with ottoman footrests were placed perfectly in front of the window to take in views of the lake.

'Over here is the bathroom,' Steve said and opened a door next to her bedroom.

Christine followed Steve into the bathroom. The bathroom was painted a warm yellow and had a freestanding antique bath, which was again placed to enjoy the views towards the hills through a large window. The floor was marble and matched the top of the vanity unit. There were stacks of fluffy towels and an inviting bathrobe. Christine was speechless.

'I'll show you to your room now.' Steve winked at Eva.

'Okay.' She felt like a little girl in a toyshop and followed him, almost skipping.

'Okay, princess,' he said when they arrived at the other end of the hall. 'This is your boudoir.'

Eva clapped her hands in excitement! She was without words when she walked into the large master bedroom. 'Steve, this is beautiful! I have never slept in a four-poster bed,' she said, as she slid her hands over the soft, deep red linens. To the left, was a fireplace covered in natural stone. Eva walked around the room, opening all the doors. Her room also had a balcony overlooking the lake.

'There's a *dressing room*?' She couldn't stop herself from giggling. This was the most fantastic place she had ever seen.

She walked to the next door and opened it. It connected to the adjacent bedroom. She quickly closed it and moved on to the next door, the bathroom. The bathroom had a Jacuzzi in the middle of the room, a separate shower room, and an enormous vanity unit with 'his and hers' sinks.

'I love this house,' Eva said to Steve. 'This bedroom is amazing.'

Steve took her in his arms. 'I'm glad you like it, as I intend to spend some considerable time with you here.'

'What are you saying, Mr. Patterson?' Eva said with big eyes. 'Are you suggesting I share this room with you?'

Steve laughed and kissed her passionately. He looked at her and stroked her hair. 'I love you,' Eva blurred out. Sensing herself blushing, she tried to walk away, but he pulled her back.

'I love you, too,' he said and kissed her again.

Eva felt dizzy. This was too much to take in. The man of her dreams told her he loves her, the beautiful house, and the stunning surroundings. She could feel her knees getting weak.

'I think I need to sit down.' While she walked over to one of the chairs to sit down, he smacked her bottom.

'Aaaah,' she laughed….

'I need to go into town for more supplies for the builders,' Steve said. 'Feel free to explore the house and the grounds.'

'Will you be long?'

'Only about an hour, I think. See you later.' Steve kissed her softly on her lips.

12

Settling In

After she unpacked, Eva knocked on Christine's door. She walked in and jumped on the bed next to Christine.

'Isn't this something? I can't believe we're here. Look at this view.'

'It is stunning,' Eva said. For a moment, they laid next to each other, just looking out the window. The last rays of sun for the day disappeared. Eva looked at Christine and gave a mischievous smile. 'Shall we explore the rest of the house? Steve went into town for supplies for the builders. We can sneak around and open all the cupboards.'

'You are wicked. But I like it.' Christine jumped off the bed and put on her shoes.

'Let's go, Sherlock.' Eva grabbed Christine by the arm. They opened all the doors on the landing. There were four more bedrooms, all in-suite. Though all the rooms were gorgeous, it was evident that Steve had given them the best rooms in the house.

They walked into the living room and let themselves flop on the two leather chairs in front of the fireplace. Both chairs were covered with soft leather and two matching ottomans sat in front of them.

They got up and walked past the large dining room table surrounded by twelve arch-back hickory armchairs and proceeded into the kitchen.

Things seemed like they were untouched and made the girls think that when Dr. and Mrs. Patterson came to the house, they had no intention of spending any time in there.

'Let's go outside,' Eva said and opened the large French doors leading to the patio.

'Oh my! Look at this!' Eva shouted. 'There's even a fireplace outside. This is amazing.'

'Fantastic! Maybe we can eat here this evening,' Christine suggested.

They took a seat on one of the teak benches. 'They say money doesn't bring happiness, but this would sure keep me smiling,' Eva said.

'I don't understand why Dr. and Mrs. Patterson don't come here more often.'

Eva shrugged her shoulders. At this moment, she couldn't care less about the Patterson's. 'Let's have a look and see if there's any wine in this house.' Eva jumped up and walked inside.

Christine was taking in the scenery. She felt peaceful and was happy she decided to come along.

Eva found a bottle of red wine and, as they were sipping their wine, they heard a car pull up and a dog barking.

'Who's that?' Christine asked

'How should I know,' Eva shrugged her shoulders and poured another glass of wine.

Christine stood up to have a look when a happy Golden Retriever came running around the corner. The dog was wagging his tail so hard his entire body was shaking.

'Come here, doggie,' Christine called him. Without hesitation, he jumped on top of her; nearly knocking over the wine.

'Max, come here!' They heard a man's voice. 'Sorry, ladies. He loves attention,' the man shouted as he walked to the house.

'No problem. He's lovely,' Christine yelled back.

As the man came closer to the house, he suddenly stopped in his tracks. 'I don't believe it,' he whispered. He had a strange look of shock and surprise on his face. Christine and Eva looked at the man and then looked over their shoulders toward the house, expecting to see someone behind them.

'Harry, I see you've met Eva and Christine,' Steve said. The man was still standing frozen on the spot. 'Harry?' Steve asked. 'You okay?'

Harry snapped out of it. He walked up to the girls and shook their hands. 'Very nice to meet you both,' he said. He looked at them for a couple of seconds, then turned around abruptly and walked away.

'What was that all about? Did you see how he looked at us?'

'I did. What a strange man.' Eva said

'Harry?' Steve interrupted. 'No way. He's a great guy. He has been with us since he was eighteen years old. I've known him all my life.'

***

'Steven, it's your mother.' Marlene was sitting in her sun-drenched Victorian conservatory; the room that had been featured in a variety of magazines. Marlene loved showing off her wealth. Rather than sitting on one of the relaxing, large, comfortable chairs, Marlene sat on a dining chair. She couldn't stand creasing her clothes.

'Good morning, mother,' Steve replied, somewhat surprised by his mother's telephone call. His mother rarely phoned him.

'How are the works progressing at the country home?'

'Very well. Harry has everything under control.' He was somewhat puzzled by his mother's interest in any of the works done to the country home.

'Oh, good. How is Harry?' she asked, with false interest.

'Very well.'

'I hope you're not getting too bored by yourself. I spoke with Annabel Malmesbury last night. She phoned to thank me for dinner; such a wonderful and sophisticated young woman. I suggested she drive up to the house and visit you. After all, the weather is marvellous, and she would enjoy the scenery.'

Steve sighed. So, this was his mother's plan. 'Mother, I am sorry, but I have already invited Eva and Christine.'

'You did *what*?'

'I invited Eva and Christine.'

'Well, I'm afraid you will have to cancel their visit.'

'It's a little late for that, mother. They're already here.'

'You do understand that the country home is *not* a hotel. I do not appreciate having strangers in my holiday home.'

'Mother, please. First of all, Eva and Christine are hardly strangers. You have known them much longer than Annabel Malmesbury. And, secondly, you never spend any time here. So, what difference does it make?' Steve said.

'The property is mine. I, *not you*, I decide who visits,' Marlene continued.

'Well, as I said, mother, they are already here. I'm not going to send them away. What is your problem with Eva and Christine anyway? You are the one who always invites them to *your* house.'

'As I said to you before Steven, I decide what I do with my properties. When you have your property, you can invite whomever you please.'

'I think you are unreasonable. Eva and Christine will stay here until Sunday,' Steve said, decisively. 'If you'll excuse me, mother, Harry needs help with the roofing. I'll speak to you when I'm back in town.'

Steve put the phone down and shook his head, sometimes his mother was unbearable.

Marlene stared at the telephone. Did her son hang up on her? She was furious. She dialled her husband's private line into the practice.

'I'm with a patient,' he answered.

'I don't care, Matthew. I need to speak with you *now*.' She heard Matthew excusing himself to his patient. A few seconds later, he picked up the call from another room in the practice.

'What is so urgent that couldn't wait fifteen minutes, Marlene?'

'Steven has invited Eva Williams and Christine Rhodes up to the country home.' Marlene spoke fast in a shallow voice. It was apparent to Matthew she was about to explode.

'Well, did you tell him that is unacceptable?'

'Of course, I did. But they are already there. They arrived last night and will stay until Sunday. That boy is really out of control. I told you we should have kept a closer eye on him growing up. He has always been a loose cannon. We should have never let him quit medical school. *You* have always spoiled him too much. You should have cut him off financially when he was young.'

'Oh, so now it's entirely my fault. Let me remind you that he is your son too and, furthermore, do you think he would have listened to me?' Matthew could feel the anger building inside him. This was her territory. He never wanted to be involved in the upbringing of their children. When they decided to have children, he made this very clear to Marlene. He would provide the finances for any number of staff and nannies Marlene needed and pay for the best schools. The rest was up to her. 'I think we should let it rest. If we interfere more, Steven may become more obstinate. Now, if there is nothing else Marlene, I have patients.'

After putting the phone down, he pulled his hand through his thick grey hair. He had to have words with Marlene this evening. He didn't care how she did it, but she had to sort that boy out.

***

Eva and Christine both slept in the following morning and were awakened by the sun streaming through their bedroom windows around ten o'clock. Eva looked around and stretched her body like a cat. She got up and walked into the beautiful bathroom. The whirlpool looked very inviting, but she desperately needed a large cup of coffee. She was unable to do anything without caffeine. She put on a pair of jeans and a light blue shirt, picked up a cream-coloured jumper and put it around her waist. She walked to Christine's room and knocked on the door. There was no answer. She opened the door and looked inside. The bed was empty and neatly made. Eva smiled. Christine was so proper. She walked downstairs and spotted Christine sitting on the patio with a big mug of coffee. 'Morning. Have you been up long?'

'No, about twenty minutes. There's coffee in the kitchen.'

'*Coffee*. The magic word.'

When she came back with a large mug of steaming hot coffee, Christine had put her legs on the table and was snuggled into the large wicker chair.

'Isn't it wonderful waking up here? I could never get tired of this view,' Christine said

'It is exceptional.'

Out of nowhere, Max came hurdling towards them. It looked like he wasn't going to stop. Both girls let out a scream. They both laughed out loud when the dog came to an abrupt stand-still just in front of them.

Eva made the same mistake Christine had made and called the dog. He jumped up next to her on the small sofa. He licked her face and Eva giggled like a little girl. 'Stop kissing me. I already have a boyfriend,' she said as she tried

90

to push the dog off her.

'What a sweetheart,' Christine said, laughing at the fuss the dog was making.

'Try kissing him.'

'Max,' they heard Harry call the dog from a distance.

'It's okay, Harry. He's with us,' Christine shouted back.

Harry came running to the house. 'I'm so sorry. Max is a bit of a ladies' man.' Both girls smiled at his remark. 'I'm sorry if I made you feel uncomfortable yesterday. It's just that you look like someone I used to know,' Harry said apologetically.

Christine and Eva both waved his apology away. 'Can Max stay with us? We'll be going for a walk in a while. Maybe Max can be our guide?' Eva asked.

'Okay, but if he gets to be too much let me know and I will put him on the lead. Have a nice day.' Harry gave them a warm smile and walked away.

'Well, at least your boss knew he was acting very strangely,' Eva said to the dog.

13

The Cabin

Steve told the girls about the path through the hills. After they had their coffee, they went for a walk. Max, obviously aware something was going on, was barking with anticipation of what was to come. Together, they walked along the beautiful path.

'I'm really sorry to bring it up again, but were you absolutely honest about taking the sleeping pills by mistake?' Eva asked.

Christine stopped and looked out over the lake. 'I really had no idea that those pills were so strong. I think I took five or six, and not even at the same time. Maybe it was the wine. I'm just incredibly lucky that Dr. Patterson came by.'

'I'm so sorry I went to stay over at Steve's. I'll never forgive myself for that.'

'Don't worry about it,' Christine reassured her. 'I'm fine now.'

'Yes. Thank God for that. Talking about Dr. Patterson, I suppose the man does have a purpose,' Eva concluded.

Christine smiled and said nothing for a while. 'There is something else that bothered me afterwards. How did he get into our house?'

Eva stopped and looked at Christine. She never thought about that. 'Maybe I left the door open?' She was desperately trying to remember.

'No, you didn't. I clearly remember locking the door. I have many flaws but forgetting to lock the door isn't one of them.'

'So how did he get into the house?' Eva asked.

Christine shrugged her shoulders. 'Dr. Patterson did find us the apartment, remember. Maybe he kept one of the keys when we moved in.'

'Don't be silly. That's the creepiest thing I've ever heard.'

'We were only eighteen. Maybe he felt we were very young and wanted to keep an eye on us. But he should have told us. Let's make sure we change the locks when we get back. I don't like the idea that he can just come into our apartment when he pleases,' Christine said.

'My, maybe he has even gone through our drawers!'

'Sure. He comes over regularly to check on your underwear,' Christine said and laughed out loud.

'Gross. Stop it.' Eva stuck out her tongue in disgust.

***

Christine and Eva spent most of the day walking and playing in the garden with Max. They enjoyed the feeling of being outside all day. They found some magazines in the house and decided to play their game, Chaser Blazer. And, after Steve made them dinner on the grill and two bottles of wine later, all three were yawning. Christine looked at her watch; it was only half past nine. 'I know it's early, but I am shattered. I'm going to sleep,' she said.

'I don't think we'll be far behind,' Eva said. She got up and gave Christine a kiss on the cheek.

'Goodnight, Steve.'

'Night, Chris. Sleep well.'

Eva and Steve stayed on the patio in front of the

fireplace. She was comfortable in his arms, staring at the fire. She felt extremely happy and relaxed. After half an hour, Steve asked if she wanted to go to sleep. She nodded, almost relieved.

After they brushed their teeth, they laid in bed just looking at each other for about five minutes. They were both very tired and fell……

***

During the night, Eva and Steve woke suddenly. They heard a shocking scream coming from Christine's bedroom. Steve jumped out of bed in a panic. Eva also jumped out of bed and was already out of the door. Christine was sitting on the side of the bed. She looked like a little girl. She was tall but the bed was so high her feet didn't reach the floor.

'You okay?' Eva asked and put her arms around her.

'I don't understand. I took a sleeping pill this evening. It shouldn't happen with the new sleeping pills. It *can't* happen. What am I going to do now?' Christine said through her tears.

'What happened?' Steve asked dazed and confused.

'Nothing, just a nightmare,' Eva said without taking her eyes off Christine. 'Can you get Chris a glass of water?'

He nodded. He came out of the bathroom and handed Christine the glass. She smiled almost apologetically.

'Go back to bed, Steve. I'll be there in a minute.'

Christine took a deep breath and told Eva she was feeling better. 'I'll need to speak to Dr. Patterson again,' she said.

'It happened to me the other night,' Eva said. 'I was at Steve's the night you…well you know what.'

'Really? And you'd taken your sleeping pill?'

Eva nodded. 'I never sleep away from home without taking my pills. We both need to speak to Dr. Patterson as soon as we get back. Maybe he can prescribe something else.'

'Yes,' Christine said. 'And maybe we can ask for our key back at the same time.'

Eva laughed. 'Try to get some sleep,' she said and kissed Christine on the top of her head.

'It must be something in the water,' Steve said when Eva walked back into the room.

'What's in the water?'

'Well, both of you are suffering from severe nightmares.'

'Must be.' Eva didn't want to talk about it and crawled back into bed. She turned off the light and snuck into Steve's arms. She felt nervous about going to sleep herself and, although she took another sleeping pill, it took her a long time to fall back into a restless sleep.

***

'Why don't you explore the grounds this afternoon?' Steve suggested to Eva and Christine. They finished lunch and were sitting on the patio enjoying the view. 'There is a great guest cabin and behind the garage is a path that leads you there. I'll leave a set of keys. That way, you can rest and enjoy the fantastic view from higher up.'

Christine looked at Eva. She couldn't really hike very far. 'Is it a long walk?' she asked.

'No. It's only about twenty minutes.' Steve told them he would be working on the roof and if they needed him to call him on his cell phone.

'He's a great guy.'

'I know.' Eva's face turned all dreamy. 'I'm truly fortunate to have found such a great man.'

'You certainly are. If I didn't love you so much, I would be jealous.'

'You will find someone who deserves you, Christine. It's only a matter of time.'

Christine jumped up from her seat. She was ready for a

good walk.

'Let me go and put on my comfortable shoes and grab a bottle of water,' Eva said and walked into the house.

They found the path behind the garage and walked through the large forest; the cedar and willow trees towered over them. The spring flowers had emerged and covered the grounds like little carpets. After five minutes, Eva began complaining about the walk. Steve failed to mention that the twenty-minute hike led steeply up into the forest; making the hike a lot heavier than expected.

Christine tried to calm her down by telling her the walk was perfect for toning her legs and bottom. She waited for Eva, who had been huffing and puffing behind her, to catch up. 'Isn't it beautiful? Look behind you,' Christine said.

Eva looked back at the landscape. They stood and took in the stunning scenery together. Christine took a deep breath - taking in the fresh air. 'It doesn't seem real. We only live five hours from here and I feel as if I'm in a different country.'

'I never imagined it would be this beautiful,' Eva replied. She took a sip of water and continued to walk in search of the guest cottage. Christine slowly followed her up the hill, dragging herself away from the striking views. They walked on for another ten minutes when they saw the outlines of a cottage. The thatched cottage was at the top of the wooded track. From the outside, it looked like a traditional green, oak timber-framed house with a thatched roof and climbing roses.

Eva looked for the key and tried several before she found the right one. She opened the door and walked into a small living room. A natural stone fireplace took up almost one entire wall. The cabin was furnished with rustic wooden furniture. The walls were left without any decorations to display the natural beauty of the wood. As romantic as the outside looked, the inside was neglected, for what looked like, many years. A thick layer of dust was everywhere.

They made their way upstairs on the squeaking stairs into an ample open space. There was only a large desk and several filing cabinets in this upstairs.

'Someone must have used this as an office,' Eva remarked.

'Probably Dr. Patterson. Even when he was in this beautiful home in this beautiful place, he probably wanted to work.'

'Wouldn't you? If only to get away from Marlene?' Eva said.

'You'd better start liking that woman. She might become your mother-in-law and you will be forced to see her on a regular basis.'

'Are you trying to make me sick? That woman is terrible,' Eva said with a horrid expression on her face.

Christine laughed, and had a coughing fit from all the dust around. 'Imagine planning your wedding together; searching for that perfect dress. You should start getting used to calling her *mother*.' Eva put her two fingers in her mouth as if to vomit.

Christine walked over to the impressive solid cherry wood desk. It overlooked the hills. The mahogany, leather upholstered chair looked inviting and Christine sat down, ignoring the dust. 'Need any re-fill prescriptions?' she asked, impersonating Dr. Patterson. Christine swung herself around in the large chair and tried to open some of the drawers of the desk. They were all were locked. 'Dr. Patterson must have secrets,' she said. 'Why would he keep all his drawers locked in a house he never visits?'

'He must have been expecting *you*.' Eva walked over with the keys. 'Maybe one of these little keys will open the drawers?' Eva tried several keys until one turned. She looked at Christine with a crafty look on her face.

'Eva, I'm not sure we should do this.'

'*What*? You let me try all these keys and you say nothing.

Then, when I find the one that fits, you all of a sudden have a conscious? I'm opening this drawer, like it or not.'

Eva opened the drawer. It was filled with paper files. The top file was named *Santa Tecla, Chile*. Eva opened it and saw what looked like a young Dr. Patterson.

'Look at this,' she shrieked and took out a photo of a group of smiling people standing outside a building that looked like a hospital. The picture had both locals and foreigners in it.

Christine picked up the photo and looked closer. 'I'm sure this is Dr. Patterson. He must have been in his late thirties here.'

Dr. Patterson was standing one step higher over three pregnant women. He was smiling and his hands were resting on the shoulders of the woman standing in the middle. The woman had long dark brown wavy hair and a happy smile. Standing next to him was a man with heavy sunglasses and red hair that was un-kept and pointing in all directions.

'Who is this?' Eva asked, pointing at the pregnant woman. She asked this more to herself than Christine. 'Did Dr. Patterson have an affair?'

'Doesn't she look familiar?' Eva asked Christine, who nodded in agreement.

The two girls looked at each other. Christine got up, took the photo, and walked over to the window to get a better look in the sun light.

'Maybe Steve will know who she is.'

'Maybe, but then we have to tell him we broke into his father's desk.'

'Good point,' Eva said nodding slowly and lifted her eyebrows. 'Maybe there are more photos in other files.' Eva opened the other files and went through the papers.

'There's a lot of information on pregnant women in this file. I didn't know Dr. Patterson worked in gynecology in the past. Look at all these names.'

All the women had miscarriages; it carefully displayed the timelines for each. The papers were filed in chronological order, depending on when they miscarried.

'This is ridiculous,' Eva said and gestured for Christine to come over. 'It says here that a woman called Teresa Santiago miscarried at ten days. Did women really know they were pregnant at ten days? I'm sure that in those days you couldn't walk to the pharmacy to buy a pregnancy test. I thought you would have to miss a cycle first for any woman to realize she was pregnant.' Eva continued reading. 'Look at this. Here's an eighteen-year-old girl who miscarried at twelve days.'

'When was this?' Christine asked.

'Let me see.' Eva kept going through the file. 'About twenty or thirty years ago.' They heard a door slam downstairs.

'Quick! Put the files away!' Christine whispered in a panicky voice.

'*Okay, okay.*' Eva said. She threw the files back in the drawer and locked it. They both ran to the window and pretended to admire the view while trying to catch their breath

The door to the study opened. 'What are you two doing here?'

Eva turned around to see Daulton standing there. 'Hello, Daulton,' she said with a big smile on her face. Eva had always been cooler than Christine, who still couldn't bring herself to turn around. 'Steve suggested we come up here. He said it was a lovely hike. He gave us the keys to the cabin so we could rest and to enjoy the views.'

'You should go back to the main house,' Daulton said, matter-of-factly.

'Sorry, Daulton. We had no idea we weren't allowed here.' Christine finally turned around.

He gestured the girls out of the room. 'I'll drive you back

to the house.'

'There's a road?' Eva asked.

'Of course, there is. You didn't expect my father would walk up here?'

Eva looked Christine with an, *I told you so,* expression. That spoilt fart wouldn't undertake any physical exercise if it weren't necessary. She and Christine walked to Daulton's car. They felt like two naughty schoolgirls who had been told off by the headmaster. They didn't speak a word the entire drive back to the main house. The tension was agonizing, and Christine let out a sigh of relieve when she recognized the entrance road to the main house. Daulton parked his car next to their car.

'Where's Steven?'

'Not sure. I think he's with Harry,' Eva said.

'I feel awful. I feel like a trespasser,' Christine whispered when Daulton walked away.

'A trespasser, no; a thief, maybe,' Eva said and took the group photo out of her trouser pocket.

'Oh, no! Why did you take it?' Christine said and frantically looked around.

'There's something about this photo. I'm not sure what, but I want to have a good look at it at home.'

'Eva, get rid of that photo. There might be something familiar about that woman, but you have no right to take it. Also, if Dr. Patterson knows it's missing, he'll know it was us.'

'Chris, relax. Nothing happened.'

14

The Photo

Christine stopped abruptly.

'That's not true, Eva. Otherwise, you would not have taken that photo.'

'Aaaa, you see,' Eva said, pointing a finger in Christine's face, 'you feel it too.'

'Maybe there is Eva, but this is not the time to get into that. For goodness sake, we're guests at your boyfriend's home, and we've just been going through his father's desk and have stolen one of his photos.'

Eva put the photo back in her pocket and made sure she buttoned it to make sure the photo would not fall out.

Christine disappeared into her room in the hope she would not have to face Daulton. Eva sat outside on the patio, waiting for Steve. What on earth was Daulton doing here? And why did he come up to the cabin before seeing Steve? She was dying to take the photo out of her pocket and study it. She was sure she recognized other people in the photo. She tapped her feet nervously on the table in front of her. She could hear Max's excited barks. He came flying around the corner and, as usual, jumped up without stopping.

'Calm down, boy. You're going to break your neck one of these days,' she said and gave him a big hug.

Steve and Daulton walked over the carefully maintained

lawn to the house. Steve waved at her when he saw her sitting on the patio. She waved back, pleased to see him. Daulton shouted back over his shoulder to Harry to keep the dog away from the main house. Max was too excited to even pay attention to him. Eva pushed the dog off her. Max understood playtime was over and ran home.

'Harry knows better than to leave that dog loose around the house,' Daulton complained to Steve.

Steve ignored his brother and smiled at Eva. 'Did you enjoy your walk?'

'It was lovely,' Eva said excitedly. 'By the way, you could have told us there was a road leading to the cottage.'

Steve laughed, 'And keep that beautiful, healthy walk from you?'

'I do apologize for going into the cabin,' Eva said to Steve, ignoring Daulton.

'Nonsense,' Steve waved his hand. 'I gave you the keys, didn't I? There's nothing in that house other than dust and a fantastic view.'

'Father's study is there,' Daulton said. 'I don't think we should let strangers loose in there.'

'Please, Daulton. *Father's study*,' he was mimicking Daulton. 'Dad has not been here in years and, on top of that, Eva and Christine are hardly strangers.'

'It's father's property, nonetheless and, as such, his privacy should be respected,' Daulton preached.

Eva was starting to feel uneasy and told Steve she was going to her room to freshen up. She kissed him on the lips and ran upstairs.

'What are you doing here?' Steve asked Daulton without looking at his brother. 'The last time you were here you were eighteen years old. Now, all of a sudden, here you are; just when Eva and Christine happen to be here too. Did mother send you?'

'I don't owe you an explanation,' Daulton replied.

'Are you staying? I'll ask Sarah to cook for an extra person.'

'I'm staying for a couple of days. I've been working a lot lately, and I think a few days of rest will do me good.'

Steve got up without answering his brother and walked back into the house. He knew for a fact that his mother had forced Daulton to check upon him. Steve walked into the bedroom, where Eva was laying on the bed, flicking through an old magazine.

'Maybe Christine and I should leave,' Eva said to Steve. 'I don't want you to get into trouble for asking us here.'

Steve took a seat on the bed next to her. 'I meant what I said to you, Eva. I love you, and I want to be with you. If my brother or anyone in my family has issues with that, then that's their problem.' He put his hand on her arm. 'Daulton had no right to speak to you like that. Now, let's do something fun.' Steve got up, walked into the bathroom, and turned on the tab of the whirlpool. 'You and I are going to take a lovely, long, hot bath together. I'm going down to the kitchen to get a bottle of wine and, when I come back; I expect to find you in the bath.'

'Yes, sir,' she saluted him and started to the bathroom.

***

'Have you arrived?' Matthew Patterson asked his son. 'Are Eva and Christine still there?'

'They are. It might be nothing,' Daulton said. 'But when I arrived, I went straight to the cottage as you said and found Christine and Eva in your study.'

'*What…?*' Matthew Patterson shouted so hard Daulton had to remove the receiver from his ear. 'What in the world were they doing there?'

'They hiked up from the main house and used the cabin to rest. When I got there, they were upstairs enjoying the view from the window.'

'That stupid brother of yours must have given them the keys.' Matthew Patterson was fuming. 'Sometimes I think he got swopped in the hospital.'

Daulton didn't respond. He knew better than to speak to his father when he was angry.

'Daulton, listen to me carefully. When you get to the cabin, go upstairs and find out if there is a key on the key holder that opens my desk. You must go up to the cottage immediately and check this for me.'

Before Daulton could answer, his father had already put the phone down. Daulton took the keys from the kitchen and walked to his car. He sped away, leaving a cloud of sand behind him.

Daulton walked upstairs to his father's old study. He tried several keys until one of them opened the drawers. Before checking the contents of the drawer, he took out his mobile and phoned his father.

'One of the keys opens the desk,' he said without greeting his father.

'Which file is on top?' Dr. Patterson asked.

Daulton got the top file out and read out the name on the front. 'It's called *Santa Tecla, Chile*.'

'%$#*^!.' He could hear his father swearing on the other end of the line. 'When you come back to town, I need you to bring that file with you. There should also be a file labelled *Jennifer Earl*. I need you to bring that too. Take them now and come straight back to town,' his father ordered.

'I was thinking of staying a couple of days,' Daulton tried to say; although he knew his father was livid and in no way interested in what someone else wanted.

'Don't argue with me, son. This is extremely important. Bring the files straight to me, *now*.' With that, Matthew Patterson slammed the phone down.

Daulton let out a sigh. He was confused and annoyed.

He was sorry he had to leave the cottage. He had forgotten how beautiful it was. He promised himself to come back soon. He walked to his car and drove off.

Sarah, Harry's wife, was preparing dinner in the main house when Christine walked into the kitchen.

'Dear me. Oh, my! We don't eat that much.'

'It turns out that Mr. Daulton decided not to stay, after all. He went back to town, leaving me with all the groceries,' Sarah responded without looking up.

Sarah turned around to get another grocery bag from the countertop and stared Christine in disbelief. 'What the…,' she said.

Christine smiled slightly embarrassed. 'I had the same effect on your husband.'

'Sorry, darling. You just remind me of someone.'

'Who?' Christine was intrigued.

'Oh…' Sarah answered, dismissing Christine's question with a hand gesture, 'someone I knew many, many years ago.' Christine was slightly disappointed. 'Can I get you anything?' Sarah asked, quickly changing the subject.

***

Daulton drove up to his parent's house and parked his car behind his father's Mercedes. He picked up the files from the passenger seat and walked to the house. He rang the doorbell and waited impatiently for one of the maids to open the door.

'Where's my father?' he asked, charging into the house, ignoring the help.

'Dr. Patterson is upstairs in his study,' the help responded timidly.

He ran upstairs and knocked on the door. He could hear an irritated, 'Yes,' coming from the room. Daulton opened the door and entered. He was surprised to see his mother also in the study. It was not often his parents spent time together, other than at functions.

'Mother,' Daulton walked up to his mother and kissed her.

'Hello, sweetheart,' his mother greeted him back.

'Did you bring me the files?' Matthew asked. He had no time for niceties.

Daulton walked over to his father's desk and placed the two files before him. Matthew immediately opened the files, running his fingers through the paperwork, glancing at every page inside. When he had finished the data, he picked up the file named *Santa Tecla, Chile*, and continued checking. He was getting anxious and went through the papers a second time.

'Are you sure you didn't drop anything?' he asked Daulton without looking up.

'Yes. I took the files as you told me,' Daulton replied.

Matthew looked up at his wife. 'The photo is missing.'

'Are you sure?' she asked him.

'You just saw me going through the files twice.'

'You think they took it?'

'*Who else*?!' he snapped.

'What are you talking about?' Daulton interrupted his parents.

'Nothing, sweetheart,' Marlene took his hand. 'This does not concern you.' Knowing his mother, Daulton decided not to ask any further questions. 'Can you give us a minute alone?' Marlene squeezed her son's hand. Daulton knew it wasn't so much a question as an order.

'I'll wait for you downstairs.'

Matthew had not taken his eyes off Marlene and, as soon as Daulton had left the room, he burst out. '*!@#!*, Marlene what are we going to do?'

'Matthew, please calm down. We don't know they took the photo. It might have fallen out, or maybe you filed it in another file.'

Matthew looked at his wife. His eyes narrowed. 'I'm sorry,' she said immediately. She knew Matthew would never misplace a document. Matthew was a perfectionist and kept accurate records.

'Matthew, let's not jump to conclusions yet. Even if they have the photo, what are they going to do with it? They might recognize you or even maybe Charles and Alan, but what does that prove? It's no secret you all worked together. Is there anything else missing other than the photo?' Matthew shook his head.

'Matthew, I think you're overreacting. We have nothing to worry about,' Marlene persisted.

He looked at his wife and wanted to believe her. He was unable, however, to ignore the uncomfortable feeling that came over him.

'Maybe I should just inform Charles and Alan.'

'No, *absolutely* not. We have always been in charge, and we will stay in charge,' Marlene said decisively. She got up from her seat and straightened her skirt. 'If you'll excuse me, I'll have tea with Daulton now. By the way,' she stopped halfway toward the door, 'I think Steven being this close to Eva and Christine is the bigger problem at the moment.' She left the room and slammed the door behind her.

Matthew opened the file *Jennifer Earl*. 'At least you can't do much damage anymore,' he said to himself.

15

Years Earlier: The Mid 1980's

Jennifer Earl was a beautiful and bright woman. At the age of thirty-five, she had come to the conclusion that something was missing. And she knew that something was a baby. She had never found a suitable man because she was always focused on her career, rather than hoping for the right man to come along. So, she had decided to have a baby by herself.

Jennifer was one of the most successful advertising executives in the city. She was a strong and independent woman who, after many years of success, won the respect of her colleagues to make a career for herself in a man's world. She proved over and over that, although she was a woman, she was tough, if not tougher, than most of her male colleagues. She had that certain something; she could pick up signals like a machine.

It had not been a smooth ride, however, for Jennifer to get where she was. She was an attractive woman and that led to many men trying to seduce, belittle, or scam her. Early in her career, Jennifer vowed to never date her colleagues or any other man in the advertising industry. She knew this would eventually work against her. Emancipation was still in baby shoes and Jennifer knew that if she wanted to make it, not only did she have to be as good as her male colleagues, but she also had to be ten times better. And she needed to watch her P's & Q's.

She worked hard and, at the age of thirty-five, she realized that if she wanted to have children, she needed to move quickly. She was already considered old. Most woman in the '80s were married by the time they were twenty-one-years-old and had children by twenty-two-years-of-age. She was lucky to have a sufficient income to hire a full-time nanny and continue working in advertising.

Jennifer had approached several doctors. However, they all dismissed her because of her age. One doctor even scolded her and said she should have considered having children at a much younger age like other women.

She was introduced to Dr. Patterson by friends. They said he was a pioneering doctor in in-vitro-fertilization (IVF). This procedure was still in baby shoes, but she decided to approach him. She wasn't sure if Dr. Patterson would consider her because of the negative reception she received from the other doctors; being a single, thirty-five-year-old woman.

Jennifer waited a long time for an appointment with Dr. Patterson. When she first tried to see him, he was working with a charity team in South America. He travelled home once a month to see patients. Jennifer was delighted to hear how Dr. Patterson dedicated his time and talents to the less fortunate.

Often, she had wanted to do something to help others. However, her line of work did not allow for such 'luxuries.' She was expected to produce and meet high goals and standards each month.

She looked forward to meeting Dr. Patterson and was thrilled when she was finally given an appointment on the 7th of February.

Dr. Patterson had a small practice in the suburbs. He worked with his wife, Marlene, who assisted him in a variety of capacities. She was his receptionist, secretary, and medical assistant.

When Jennifer arrived at the practice, she took a seat in a waiting area that consisted of two plastic chairs and an old black coffee table. Marlene came out from the office to make sure Jennifer was comfortable.

Jennifer was surprised to see someone like Marlene in a doctor's practice. Marlene was stunning. She was tall and slim with long, blond hair tied back in a ponytail. She had defined cheekbones, full lips, and strikingly piercing blue eyes. Jennifer thought Marlene belonged on the cover of a fashion magazine or the arm of a wealthy millionaire, not in some shabby doctor's practice.

After about ten minutes, Marlene called her into the office. Dr. Patterson's office was a tiny old room with a small dark brown desk that was, without a doubt, second hand, two chairs, and a gynaecological table with stirrups. The room had one small window that was covered by a green curtain for privacy.

Jennifer introduced herself to Dr. Patterson. He was a tall man with dark brown hair and probing brown eyes. Jennifer did not consider him handsome, but he had a certain natural arrogance that made everyone pay attention to him. *What a strange couple*, Jennifer thought. She immediately tried to shake off her judgemental feelings.

After explaining her plans to him, he examined her and took several blood samples. He told her he would contact her the following month after all the tests were completed. He said they would discuss the insemination procedure and set a date at that time.

Dr. Patterson gave her medication to stimulate egg production and avoid early follicle ovulation. He told her she may gain some weight, but this was a good sign. He put his hand on her shoulder and said, 'Babies need to grow in the bellies of a healthy woman.' Jennifer left the practice thrilled that she found a doctor who was willing to help her.

As soon as Jennifer left, Dr. Patterson picked up the phone. 'I think we found ourselves the perfect subject,' he said to the person on the other end. 'Marlene has finished checking her background. She has no living relatives other than an aunt who's ninety-two-years-old. I'll run the tests, but I think we can proceed.' He put down the phone and looked at his wife standing in the doorway.

'Finally. At least we won't have to use this horrible office as a front any longer. I hate coming here,' she said.

Matthew nodded with a big smile on his face. 'This is it, Marlene. Our dreams will come true.'

One month later, Jennifer received a telephone call from Marlene Patterson. 'Jennifer. It's Marlene Patterson. How are you?'

'Marlene, hello. I'm very well, thank you.'

'We have the results of your tests and my husband would like to discuss them with you.'

'Sure. I hope everything is in order.'

'Don't worry. Everything is fine. Rather than meeting Matthew at the practice, we want to invite you for the weekend. Matthew and I recently bought a property north of the city. You can relax and enjoy the fantastic views.'

'That's very kind, Marlene. Are you sure it's not too much of an inconvenience?'

'Absolutely not,' Marlene lied. Jennifer agreed and wrote down the address.

Jennifer arrived at the Patterson's country home that weekend. She was stunned by the beauty of the property. The practice seemed so scruffy that she wasn't expecting such an impressive property. The country home was a dream. She was greeted by a young man who introduced himself as Harry Theakston. His wife, Sarah, was in the kitchen preparing dinner for that evening.

'Jennifer, welcome,' Marlene said, walking down the

stairs. She walked to Jennifer and gave her a hug and a kiss. Jennifer was slightly taken aback by this familiarity. 'Please, let me take you to Matthew's cottage. He likes his privacy when he works.'

Marlene drove her up to a quaint little cottage. Dr. Patterson was in his study on the first floor and greeted Jennifer with the same enthusiasm as Marlene.

Jennifer was excited to have found Dr. Patterson and his wife. They didn't judge her and seemed perfectly happy with her decision to raise a child by herself. Dr. Patterson motioned for Jennifer to sit with him on the sofa.

'Jennifer, I'm pleased to say all your tests are in order. I just have to ask you some further questions.'

'Fire away,' Jennifer said.

He asked her some questions about *hereditary diseases* in her family and about any childhood diseases she had suffered. The questions went as far as what her current diet was. Jennifer answered the questions to the best of her knowledge. Dr. Patterson seemed satisfied.

After finishing his notes, he sat back and told Jennifer there was something else he wanted to discuss with her. 'As you know, I do charity work in South America. Chile, to be precise.'

'Yes. You told me,' Jennifer answered.

'Let me come straight to the point. I would like you to join me. This way I can follow your pregnancy closely. I must be honest; I've never performed IVF on a woman your age. And, on top of that, you're single. Although I believe there are absolutely no problems and you are healthy, I would feel happier if you were a bit closer in order to give you my undivided attention.'

'I'm not sure, Dr. Patterson. This is a bit sudden. I have a job, an apartment, and many friends here.'

'Needless to say, I can offer you an administrative position in the hospital. That would allow you to cover your costs for an apartment. But let's not discuss that now. Let's go back to the house. I'm sure dinner is ready.'

During dinner, Marlene Patterson talked about her experiences in Chile. She talked about how she worked alongside her husband in the hospital and the great satisfaction she felt as she helped the local women. But, in reality, Marlene Patterson was only in Chile once and refused to be anywhere near the local women.

They all spoke more and at half-past-nine, Marlene suggested she show Jennifer to her room.

'Thank you both for inviting me here. This is a magical place,' Jennifer said and retired to her room.

'Please, Jennifer, Matthew and I have little time to visit. You are more than welcome to use the house whenever you want. Just phone Sarah before you arrive, and she will prepare everything.'

'You are too kind, Marlene. I'm really touched by your generosity.'

Matthew and Marlene looked at each other when Jennifer left the room. 'She'll come to Chile. Mark my words,' Marlene said whilst smoking a *Lucky Strike*.

'How can you be so sure?'

'She is one of those do-gooders. I can smell them from afar.' Matthew looked at his wife with an amusing smile on his face.

Jennifer woke the following day and was surprised to hear that Marlene had left for the city to collect the children. Sarah Theakston told her that Dr. Patterson was working in the cottage. She helped Sarah clean up. The two women hit it off as if they were old friends. Sarah invited Jennifer for lunch in their small cottage.

Marlene Patterson returned late that afternoon with her two children. The two boys were neatly dressed. Jennifer introduced herself. They were extremely polite and tiptoed around their mother.

'They are good-looking boys,' Jennifer said to Marlene.

'They are. If you'll excuse me, Jennifer, I'm going to go to my room to rest.' Marlene hardly showed her face for the remainder of the weekend. She told Jennifer she suffered severe migraines and needed to stay in a dark room. Jennifer spent the rest of the weekend playing with Steven and Daulton.

The following day, the three of them had lunch at the Theakston's. It was a fantastic afternoon. They walked by the lake and played hide and seek until both boys were exhausted.

'Jennifer, it was lovely having you. Please make sure you stay in touch.' Sarah hugged Jennifer on Sunday evening.

'I will try and come again soon.'

'Bye, Jennifer,' Harry said and gave her a hug.

'See you, Harry. Look after your lovely wife. Can you say goodbye to Marlene and the boys for me?' Jennifer asked Sarah. 'I don't want to disturb her.'

'I will. Don't worry. Drive safe.'

***

Jennifer sat behind her desk at the Butch Everest Advertising Agency. She had just finished a meeting with a client who was introducing a new cleaning product on the market. She was put in charge of their account, so she had to create an advertising campaign for the product. She took the sample spray she was given and sprayed it in the air. The potent smell almost made her choke. She ran to the window, opened it, and put her head outside for fresh air. 'What the heck…? How am I supposed to sell a product like this?' she yelled, outraged.

She went to Mr. Everest's office; one of the owners of the agency. 'Mr. Everest, may I speak with you?'

'What do you want?'

'I have a problem with the new cleaning spray. I really think it's an awful product.'

'Jennifer, may I remind you that we are not in the business of judging products. We are here to sell them.'

'Mr. Everest, this product will put housewives in the hospital. That's how potent it is.'

'Just do your job,' he said and gestured for her to leave his office.

Jennifer thought for a moment and decided that Mr. Everest should experience the product himself. So, she sprayed in the air.

Mr. Everest started coughing loudly. 'Open the window *NOW!*' he yelled.

He was still coughing as his secretary ran in with a glass of water. She shot Jennifer a dirty look. Mr. Everest was livid and slammed his fist on his desk. Jennifer was shocked by Mr. Everest's reaction. It was never her intention to upset him this much.

'I told you to market that blasted spray! If you can't do that, I suggest you look for a job elsewhere!'

'I'm sorry Mr. Everest, but I have been with the agency for eight years and am one of your top employees. Maybe I do have some insight about what will sell and what will not.'

'Don't be such a little girl, Earl. Just do your job! You women are so emotional!'

As Jennifer walked back to her desk, she thought about what just happened. Over the years, she had seen her male colleagues blow up for less significant matters. But, because she was a woman, she was emotional. After a few seconds, she picked up the phone and called Dr. Patterson to tell him she was ready to move to Chile.

16

The Search

Steve loaded the suitcases into the rental car. Eva walked from the house, carrying a blue denim jacket in her hand.

'I can't believe we have to leave already. It has been a wonderful couple of days,' she said. She walked up to Steve and put her arms around his waist.

'I'm glad you both had a good time. Sorry again for Daulton. I'm sure he was acting solely on behalf of my mother.'

Christine kissed Steve on the cheek, 'Thank you for a wonderful time.' She slipped into the car to allow Eva and Steve some privacy to say goodbye.

'When will you come back to town?' Eva asked after a long kiss.

'Either Thursday or Friday. Call me when you get home,' Steve said as he opened the door.

She smiled at him and opened the window. He leaned down to give her another kiss. Then, he tapped the roof of the car twice and Christine and Eva drove off.

They arrived back to their apartment around nine that evening. There was a great deal of traffic as they drove back into the city. This made the five-hour drive turn into a seven-hour drive.

'I'm absolutely exhausted. We were so relaxed.'

Christine let herself fall on the sofa.

'We were extremely lucky. I'll call Steve to let him know we finally made it home.'

Christine picked up her things and walked to her bedroom to unpack. She stopped at the bathroom and looked inside. 'Did you see this bathroom? It feels like a shoe box compared to the bathrooms at the country house.'

'We were born for luxury. It's an absolute sin that we live in this apartment.'

Christine laughed and said, 'I couldn't agree more.'

***

At work, Christine was busy researching newly released publications for the library's resources. She was so concentrated on her tasks that she didn't see or hear Eva standing in front of her desk.

Eva was standing impatiently with one hand on her hip. 'Busy, are we?' she asked abruptly.

Christine jumped in her seat. She let out a startled shriek and moved her head back. 'Eva, you scared me half to death!' Christine picked up her reading glasses that had fallen to the floor.

'Sorry about that,' Eva said with wicked smile on her face.

'What are you doing here? Shouldn't you be promoting anorexia at the modelling agency?'

'I took the afternoon off to do some research.'

'Research on what?'

Eva reached into her moon shaped handbag and took out the photo she had taken from Dr. Patterson's desk at the country home.

'On this!' Eva showed Christine the photo. 'The library keeps a large database on prominent people and their past, don't they? I thought I'd have a look into Dr. Patterson and his charity work in South America.'

Christine took a deep breath. 'What do you expect to find.'

'Not sure,' Eva shrugged her shoulders. 'But I'm curious. He doesn't strike me as a man who would do something for someone else for nothing.'

'He looked and still looks after us.' Christine was always defending Dr. Patterson.

'Yeah great, Christine. He put us in an orphanage. Yoo-hoo for Dr. Patterson,' Eva responded, raising her arms as if to support him.

Christine smiled, 'Come. Follow me.' She got up and walked to the back of the library to the monitors for public use. Christine wore comfortable pump shoes that made no sound whilst she walked through the library. Eva felt somewhat self-conscious as she followed Christine with her noisy ankle boots. They were not so quiet. She tried to walk on her toes as much as possible.

'Knock yourself out,' Christine said, pointing to the computer. 'The system works like a normal search engine.'

'Great. Thanks.' She took off her second-hand jean jacket and hung it on the back of the old desk chair. The chair was uncomfortable and offered no support. Eva knew she would have a backache this evening because of that chair.

She started researching Dr. Patterson. She was surprised at the amount of information that was available. He had an extensive bibliography of publications and presentations; all regarding in-vitro-fertilization treatment and techniques. Eva quickly realized that it would take her weeks to read through all the clippings.

She decided search, '*Santa Tecla, Chile*' instead. Little information came up on her search. The remote village of Santa Tecla consisted of no more than sixty wooden houses and a church. It was surrounded by mountains and green fields. It was pretty much cut off from the rest of the world.

The nearest large city was about an eight-hour drive away. It was obvious that Santa Tecla was a poor village, surviving only on agriculture and llama farming.

During her search, she noticed there was no mention of any hospital. Eva took the photo out of her handbag and studied it carefully. In the background, she could see the hospital had a name, but it was obscured by the people standing in front of it. She could make out the first three letters - *'cen'* - and the four last letters *'ario.'* She decided to type in the letters followed by *'Chile.* Even with this, however, she still didn't find anything interesting.

She tried by swopping the words around - *'Chile' 'Bar' 'Ario'* - which came up blank as well. She sighed and decided she would try one more time to search *'Dr. Patterson,'* 'Bar,' *'Ario,'* and *'hospital.'*

To her surprise, she found two listings. One with a photo of the hospital. She barely recognized the building from the photo, however, because the structure had collapsed. And, from the peeling paint and plant growth in and around the collapsed walls, Eva concluded that the hospital was in ruins for many years when this photo was taken. She read the print underneath the photo, *'Vistas de hospital Barros Rosario después del terremoto 1983.'* Nothing else was written.

'How odd. There's no further information on the earthquake. Santa Tecla is a small village, but weren't scientists who researched all the earthquaked areas around the world interested?' she asked, out loud.

The next article only consisted of a few lines. *'Dr. Patterson and staff were forced to leave Chile after his hospital Barros Rosario was destroyed by an earthquake.'* It was interesting that they referred to the hospital as 'his.' She assumed he had worked there, but not that he actually *owned it.* She felt frustrated that no other information was available.

She looked at the photo again and stared at it closely. She decided to scan the photo into the computer. That way, she could zoom in and study it even more carefully. She walked back to Christine, who was assisting people looking for the psychology sector of the library. Eva waited patiently for her turn.

'Find anything interesting?' Christine asked whilst putting several books on the filing cart.

'Only the name of the hospital. Did you know that Dr. Patterson actually owned the hospital?'

'Really…? I thought he worked there as a volunteer?'

'Me too. But it says in one of the articles that he owned it.'

'So, who runs it now?' Christine asked.

'It was destroyed in an earthquake back in '83. The hospital was in a village that had no more than sixty houses and is totally cut off from the rest of the world. Why would anyone want to open a fertility clinic in a village with maybe one hundred women? Can you help me to scan the photo? I want to have a closer look.'

Christine took the photo and put it into her scanner. She pressed the start button and watched her screen. 'Done,' she said after a minute. 'I'll send it to the monitor where you're working. It's called, '*photo*' and it's on the desktop.'

'Much appreciated,' Eva said. She made a courtesy bow and tiptoed back to the workstation. She opened the photo and examined it carefully. She looked at the faces and zoomed-in to allow her a closer look. She started in the left-hand corner and zoomed in on what were no doubt local nurses.

Suddenly, she stopped on one of the faces. She recognized him. She felt herself getting excited and explored the photo further. When she recognized a second person, she jumped up from her seat. 'Christine!' she yelled.

Christine was annoyed as she stood at her workspace. She gestured to Eva to be quiet. When she arrived at Eva's desk, she was whispering angrily, 'In case you haven't noticed, this is a library!'

At this particular moment, she looked like a true old-fashioned, but beautiful, librarian. A dark-coloured dress covered her knees, and she wore a soft blue cardigan. Her hair was tied back in a low knot. No matter how she tried, Christine was an incredibly attractive woman with a figure most women would kill for.

'Okay, okay,' Eva said and pulled Christine impatiently by the arm towards the screen. 'Look at this,' she said, as she zoomed in to show Christine the two faces she recognized.

'But, that's Dr. Charles Alamilla and Dr. Alan Abrahams,' Christine said, surprised.

They met Dr. Abrahams and Dr. Alamilla several times at the Patterson's house. In fact, whenever Christine and Eva were invited, they were always there.

'Other than a few wrinkles and some grey hairs, they really haven't changed that much,' Eva said.

'Just out of curiosity, what are they doing now?' Christine asked.

'Let me see.' Eva typed Dr. Alamilla's name into the search engine. He showed up as one of the directors of a large pharmaceutical company. Eva typed Dr. Alan Abrahams next. His profile came up under the same pharmaceutical company. It stated his position and responsibilities. Within the structure of the company, it mentioned Dr. Abrahams as Chief Medical Executive with Dr. Eric Woodlands as Assistant Medical Executive.

'*Stop!* Wait a minute…' Christine said, 'Eric is Dr. Abrahams number two?' She felt herself shaking. Eva took over the mouse when she saw Christine's reaction. 'This must be the reason why Marlene Patterson knows Eric. This is crazy. Why didn't he ever mention anything?' Christine was asking herself more so than Eva.

17

The Mystery Continues

'So, they worked together in Chile and still work together here,' Eva mumbled and wanted to search further.

'I wonder why Dr. Patterson isn't working there. They were together in Chile and are still exceptionally good friends.'

Eva typed in '*Matthew Patterson*' and, to their surprise, Dr. Patterson came up as C.E.O. 'What the heck. I never knew Dr. Patterson owned a pharmaceutical company,' Eva said out loud.

'Shhhh. Please, Eva. This means that Eric must know Dr. Patterson as well,' Christine said.

'What's going on here?' Eva asked, shaking her head.

Christine thought about what she just read for a minute. 'I'll print these pages on A3 paper. I'd like to read them at home when I have more time. If you wait about twenty minutes, we can drive home together,' Christine said to Eva, looking back over her shoulder at her.

***

The moment they arrived home, they immediately laid the A3 copy of the photo on the kitchen table and studied it up close. There were twelve people in the photo. The three women in the middle held both hands on their bellies, proudly showing off their pregnancies.

'Who do you think they are?' Eva asked.

'Not sure. I think the two western women must be nurses or married to the doctors. I can't imagine anyone going to a remote village in South America to have a baby.'

Christine suggested taking the original photo to a photographer to have it enlarged professionally. The copied version, although larger, had lost much of its clarity. She looked at her watch. 'I still have time. I can try the photographer on Lind Avenue.' Christine put on her coat.

'What has gotten into you all of a sudden? I thought I was the nosy one in the house.'

Christine smiled and walked out. Eva continued examining the A3 copy. Something about the woman in the front looked familiar. She already felt it when she first saw the photo in the country home. That was the real reason she took it. She couldn't care less about Dr. Patterson and his pathetic doctor friends. She kept staring at the woman's face. She looked so happy and so proud of her pregnant belly.

'Who are you?' Eva asked out loud.

Twenty minutes later, Christine walked back into the kitchen. 'Good news. The photographer told me they could do an A3 size of the photo without losing any of the clarity. It should stay as clear as the original. We can collect it in two days.' Christine sat at the kitchen table. She had picked up a bottle of red wine on her way back and was unscrewing the cork. 'I am very tempted to phone Eric,' she said, while she poured two glasses.

'Why would you do that?' Eva said with a questioning face.

'Well, obviously he knows Dr. Patterson and the other doctors well. Maybe he could recognize someone else in the photo.'

'What a wonderful idea. That way, he can go straight to

Dr. Patterson and tell him that we stole a photo from his locked desk. Remember, these doctors are all well-established and respected doctors. No one will believe us over them. Any more bright ideas, Sherlock?' Eva said in a sarcastic tone.

'Okay. Keep calm. I get it. But how else are we going to find out anything?'

'It might be safer to ask Steve. At least we know he won't rat us out.'

Christine nodded as she handed Eva a glass of wine. Both girls sipped their wine while they looked at the brunette standing in the centre of the photo.

***

Eva met Steve for dinner at a local steak house. He finally returned from the country home. When she arrived, Steve was already sitting in the restaurant and waived to her from his window table. She ran into his arms and kissed him.

'I've missed you,' she said, looking into his beautiful blue eyes.

'Me too,' he said and squeezed her tightly against his chest.

Eva took a seat and picked up a menu. She wasn't hungry; all she really wanted to do was go to Steve's apartment. She was surprised at her passionate feelings. She knew she loved him, but the feelings she had for him were so intense that they almost scared her.

What if he changed his mind about her? So many thoughts raced through her mind and left her feeling dreadfully insecure. Eva wasn't used to this. Up until now she had always been in control. Yes, she loved some of her previous boyfriends, but realized now that it had been nothing more than infatuation. This was the real thing, and she wasn't sure if she was ready for this overwhelming sensation. She thought of Christine and, all the sudden, she understood the pain she

127

must have felt when Eric broke off the engagement so suddenly.

'Ready to order?' Steve asked.

Eva snapped out of her thoughts. She had been oblivious to the waitress who was ready to take their order. 'Yes, yes,' she said quickly. She had no idea what she wanted, so she decided to go with the first thing that caught her eye. The unprofessional, but beautiful, waitress snatched the menu out of her hands. Surely, she was yet another actress, artist, model-type not able to make a living from her 'art.'

'You okay?' Steve asked. 'You seem a bit distracted.'

'No. I'm fine... Did you finish all the work? Or will you have to go back to fix the plumbing?'

'No. I think my mother is content to leave the house uninhabited for at least another year.' Steve took her hand and pressed it softly. Eva could feel her heart skip a beat. She said a little prayer. *Dear God, make him love me forever.* 'It's good to be back home,' he said. 'I love staying at the country home but when you left, it wasn't the same.'

She looked at him and smiled. She wanted to say something but didn't know what.

'We should go back again together, just you and me. We can take long walks with Max and…. have romance…..'

Eva couldn't contain herself any longer. 'I'm not that hungry. Shall we go to your place?'

Steve's face lit up. 'Perfect plan,' he said and took out his wallet and left enough to cover the bill and they quickly left the restaurant. Once outside, Eva turned around and kissed Steve passionately.

Eva was sitting on the bed when Steve came into the room with two peanut butter sandwiches and a bottle of wine. 'Dinner is served, my lady.'

'Great. I'm starving,' she said and picked up one of the sandwiches. 'I want you to have a look at something,' Eva said and walked over to her handbag as she ate her sandwich.

'What is it?' he asked and started to open the A3 copy of the photo. 'That's my father. Where did you get this?' he asked her, surprised.

'Doesn't matter. Do you know any of the other people, besides Dr. Abrahams and Dr. Alamilla?'

'Not sure. Let me have a look.' Steve put the paper under the bedside table lamp and studied it carefully. 'Dr. Abrahams, Dr. Alamilla....'

Eva was looking over Steve's shoulder when he pointed at a face on the second row of people in the photo. 'I don't know who that is; probably one of the nurses. Oh, here is Dr. Bernard...' Eva took the photo from his hand and studied it carefully.

'I'll be! So, it is. I didn't recognize him with all that crazy red hair. Do you know who any of the pregnant women at the front are?'

'I think this is Mrs. Eastman. She was Dr. Eastman's wife.' He pointed at the man standing behind her.

'Was...? Are they divorced?'

'No. They were killed in a car accident. I think it must have been something like twenty years ago. The other women I don't know.... she looks familiar,' he said as he pointed at the brown-haired woman. 'Where did you get this photo? This is at least twenty-six or twenty-seven-years-old.' Steve was puzzled.

Eva decided to come clean, at least partly. She told him how they found the photo in his father's study. Steve took another look at the photo and handed it back to Eva. She felt embarrassed and didn't know what to say. She folded the A3 copy and put it back into her handbag. She was taking more time than necessary closing her bag. She was nervous to face Steve but, when she turned around, he was smiling.

'What is your certain interest in my father?'

'Don't know. I just have the feeling I know that pregnant

lady at the front,' she said, and shrugged her shoulders innocently.

'Make sure my father never finds out you took something from his office. He will go insane with anger.'

Eva smiled uncomfortably. If only he knew she had stolen it from a locked desk.

'Come to bed. Let's go to sleep. I'm shattered.' Eva climbed next to him and fell asleep immediately.

18

The Coffee House

Christine walked to the library. She had picked up the enhanced photo earlier that morning and couldn't wait to have a good look at it. She stopped at a café; she needed a coffee.

She enjoyed the aroma of freshly brewed coffee as she walked into the *Italian Job*. It was a busy coffee house that served the best cappuccino in town. She took a seat at one of the small, dark brown tables close to the window.

The place was buzzing with people at the counter. All of them ordered a coffee and croissant to go. The noise of the coffee grinding machine was deafening. Christine thought, *This must be what a real bar in Italy sounds like*. She raised her hand, trying to get the attention of the waiter who was frantically running around, without achieving much. He looked irritated and visibly sighed, annoyed when he spotted Christine. He walked over to her table.

'Yes?' he asked in an irritated voice.

'Good morning. I would like a large cappuccino and a chocolate muffin please.'

Without saying a word, he walked back to the counter and barked the order to the barista. Christine smiled. *He is going to have an awfully long day*, she thought.

She picked up the envelope and slid the photo out a bit.

The photo was extremely clear. She slipped it back into the pouch quickly when the waiter placed the coffee and muffin in front of her. He scribbled out the bill and slammed it on the table in front of her.

'Pay at the till,' he said and walked away.

'No tip for you, friend,' she said to herself while stirring her coffee.

As she enjoyed her breakfast, she stared out of the window at nothing in particular. She was so caught up in her thoughts, she was unaware that someone was standing next to her table. 'Hello Christine,' she heard a well-known voice, and nearly choked on her muffin.

'Oh…, hello, Eric. How are you?' she asked, anxiously.

'Not bad. You?'

'I'm doing well,' she answered quickly

'You mind if I join you for a coffee?'

She gestured at the empty chair. Eric called the waiter and ordered himself a coffee and a chocolate croissant.

'What are you doing in this part of town? I thought your office was on the other side?'

'We've opened an office across the street.'

Christine was debating if she should ask Eric about Marlene and Dr. Patterson. Eva could be right, though. Maybe Eric would tell Dr. Patterson immediately. 'You must be doing well for yourself. I heard you are Dr. Abrahams' 'number two' now.' Christine decided to have a go and probe.

Eric didn't answer, but she noticed he was slightly nervous. However, he put himself together immediately. He gave Christine one of his charming smiles and took a sip of his hot coffee.

'You never told me you knew Dr. Abrahams. Do you know that he is always at the gatherings at Dr. Patterson's home? You must know Dr. Patterson as well. You are an ambitious man. Why didn't you ever join me to one of the parties?' She took a sip from her coffee. 'I asked you several times. It must have been a perfect opportunity for you to mingle with the top executives; not to mention the owner of your company?'

Christine felt good. She wasn't afraid of Eric's reaction. This was the first time she ever confronted him. Eric gave her a suspicious look, but quickly corrected himself. 'I never wanted to mix work with pleasure.'

Christine took another sip from her coffee. 'Pleasure... ah,' she said and smiled.

'Sorry, Christine. I must run. I'm already late for a meeting,' Eric said, while looking at his watch. 'It was terrific seeing you again and, by the way, you look wonderful.' He kissed her on the cheek and quickly walked out of the coffee shop. He gave her a quick wave outside and ran towards the crossing to make the green pedestrian light.

Christine watched him disappear in the sea of people crossing the busy road. She touched her cheek where he kissed her and wiped it away as if something dirty had touched her.

As she walked to the library, she realized she had a silly smile on her face. Her meeting with Eric after their break-up left her with a strange, but satisfying, feeling. She felt she was in control and didn't need him anymore. He commented on how wonderful she looked, and he was not wrong about that. She wore her hair loose at this time and she looked healthy and sun-kissed. She felt like she owned that moment. *One-nil for me*, she thought.

***

Eva sat at her desk, staring at her computer. She was oblivious to the commotion around her. A group of models was seated on a large sofa. They were trying to impress each other with their work experience. One very skinny looking girl, who couldn't be more than seventeen-years-old, was showing off her portfolio to the rest of the group, explaining every photo in detail.

Eva opened the search engine on her computer and began researching the hospital again. She couldn't seem to find any additional information. She thought about what Steve said and typed in the name 'Dr. Eastman.'

There was an old entry that listed him as a member of the *Society for Assisted Reproductive Technologies* - specializing in infertility treatment, IUI (in-utero-insemination) and IVF (in-vitro-fertilization – meaning test-tube-babies). This must have been one of the first organizations because IVF was so new at that time. She read further and saw mention of the accident. She double-clicked on the article:

'Dr. and Mrs. Eastman died Saturday night after Dr. Eastman lost control of the wheel sending the car into an oak tree at an estimated 60 mph. The police investigation remains ongoing,' said Inspector Peter McMillan.

Eva stared at the article. She read it over and over again. Didn't Steve say the Eastman's died after leaving a party at his parents' house? She pressed the print button, took the printed page off the printer, and put it in her handbag. She tried a new search.

Eva discovered that the internet wasn't particularly useful when looking for people or news items from some twenty years ago. She decided to have one more go and looked up *'Mrs. Eastman.'*

To her surprise, Mrs. Eastman had more available information than her husband. There were several old listings mentioning her under several Ladies Charity Luncheons and Fund-Raising Groups. Eva pressed the 'images' button, and several photos of Mrs. Eastman popped up. Eva recognized her from the photo.

Eva picked up the phone and dialled Christine's work number. 'The man with the silly red hair is Dr. Bernard and I know who one of the pregnant ladies is,' she said without introducing herself.

'Who?' Christine asked hurriedly.

'Her name is Mrs. Eastman. She's the blond lady.'

'Hang on. I have the photo. Let me fetch it.' Christine took the freshly developed photo from her bag.

'The clown with the crazy red hair next to Dr. Patterson is Dr. Bernard.'

'Ohhh, you're right! He doesn't even look like himself.' Christine smiled when she recognized Dr. Bernard in the photo. 'And who is Mrs. Eastman?' she asked.

'Mrs. Eastman was married to Dr. Eastman. I showed the copy to Steve,' she said quickly. 'He told me about Mrs. Eastman.'

'Why did you…'

'Stop. Let me finish,' Eva interrupted. 'Steve told me that they died in an accident after they left a party at Dr. Patterson's house.' There was a long silence. 'You still there…'

'Yes, I'm getting a bit nervous. Maybe we should just drop this entire thing.'

'I want to know who the brunette is,' Eva said abruptly.

'So where do we go from here?'

'Maybe I could contact the detective who was in charge of the accident investigation. His name is in the article.'

'Okay, Let's see what you can find out.…'

Eva put the phone down. She felt they were getting somewhere now. She looked at the photo again and, as always, stared at the brown-haired lady in the front.

***

On her way to the library a few days later, Christine passed the *Italian Job* coffee house and debated whether to order a coffee when she heard knocking on the window. She saw Eric sitting by the window, gesturing for her to come in.

Christine wasn't sure what to think of this. She hadn't seen him in months and, all a sudden, she saw him twice in one week. 'Good morning,' he greeted her with a big smile when she walked to his table.

'Hello, Eric. Is this becoming your local?' she asked and sat down on the edge of the chair without taking her coat off.

'Can I get you a cappuccino?'

'Well… I may as well.'

There was an uncomfortable silence, which was broken by the waiter placing a coffee on the table. 'I remembered that I left the other day without paying for my coffee and I was hoping I could treat you this time.' Christine waved away his apology. 'How have you been?' he asked.

'Okay,' she said, shrugging her shoulders.

'No, really. I have been a real creep to you. You didn't deserve to be treated that way. I'm not sure what I was thinking.' He paused for a moment. 'I can only blame it on the stress of work. I was waiting for my promotion, which seemed to be taking forever and we were in the middle of moving to our new offices. I know this is not an excuse, but I want you to know that I never meant to hurt you intentionally.'

Christine sat quietly, drinking her coffee. What was she supposed to say? Was he expecting her to say it was okay and not to worry about it? She couldn't get any words out and felt trapped for a moment. She hadn't expected Eric to bring all of this up.

'I understand if you're angry. I deserve it,' Eric continued.

'I have to go to work.' Christine got up suddenly.

Eric grabbed her wrist. 'Please, Christine, you have to

believe me when I say I'm sorry.'

Christine nodded and walked out. She turned the corner towards the library and stood still for a moment. The emotions that rushed through her head were overwhelming. She felt a surge of electricity when Eric had grabbed her wrist. *Was she still in love with him?* Anger took over the confusion. *Who in the world did he think he was, breaking her heart without any consideration for her feelings,* and now, only months later, he was expecting her to forgive him?

Christine felt the tears welling up in her eyes. *Why couldn't he leave her alone?* She dealt reasonably well with the break-up. She thought she was finally getting over him. She no longer spent every evening looking at photos and crying. She felt real feelings of hate towards him, which, according to Eva, was a good thing. She called them the stages of mourning. It was a sign she was getting over him. Now, he was working near the library and had made her favourite coffee house his own.

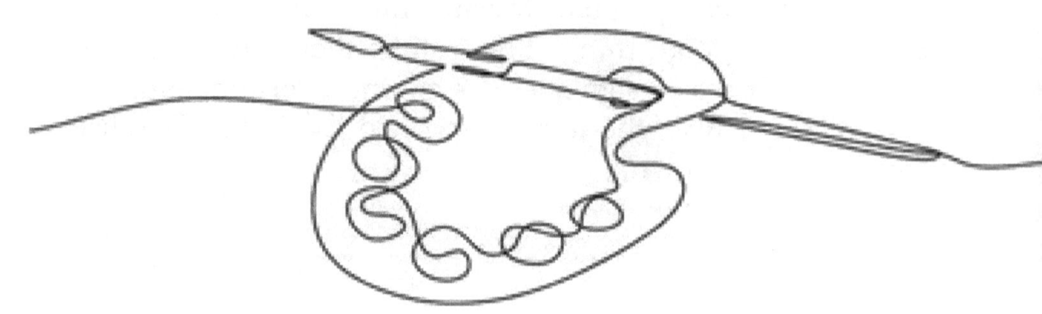

19

Eva's Nightmare

Eva woke distraught. Her sleeping t-shirt was drenched with perspiration. She sat up straight, turned around, and stared at her bottle of sleeping pills. This was the third time now that she had a nightmare while taking her medication.

She dragged herself out of bed, took off her t-shirt, and walked into the bathroom. She looked in the mirror. Her dark brown, rich, curly hair hung in wet strands over her shoulders. Eva opened the tap and rinsed her face, neck, and body with cold water. While she was drying herself, she knew she would have to visit Dr. Patterson to get other medication. Ever since the first time she had the nightmare at Steve's, she was nervous to go to sleep. Now, after the third episode, she felt outright panicky.

She knew she wouldn't be able to fall back asleep. She looked at the small clock on the shelf behind her. It was twenty minutes past five. She walked back to her bedroom and picked out her clothes for the day. After she showered, she made herself breakfast. It was seven o'clock when she left the house for work. The entire way to work she kept thinking about her forced visit to see Dr. Patterson.

As soon as the clock hit nine, Eva picked up the phone and called Dr. Patterson's office. She scheduled an appointment for eleven. She decided to phone Christine. 'I'm going to see Dr. Patterson this morning.'

'Eva, you left early this morning. I was up at a quarter past seven and you'd already left the house. Is everything okay?'

'I had a nightmare again. This is the third time it's happened now – and with medication. I think I need something a little bit stronger too. I was wondering, since you also had another nightmare, maybe you wanted to join me?'

'I'm not sure. It has only happened to me once. I have been sleeping reasonably well.'

'Do you need a refill?' Eva asked in a disappointed voice.

'You know what? I will come with you.'

'Sorry Christine, I'm not a child. I can go alone – forget about it.'

'No. I'm coming. What time is the appointment?

'Eleven o'clock. Are you sure?'

'I'll meet you outside the practice.'

***

Eva waited for Christine outside Dr. Patterson's practice. She wished she was a smoker. She could certainly do with a cigarette. She was wearing black leggings with cherry red *Dr. Martin* boots, a green wool coat, and a large brown scarf.

'Hi. Have you been waiting long?' Christine asked, slightly out of breath.

'No. I just arrived.'

They made their way into the office. As soon as they walked through the door, Rebecca greeted them. As usual, Rebecca looked like she was going to a chic event. 'Dr. Patterson will only be a minute. Please take a seat. Can I get you anything to drink?'

'No. We're fine. Thank you,' Christine replied for both

of them.

Dr. Patterson opened the door to his office. This was the first time the girls had ever seen him do this. Usually, they had to wait for at least ten minutes before he buzzed Rebecca to show them in.

'Good morning, ladies. Please, come in.'

'Good morning, Dr. Patterson.'

Eva and Christine took a seat in front of Dr. Patterson's desk. They noticed a new, rather large, photo of Marlene on his desk. She obviously went to an outstanding photographer who was a master at retouching. She looked flawless. She didn't have a single line, shadow, or blemish on her face. Eva thought they must have spent days retouching that photo.

'I heard you both visited the country home. I hope you enjoyed it. Marlene and I hardly have the chance to visit anymore. With all our commitments in the city, there is little time left for us to go.'

'It was fantastic; almost like a mini-vacation,' Christine responded enthusiastically. 'If it was my house, I would be there every weekend.'

'I'm sure you would, but I'm afraid my work takes up 99% of my time.' With that, he stopped the niceties. 'What can I do for you girls?'

'My nightmare has come back even with the medication, just like Christine. It has happened three times over the past month and I was wondering if you could prescribe something else; maybe something a bit stronger?'

'What about you, Christine?'

'It has only happened once with the new medication; while we were at the country home to be exact.'

'I wish you girls would consider the hypnotherapy. I suggested it for good reasons. If we want to get to the root of the problem, I think this is the only way forward. I can prescribe something stronger, but I'm not sure how this will affect you during the day. Sleeping aids are not something to take lightly. They can keep you tired the following day, not to mention that they are highly addictive.'

Eva and Christine looked at each other. Neither of them were very keen on the hypnotherapy Dr. Patterson suggested; more so now that they knew that Dr. Patterson was so closely connected with Dr. Bernard.

'I think we should start with you, Christine. Obviously, your nightmares are starting to affect your life.'

'I don't understand. In what way are they affecting my life? I just don't understand why you believe hypnotherapy is so important now, why not ten years ago when we both started to have them?' Christine asked.

'The nightmares are becoming more apparent. You are here to get other medication, are you not?' He gave Christine a condescending smile.

'We'll think about it,' Eva quickly intervened. 'Maybe I can see how I react to the other pills and we can take it from there.'

Dr. Patterson was already writing out a prescription. His pen was pressing hard into the pad. It was apparent he was outraged that they didn't want to follow his advice immediately.

'I gather that you know my ex-finance, Eric Woodland,' Christine asked boldly.

'I don't think I've had the pleasure.'

'That's strange because he is 'number two' to Dr. Abrahams at PharmaTech. I thought you would be familiar with all the management of your company.'

'What do you mean *my company*?' Dr. Patterson asked without looking up.

'We read on the internet that you are the owner and chairman of PharmaTech. I understand how all your time is taken up by your work and why you and Mrs. Patterson have so little time to enjoy weekends together. Eva and I always assumed you were only working as a medical doctor, but to run a business next to this must be dreadfully strenuous.'

Eva looked at Christine with big eyes. *What was she doing? Was she going to ask him about Chile? Or maybe even tell him that she had taken a photo from his desk.* She kicked Christine's leg, but Christine was undeterred.

Dr. Patterson looked at Christine for some time. It was as if he was thinking about what route to take; get angry or ignore her.

'Don't you worry about me. I've been working this hard since I can remember. And Mrs. Patterson is fully supportive.' Dr. Patterson was back to his usual pedantic self.

Christine, however, couldn't stop herself, 'I'm sure Eric is a close acquaintance of Mrs. Patterson. I saw them some weeks ago exchanging niceties and then they got into a car together.'

'I am only the chairman of PharmaTech on paper. I'm not physically involved. This is why I don't know this Eric character and my wife chooses her friends as she pleases. I suggest you think about yourself. I'll worry about my issues as you do about yours.'

Eva picked up the prescription and stood up. 'Thank you, Dr. Patterson. Please say *hello* to Mrs. Patterson for us.'

'I hope you will seriously consider my suggestion about hypnotherapy.'

'We will,' Eva said and grabbed Christine by the arm and dragged her outside. 'What on earth were you doing in there? Are you insane?'

'I had to see his reaction. I went out with Eric for three years. Why would he and Dr. Patterson want to keep this a secret from me? In case you didn't notice, he still denied knowing Eric. He also denies knowing Mrs. Patterson knows and spends time with Eric. And, on top of everything, he denied he owns PharmaTech. *Why* would he do that?'

'Not sure,' Eva shrugged. 'I thought you had gone mad and that you were going to tell him about the photo.'

Eva saw a side of Christine she had never seen before. Christine was usually shy and tense around Dr. Patterson. This time, she showed no fear. Eva was also surprised at how Christine had shown no respect.

As Eva and Christine talked outside, they noticed Dr. Patterson looking at them from his office window. He squinted his eyes and concentrated as if he was trying to hear what they were saying. He had hoped that both girls were open to the hypnotherapy. He realized he had to pressure them more. He also had to speak to Marlene. She had to be more careful.

20

A Possible Connection

'Why *did* you go to medical school?' Eva was at Steve's place. He offered to cook her Roman Gnocchi, a typical Italian dish that was historically eaten only on Thursdays. 'Did your father want you to take over his practice?'

Steve started laughing as he prepared the tomato and basil sauce. 'I don't think my father will ever let anyone take over his practice. He thinks he's going to live forever. Look at Daulton. He's not working for my father. If anyone was considered good enough to take over his practice, it would have been him.'

'Then why were they so upset when you left medical school?'

'I think my parents wanted both Daulton and me to have a secure future and the only thing they know is medicine.'

'But you are doing well for yourself now. Why are they still so upset about it? I could understand if they wanted you to take over your father's practice, but if that is not the case, then why? You have a successful business. You're not trying to start a band or become a ballet dancer.'

'*Seriously*? Social status. That's all my parents think of.'

Eva considered bringing up PharmaTech, but she was worried. What if Steve didn't know about his father's company? It was becoming clear to Eva that the Patterson's were not exactly a close bunch. On the surface, people thought them to be remarkably close. Both sons were always on their best behaviour and displayed, what Eva now understood was, a rehearsed and ordered interest in their parent's lives. At least the part their parents wanted them to know. Both of them were moulded into their roles. It wouldn't surprise Eva if Steve had no idea about his father's company, or his past for that matter. Steve was the black sheep of the family. He had strayed from medicine and was building his own life. She was grateful that Steve had liberated himself from their claws. Eva looked at Steve while he was cooking and smiled.

'Why are you looking at me like that?'

'Because you are handsome, sweet, and gorgeous and I love you,' she said and walked over to him stood behind him and hugged him.

While they were enjoying their meal, Eva couldn't stop thinking about PharmaTech, the photo, and especially the lady with the brown hair. 'When I showed you the photo I found in the cabin, you said that one of the pregnant ladies looked familiar to you. Do you remember anything about her?'

'Again, why is this so important to you?'

'It's just that she looks familiar to me too. Isn't that crazy? We have nothing in common other than your father, and I've been thinking and thinking, but I can't recall ever meeting her.' Eva played with her food, eager to see what Steve's reaction might be.

'Maybe she was someone who used to visit the orphanage where you and Christine were brought up. Think about it. It's the only place in the past where you and my father have a connection. If my father knew her, and you think you do too, then that would be the only place.'

'You might be right. I never thought about that. I must find out if any of the caregivers are still around as they closed the place down years ago. I'm sorry, Steve. You must think I am possessed.'

'Not at all. I think it's because you're an orphan. Anything that jogs a memory must be significant to you. I'll help you with anything if it brings you closer to who you are.'

Eva took Steve's hand and squeezed it. 'Have I told you that I love you?'

'You have. But I never, never get tired of hearing it,' Steve answered with a wink.

***

Eva flicked through the telephone directory, hoping to find any of the care assistants she remembered. She promised herself to buy a computer the moment she had some extra money to spend. She did her research on-line at work and discovered that the director and two of the care assistants died several years ago. She ticked their names off a list of names she remembered.

Neither she nor Christine stayed in touch with any of the employees or children from the orphanage. It was not because they were treated poorly or didn't like any of the other children, but because it was easier to not be reminded of that time in their life.

Memories of the orphanage stirred up questions like, *Who are we?* and, *Where are our parents?* They learned very early on that being reunited with their birth parents was highly unlikely. Few children in the orphanage ever managed to find their roots.

Even if a reunion with parents was possible, it was not always welcomed; no matter how romantically films or books portrayed it. Mothers left their children because they couldn't or wouldn't take care of them. By the time the child grew up, the mothers and fathers moved on and were living different lives, often with other children and husbands or wives who didn't know about their past. The difficult reality was that even though the mothers and fathers felt guilty and cried over their past decisions, living happily-ever-after was not the typical outcome.

***

Eva picked up the phone when she found a listing for a Jane Gimble. Jane Gimble was one of the volunteers who was always truly kind to both Eva and Christine. Eva's hands were clammy when she dialled the number listed in the telephone directory. She grew more and more nervous with every ring.

'Hello?' a woman's voice answered

'Hello. Good afternoon. My name is Eva Williams. Are you, by any chance, Ms. Jane Gimble, who volunteered at the Mercy Home orphanage?'

'I am … Are you Eva Williams who shared a room with Christine Rhodes?'

'I am,' Eva said. She was amazed that the woman remembered her and felt a pang of guilt that she never stayed in contact with anyone.

'What can I do for you, Eva?'

'I have some questions.' Eva paused for a moment. She didn't know how to continue. 'Rather than my explaining everything over the phone, could I meet you somewhere? I prefer to speak with you face to face. I'm sure I'm not making much sense and hope I'm not the first resident of the orphanage to contact you, uhhhm,' she hesitated, 'but I have some questions, about myself, Christine, and,' she hesitated again, 'uhhhm, a photo I found.' Eva felt ridiculous. She couldn't even form a proper sentence.

'Sure. I can meet you. You can come and visit me at my home if you want to. It'll be lovely to see you again,' Ms. Gimble said with a kind and calm voice.

Eva was extremely grateful. 'May I come and see you tomorrow? Maybe late afternoon? Christine and I still share, I mean, we rent an apartment together. Maybe we can come together; if that's okay?'

'That will be lovely. I look forward to it. Do you have my address?'

Eva confirmed the address and, after saying *goodbye*, put the phone down. She stroked her palms over her skinny jeans. She was shocked by the reaction she felt. She and Christine never discussed the orphanage. They pretended their lives started when they moved into their apartment. They moved out of the orphanage the day Christine turned eighteen. Although Eva's birthday was eight days later, the orphanage allowed them to move out together.

Eva realized she had a great deal of built-up emotions regarding her past. As she opened a bottle of soda, she heard Christine coming through the front door. She took a large sip. Eva had no idea how Christine would react to her detective work.

'I'm in the living room, Chris. Can you come here for a second?'

'What a day. The entire city decided to come to the library today,' Christine said. She poured herself a glass of wine and let herself flop on the sofa.

'I spoke with Jane Gimble today.'

'What? Jane Gimble from the orphanage? Why?'

'Yes. I'm going to meet her tomorrow after work. She still lives in town. You know she remembered both of us very clearly.'

'What on earth would you want to go and see her for?'

'Yesterday, when I was at Steve's, we spoke about the photo again. Steve suggested we try talking to someone at the orphanage.' Eva looked nervously at Christine. 'It does make sense. He thinks the woman in the photo looks familiar too. She knows Dr. Patterson. Otherwise, she would not have been in South America. The only logical place where we could have met her is in the orphanage. I have been going over the people I remembered. Some of them passed away, but Jane Gimble is alive and kicking and lives in the city.'

Christine looked intently at her glass. She was not impressed with what she was hearing. Like Eva, Christine wanted to erase the orphanage from her memory. As long as she didn't think about being dumped there, she could pretend her life was as normal as the next person's.

She didn't want to be reminded of the scars she felt would never heal. But, with the emotional band-aid she put over them, it was almost as if they didn't exist. She felt herself getting emotional. She considered herself a very calm and rational person, but when it came to her past, she always broke down. 'Why in the world do you need to start digging there?' she shouted.

Eva was shocked by Christine's outburst. She wasn't sure what Christine's reaction would be, but she hadn't expected this. This was one of the few occasions she heard Christine raise her voice.

'I'm so sorry, Christine. I am. I'm not keen on the idea either. But I think it's the only place where we can find some answers. Ms. Gimble always was a genuinely nice lady. She was excited we would come and see her.'

'*We*? I want nothing to do with it. And I don't want to talk about it. You are on your own with this mess! You are stupid if you think I would come along and hold your hand!' Christine got up and slammed the living room door shut behind her.

Eva looked at the door in a trance. She knew she had upset Christine badly and felt guilty. She poured herself another glass of wine and finished it in one go.

Christine threw herself on the bed; tears were running down her face. She was unable to control her emotions. The anger, the pain, and the memories were just too much.

As a little girl, she spent nights fantasizing about her parents and how they would come and pick her up in their beautiful car. They would cry when they saw her and tell her how someone had kidnapped her and, after years and years of desperate search, they had finally found their little girl. They would shower her with gifts, pretty dresses, and dolls. Of course, a pony would be waiting for her when she arrived at her home. She would have a beautiful bedroom; all in pink. And they would all live happily ever after. She waited and waited until she realized at the age of thirteen that no one was coming for her.

Now that she was an adult, she knew that looking for her parents was impossible. She never really stopped hoping for her parents to show up and take her in their arms. When she was eighteen, she had tried to find as much information about her situation as possible. Other than being left at the orphanage, no one was able to tell her anything about where she came from. She was left in an ordinary basket with blankets from a large department store. Nothing could be traced. It was then that she shut the door on her emotions regarding her parents and tucked her past safely away.

Christine spent another hour in her bedroom crying and yelling at Eva. After that, she took a shower, grabbed a bag of potato chips from the kitchen, and stayed in her room the rest of the evening.

21

Ms. Gimble

'Large cappuccino with double espresso to go, please.' Christine stopped in at the *Italian Job* coffee house. After the episode with Eva last night, she hadn't slept very well and needed some caffeine to help her through the day.

'Someone had a late night.'

Eva turned around and looked straight into Eric's smiling eyes. 'Oh… hi, Eric. Yes, I'm afraid I need some help waking up.' She dreaded this moment. She had glanced inside to make sure he wasn't there, didn't see him, and thought she would be able to sneak in to get a coffee to go. She looked drained and tired and hated that Eric saw her like this.

'You're not staying for a quick breakfast?'

'No. Not today. I have a meeting in five minutes. So, I'd better run.'

Before Eric could say another word, Christine was already outside, almost running to the library. She turned her computer on the moment she walked in, sipped her coffee, and thought about last night. She realized that overreacting was not the right word for her behaviour; insanity was more like it. She felt sorry for shouting at Eva like that. *My, I must have sounded like a crazed woman*, she thought. She picked up the phone and dialled Eva's work number.

'Hi. It's the crazy chick from last night. I'm so sorry. I didn't mean to go off on you like that.' Christine hesitated for a moment. 'I'm not sure why, but the thought of my… *our* past is something I can't cope with. Maybe I should start seeing a psychologist. My reaction was uncalled for. Do you forgive me?'

'Of course, I do. I'm sorry I sprung this on you. You're not the only one who overreacted. I was a nervous wreck on the phone with Ms. Gimble. I couldn't even form a proper sentence, and that was when I was fully prepared. So, believe me, I don't blame you. That doesn't mean, however, that I'm not shocked. Jeez, I never thought you had it in you. Are you sure you don't want to start working in the harbour as a fish wife?'

'Yeah, yeah. Make fun of me,' Christine said and laughed out loud. 'What time do you want me to pick you up?'

'You're coming with me?' Eva said with a sigh of relief.

'Sure am. Two neurotic women are better than one…. no?'

'That's my girl. Thanks so much, Christine. See you this afternoon.'

***

They took the Piccadilly line to Hounslow west where Ms. Gimble lived. The road was typical of the areas around the airport. The houses were considerably less expensive compared to the areas closer the centre of London. They were in zone five, which made travel into town, however, expensive. Eva was reading the house numbers out loud.

'It must be the next block. Yes. Here it is.'

They stood in front of a small, uninviting apartment block that was extensively refurbished. It was apparent the windows were recently replaced, and the block had been repainted. The intercom listed the names of the inhabitants and the building had cameras; one in the phone the other on the first floor.

'I'm terrified. How ridiculous is that?' Christine said, while searching for Ms. Gimble's name at the entrance door.

'So am I. I'm secretly hoping she's not home.'

Christine pressed the bell and waited, biting her lip. 'Third floor on the left,' a metallic voice answered over the intercom.

Christine looked into Eva's eyes intensely for a few seconds. Eva looked away, took Christine by the arm, and pulled her inside the apartment block. The hall seemed welcoming. There were colourful prints lining the walls and several well-looked-after plants were placed along the corridor to the lift.

Eva pressed the call button and waited without speaking. As they walked out of the lift, a door on the left-hand side was open, and a lady in her late fifties came out with open arms. 'It's so wonderful to see you again,' she almost sang.

She walked toward them and gave each of them a hug. Jane Gimble hadn't aged well. She had put on a considerable amount of weight and her face showed her deep age lines. Jane seemed to have no problem with her appearance. There was no sign of make-up and she made no attempt to cover her many grey hairs. What had not changed were her warm eyes and gentle smile. Both Christine and Eva felt comfortable immediately meeting Jane again after so many years.

'Please come inside, girls. I've made tea.'

They walked into her apartment. Her apartment had 'her' stamped all over it. It was painted in warm red and orange colours and there were large comfortable chairs in the living room. The wood furniture and her many plants gave the room a cosy feel. Newspapers and magazines were scattered around. Two cats walked up to stroke themselves against Christine's leg, purring contentedly.

'Please take a seat and let me take a look at you,' Jane said and took a seat opposite them. 'I can't believe my eyes. Look at you. You look even more beautiful than you did when you were children. The two of you were always my favourites. You look so different, yet I see something similar in you; old age probably,' Jane continued and nodded approvingly.

Christine and Eva smiled and felt strangely embarrassed by Jane's compliments.

'So, what can I help you with?' Jane asked.

'We have some questions,' Christine started, hesitantly. 'We found a photo and one of the ladies in the photo looks familiar.'

Christine took the photo from her handbag and placed it on the table. 'We recognized some of the people, but we both feel we know the woman. We were hoping you may know who she is,' Christine said, while pointing at the brunette.

'I only recognize Dr. Patterson,' she said without looking up.

'I'm dating Dr. Patterson's son, Steve, and he told me he recognized the lady. The only thing we have in common in the past with Dr. Patterson and his family is the orphanage. We thought that she may be connected to the home.'

Jane looked up from the photo and sighed, 'I don't recognize any of the other people in the photo. I'm terribly sorry.' She handed the photo back to Christine and then poured them a cup of tea.

'Dr. Patterson only started to work at the orphanage a few weeks after you were left with us. He never paid much attention to the orphanage itself.'

'I thought Dr. Patterson was the orphanage's resident doctor for years?' Christine asked.

'No. Dr. Patterson was never the resident doctor for the

orphanage,' Jane said and shook her head, while stirring her tea.

'What do you mean? He told us he worked at the orphanage for years and years,' Eva said with a puzzled look on her face. Jane sat back in her chair and lit a cigarette.

'Dr. Patterson is still our doctor now,' Christine said.

'A week after you were left at the orphanage, we received a telephone call from Dr. Patterson. He told us he had read in the paper that two girls were left at the home and he wanted to offer his services. Dr. Patterson was, and still is, an influential and pioneering doctor who specialized in fertility treatments. His interest in working at the orphanage seemed strange to us. Mr. Albright, the director of the orphanage, agreed to meet with Dr. Patterson.' Jane put her cigarette out in the ashtray next to her chair and immediately lit another.

'After the meeting, Mr. Albright called all the staff and gave us the usual story about how Dr. Patterson wanted to give back to the community and so on. We were all thrilled that such a leading physician had decided to offer us his services. It was then that we were told that Dr. Patterson would only look after two patients. Namely, the two of you.' Jane pointed at them as she said the words.

'What do you mean? Are you saying he never looked after any of the other children?'

'That's right. Even when he visited you, and some other children needed medical attention, he refused to see them. He was a heartless man. But, for the two of you, we could call him day or night. For the other children, he wouldn't even write a prescription.'

'Why was that? Were we some publicity stunt to him?' Eva asked. She was stunned by what she was hearing. She had always been uncomfortable around Dr. Patterson, but she had appreciated his devotion to looking after the children.

'I don't think so,' Jane said, while inhaling deeply. 'We

never received calls from reporters. He never mentioned the orphanage in any of his articles or interviews. I always wanted to believe he was offering his services out of the goodness of his heart. That was until one evening when one of the children, little James Portman, who was only five years old, broke his leg when he fell down the stairs. I remember running to Dr. Patterson, who was visiting you, Christine, for a mild flu and asked him to take a look at James.'

Jane took a moment and then pointed her finger at Christine, 'I clearly remember his cold eyes when he told me that he was not the resident doctor and that I should take the child to the hospital. I never found out why he only looked after you two. Mr. Albright retired two months after you arrived. He never left a forwarding address, and nobody knew where he went.'

Eva leaned forward and took one of Jane's cigarettes.

'You don't smoke!' Christine exclaimed.

'It seems like the right thing to do,' Eva inhaled. She didn't like it but, rather than putting it out, she held it in her hand until it burned out by itself.

'Cigarettes, like alcohol or drugs, are never the answer,' Jane said, smiling compassionately.

'What happened when we left?' Christine asked.

'We never saw him again. He asked for your files – which we refused.'

Both of the girls were shocked by what Jane told them and couldn't speak for several minutes. The silence in the room didn't bother them. They were so deep in thought that they almost forgot where they were.

'I'm sorry to have sprung this on you,' Jane broke the silence. 'I'm pleased you contacted me. I wanted to tell you this for so long.'

'We need to go now. Thank you very much, Jane. We'll invite you to our place for dinner soon,' Christine said sincerely. Suddenly, she felt the need to leave Jane's apartment. She felt overcome by panic and was scared that if she didn't get out, she wouldn't be able to breath. She ran down the stairs, desperate for some fresh air. As she leaned against the apartment building outside.

Eva ran to her. 'What happened? Are you okay?'

'Yeah. I'm fine now...let's walk to the tube and get some fresh air.'

22

In Love Again

Back at home, Christine walked straight to the kitchen and pulled a bottle of wine from the wine rack. She poured two big glasses and handed one to Eva. 'If we continue like this, we'll be joining an AA meeting soon.'

Christine gave her a measly smile. 'Can you believe Dr. Patterson? He lied to us all those years. And why is he so interested in us?' Christine said and gulped her wine. 'I trusted him like a father. Do you think he knows who we are? Even if he does, he's certainly not going to tell us. If he knew and wanted to tell us, he would have done so many years ago. I think it's time we start looking for another doctor. I don't want to see that man again.'

'I know what you mean. But, if he knows who we are, he's the only one who can help us. If we cut off all contact, we'll never find out. We have to play the part and try and find out as much as we possibly can. Think about the next gathering at his house. All the other doctors in the photo will be there. I hate that man more than you can imagine, but right now, he's the only hope we have.'

'Hope of what?' Christine asked.

'To find out where we came from and who our parents are?'

'Eva, I spent half my life thinking about that. I have

come to terms with who I am. I'm not interested anymore.'

'You keep telling yourself that. If you're so comfortable with yourself, why did you have a panic attack at Jane Gimble's house?'

Christine was unable to answer. She shrugged her shoulders and shook her head. She realized Eva saw through her *bravado*.

'This is something we have to do, Chris. No matter how hard it's going to be. If nothing comes from it, then we can start being disinterested. For now, it's the only way forward. We have to be brave.'

Christine looked at Eva and nodded. Eva was right. She couldn't run from this; no matter how painful it was going to be.

***

Christine was filing books in the library when one of her colleagues told her she had a telephone call. She walked over to the telephone. 'Christine Williams speaking,' she said politely.

'Christine. Hi, it's Eric.' Christine felt unable to respond. 'Christine, are you still there?'

'Uhmm, yes. I'm not sure, Eric. You caught me a little off guard'

'I'm sorry. I thought we could have a quick drink and catch up. I would really like to talk to you.'

'Eric, I don't think it's a good idea.'

'Chris, please. I need to talk to you; if only for a few minutes.'

She gave in and said, 'Well, I suppose I could meet you for a quick drink at the *Atlantic Café* around six.'

'Perfect. And, thanks, Christine. I look forward to it.' Christine put the phone down and felt overwhelmed. *What just happened?* It seemed like Eric was everywhere lately.

Maybe a drink this evening wasn't such a bad idea; she needed closure.

Christine felt tense as she walked to the bar that evening. Her life was quite different from six months ago. Six months ago, her life seemed tranquil, predictable, almost boring. In her mind, she was convinced she was getting married, having children, and had her entire life mapped out. Over the past six months, ever since the break-up, she felt more ups and downs than she had ever felt in her whole life. Now, every day held something shocking.

She walked into the modern bar. Everything was white and chrome. It was impressive when she entered, but after a while, it all became a bit too sterile, almost hospital-like. Christine walked to the bar area and saw Eric sitting on a bar stool. She made her way to him and tapped him on the shoulder.

'Christine.' He kissed her on both cheeks. 'You look wonderful.'

After the break-up, she lost over ten pounds. She was wearing a tight fitted skirt, a shirt with bright stripes, and a pair of boots with high heels. 'Thank you.'

'What can I get you to drink?'

'A Margarita.' Christine pulled up a bar stool and climbed up next to Eric. They didn't speak as they waited for their drinks. Christine fiddled with her hair. The silence made her uncomfortable. When her cocktail arrived, she took a large sip from the wonderfully refreshing and robust drink.

'What did you want to talk to me about?' Christine asked. She was shocked by her bravery.

'Straight to the point. I like it,' Eric said. He didn't take his eyes off her as he sipped his scotch. 'Running into you has left me confused.' Christine looked at Eric without saying anything. She kept sipping her drink waiting for him to continue.

'I think I'd better come out with it. I still love you,

Christine. I never stopped loving you.' He paused for a moment, as if he was looking for the right words. 'When I saw you at the coffee shop, I couldn't deny that I still have very strong feelings for you.'

Christine was stunned. She didn't know how to react. She dreamt about this moment. She fantasized about this before going to sleep. Now, her dream had become a reality, only the amazing feeling she had always imagined wasn't there. 'This is all a bit sudden. I'm not sure what to say.'

'I'm sorry. I didn't mean to embarrass you. But I need you to know how I feel about you. I have made a terrible mistake. I'm not expecting you to jump up and tell me you love me too. I want you to think about what I said. I can make you happy, Christine. I know I can. This time, I won't let work or anything else get in the way. I will be there for you and will make you the happiest woman in the world.'

'Eric, I'm not sure. This is too sudden.'

'Please, Chris, I told you it was the stress of the office and I felt bad and horrible breaking up with you. Something inside me always knew it was the wrong thing to do. I knew I could never stop loving you, but I blamed you for all the stress in my life, and I am so sorry. Please, Chris, tell me you'll think about it.' He took both her hands and held them while he looked deeply into her eyes.

'I suppose I could think about it.' She desperately wanted to understand how she felt, but her nerves made it impossible for her to focus on anything.

'Maybe you'll let me take you on a date? We can start anew. I have tickets to a theatre play everyone is raving about. Perhaps you want to join me?'

'I suppose we can see a show,' Christine said, and smiled at him.

'Great!' Eric kissed her on the cheek and ordered two more drinks.

That evening, Christine laid in bed thinking about what

Eric said. She felt so many emotions. She felt flattered that Eric still loved her. She also felt angry that he had so unexpectedly waltzed back into her life. She was mad that he could approach her so easily. When he broke up with her, it had been impossible for her to contact him. She had never been able to ask him questions about why he broke up with her and why he had never considered her feelings.

Most importantly, she felt confused. She expected butterflies. Instead, she felt offended by Eric's confidence, or rather her insecurity. It was as though he didn't expect her to refuse him. He was so cocky and smug. Christine was not sure she made the right decision accepting Eric's invitation. She decided to not tell Eva. She knew exactly what her response would be.

Christine woke in the middle of the night by the sound of Eva crying in the bathroom. She jumped out of bed and knocked on the door. 'What's the matter? Eva, open the door, please!'

Eva opened the door and looked dreadful. Her eyes were red and swollen from crying. 'I'm okay. I just had that stupid nightmare again. It's getting worse, Chris. It's happening more often, and it's so much more intense than before.'

'I know. I feel it too. Come to the kitchen and I'll make you some hot milk.'

'Do you think there's a reason we're having the nightmares more often and they're more intense?' Eva asked.

'I'm not sure. I wish I had some answers.'

23

Liz and Monica

Eva was excited to meet her friends, Liz and Monica, for drinks. She loved crowded bars; the lights, the new and exciting people, and, most of all, the attention everyone gave her.

Liz and Monica were already at the wine bar when she walked in. Eva was wearing a little black dress that showed off her curves without making her look cheap. Her strappy sandals were covered with little brass stones. She looked elegant. The moment she entered, she knew she was getting glances and loved it. She let her hair loose tonight and the cork curls gave her an untamed look. She sat down with the girls, who were already on their second glass of wine.

'Hey, girls. Sorry I'm late. There were delays on the tube.' Eva greeted the girls with a quick kiss.

They waved away her apology. 'What are you drinking? Do you want a glass of wine?'

'Yes. That would be lovely,' Eva replied as she put her little handbag next to her seat.

'So, tell us about the new man in your life. We haven't seen you for ages. We thought you'd left town or were abducted by aliens,' Monica said to Eva, her eyes were teasing.

'I'm not going to lie to you. I think I'm in love.' Eva

giggled and glowed at the same time.

Monica and Liz laughed and made whistling and 'oooh'-ing noises.

'Tell us everything. What's his name? What does he do?' Monica asked.

'His name is Steve. He's the most handsome and perfect man I have ever met.'

'I can hear wedding bells…! But, whatever you do, don't make us wear any silly bridesmaids' dresses,' Liz said.

'Take it easy. Don't jinx it. I intend to date this man for a long, long time before I'll commit to marriage. The thought of a ring on my finger makes me all jumpy. I'll enjoy this beautiful thing we've got going for a long time.' She took a sip of the wine the waitress placed before her and wondered if she was being sincere. 'Enough about me. Did you go for that job interview?' Eva asked Monica.

'I did. They'll let me know next week. I'm keeping my fingers crossed; if not only for the money. I'm already two weeks behind on my rent. On top of it, this job should be a cosy number. Not too much stress, decent pay, and a lot of single men. I might even get married before you.'

Eva laughed. She loved Monica. She was the total opposite of Liz, who was dedicated and enjoyed hard work. Monica, on the other hand, didn't care that much for any job. She just wanted to make enough money to cover her rent, buy clothes, and enjoy herself. Eva had always considered herself somewhere in the middle of the two. She was by no means dedicated like Liz but wanted a bit more job satisfaction than Monica.

The three of them were all vastly different, which was probably why they got on so well. They met six years ago during an aerobics class. They connected immediately. All three hated exercise and left the course halfway through to go to a pub around the corner. They stayed, talking and drinking, well into the night.

'How's your job going?' Eva asked Liz.

Liz worked as a nurse in a nursing home just outside the city. Liz was one of those people that you had to admire. She loved her job and was 100% dedicated to her patients. 'Everything's going great.'

'I don't know how you do it. What do you talk about with your patients? Do they even remember who you are?'

'Most of them do. And I talk to them about everything.' Liz looked at Eva with a questioning look on her face. 'My patients were young once. Some of them have fantastic stories to share. I like helping them. It's not pleasant that after a life of being independent and active in society, one is forced to live in a nursing home, not remember words or family members, and are reliant on other people. The least I can do is listen to them and give them the respect they deserve.'

Liz poured the remainder of her wine in the new glass the waitress put on their table. She continued, 'Obviously, there are also people I don't like very much, but I have formed some close relationships with many of my patients. For example, I look after a lady who has been in the nursing home for years now. She's the sweetest lady, only in her early sixties. Unfortunately, she's prescribed hefty medication. I don't like to second guess the doctors, but I'm confident that in her case, they got it wrong.'

'What about this lady?' Eva asked politely. She wasn't all that interested, but Liz was a good friend and she loved to talk about – what she referred to as – her extended family.

'She's been with us for five years. Before the doctors started prescribing her stronger and stronger medication, I had the most wonderful conversations with her. She was a pioneering businesswoman in the advertising world and travelled all over the world. Unfortunately, she suffers from the most horrendous nightmares. I've never seen anything like it. She's in total shock when she wakes up. The doctor told me that's why she's prescribed strong medication. I suppose something terrible must have happened in her past.'

Eva shrugged her shoulders and tried to look disinterested.

'I'm not kidding, Eva. The woman is terrified, and all the doctor does is give her stronger medication. They may as well put her in a coma. She's completely out of it, but the nightmares keep coming.'

'Has she told you what the nightmares are about?' Eva asked. She tried hard to sound bored but was totally intrigued.

'The poor woman can't even talk about them properly. Not only is she petrified when she wakes up, but she is also totally drugged. She mumbles something to do with earthquakes and blue lights.' Eva froze and was unable to breathe.

'Are you okay there, Eva? What's going on?' Monica was worried.

Eva didn't respond. She felt herself getting nauseous. She knew she was going to be sick. She got up, ran to the bathroom, and vomited violently. Her head was spinning, and she let herself fall back against the wall. She sat on the floor with her head in her hands, rocking back and forth. Liz and Monica followed her and were banging on the bathroom door.

'What's going on? Open the door! Eva, *say* something!'

Eva was unable to respond and sat in disbelief. After several minutes, she got her speech back and pulled herself up from the floor. She opened the door and walked to the basin to rinse her face. 'Sorry, girls. I think I've got a bug. I need to go home.'

Without saying another word, she left the bathroom and dashed out of the bar. She almost fell over running down the road. When she got to the pedestrian crossing, she finally stopped and leaned forward to catch her breath. After a minute, she stood straight up and, for a moment, thought about what just happened. *What is going on? Why am I so upset? Who is to say this woman has the same nightmare? It could be about anything. Maybe Liz hadn't even heard correctly. After all, she did say the woman couldn't speak properly and was always heavily medicated.*

Eva decided to get a cup of tea to calm down before going home. Although she kept telling herself this was a freak coincidence, she was unable to shed the unnerving feeling it wasn't.

***

Eva stormed into the apartment. Before she closed the door, she was already calling for Christine.

'I'm in the bathroom,' Christine yelled back.

'I need to talk to you, Chris. *Now!*'

Christine opened the bathroom door, 'This better be important.'

'I just met with Liz. She told me there's a woman in the nursing home where she works who suffers from terrible nightmares even though she's taking heavy medication.'

'And...? I'm sure there are lots of people in the world with nightmares. Eva, you scared me. Don't come running in like that again.'

'I haven't finished.' Eva put her hand nearly in Christine's face to stop her from speaking or walking away. 'She has nightmares about earthquakes and blue lights.' Christine looked at Eva with wary eyes.

'I was sick in the bathroom of the pub when she told me. I know people have nightmares, even nightmares about earthquakes; but blue lights...? Christine, it *has* to be the same nightmare.'

'Are you sure about this? Did Liz specifically mention earthquakes and blue lights?'

'Yes. The woman is under heavy medication. When she

wakes up, she is terrified but, because of the medication, she can't explain the nightmare in the detail she once did, however, she mentions the earthquake and the blue light.'

'If this is true, we'll have to visit her.' Christine walked into the living room and sat down. Eva followed her closely.

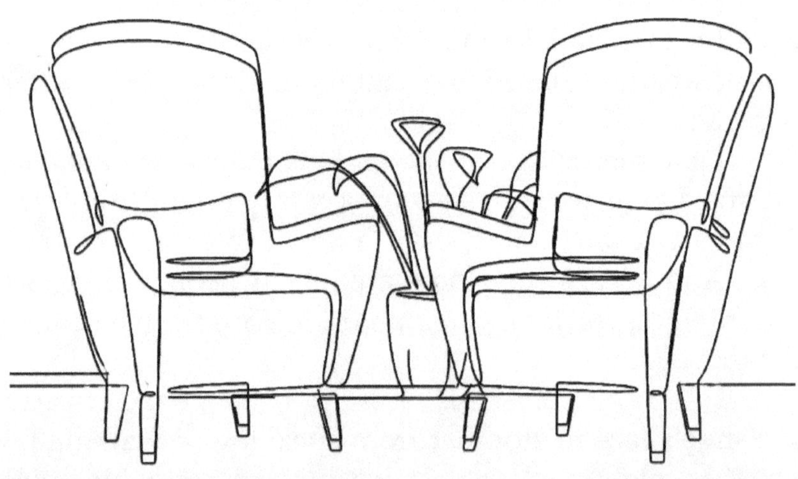

<h1 style="text-align:center">24</h1>

Confessing and Hair-Do's

Eva was sipping her beer as she waited for Steve. She thought of their first date. She still couldn't believe how close they'd become in such a short time. For Eva, it was impossible to consider life without Steve. She secretly started to fantasize about their future together. Where would they live? Would they get married and perhaps have children in the future?

Eva never had these feelings before and, even though she enjoyed being in love, she couldn't help feeling anxious. She couldn't shake the feeling that Steve would get bored or fall out of love. Liz and Monica told her these feelings were perfectly normal at the beginning of a relationship, but it didn't help her at all.

She stared out of the window and watched Steve walking toward the restaurant. Eva got up and put her hands around his neck and kissed him when he reached her. 'I missed you,' she said, her hands still around him.

'Me too.' Steve kissed her again.

Eva was wearing an off-shoulder jumper dress that showed off her curvy body and accentuated her tiny waist. As Steve looked at her, Eva could see his eyes going over her. 'Like what you see?' she asked.

'Very much so.' He grinned. Before looking at the menu, Steve gestured for one of the waiters and ordered a beer. 'I've been looking forward to this all day. I'm starving.' Steve picked up a menu. 'I'll have the usual.' He smiled and put his menu down. 'How have you been? How's work?'

'Pretty good.' She shrugged her shoulders. 'Not a lot going on other than starving teenagers who want to become famous and marry a football player or a rock star.' Eva stared down at her plate and took another sip of beer. 'Christine and I went to see one of the people from the orphanage, just as you suggested.'

'And…?'

'Nothing. She only recognized your father. She didn't even know Dr. Abrahams or Dr. Bernard. I don't think there's a link to the orphanage. We did find out something interesting. Jane, the woman we went to see, told us that your father only looked after Christine and me. She said he refused to see the other children.'

'That's odd. Are you sure that's right? My father boasts about his charity work whenever he talks to Daulton and me.'

'She seemed fairly sure. She said your father contacted the orphanage two weeks after we were left there. He said he read in the paper that two girls were left on the steps of the orphanage one week of each other and said he wanted to donate his time and talent to look after us.'

The waitress came to their table and Steve ordered for both of them. 'The next time I see my father; I can ask him about it.'

'I'm not sure that's such a good idea. He might think we're checking up on him.'

'Isn't that what you're doing?'

'Yes. But he doesn't need to know that.'

'I didn't know you and Christine were left separately. I always assumed you were left together.'

'No. There was a week, eight days to be exact, in-between. First, Christine. And, a week later, yours truly.'

'You know, when I first met the two of you, I was

convinced you were sisters. You are darker than Christine, but there is something similar.'

'A lot of people say that. Maybe it's because we've been living together for too long,' Eva giggled. 'You know what they say about dogs and their owners. Maybe Christine and I slowly started to mimic each other. I don't see the resemblance.'

Their conversation was interrupted by their starters being brought to the table; hot and sour soup for Eva and dumplings for Steve.

'We have something in common though,' Eva said while eating her soup carefully, so she didn't burn her tongue. 'It's very odd. I've never told anyone other than your father about this, but we have the same nightmare; ever since we were fifteen. It has always the been the same and very scary. In the beginning, we thought we were unlucky, but one day when we were talking, we found out that our nightmares are identical…isn't that something?' Eva made some science fiction noises and waved her fingers in front of her.

'That's crazy!' Steve exclaimed. 'What does my father say?'

'He doesn't know what to suggest. He prescribes sleeping pills; which we have been taking for years now. He suggested we take a hypnotherapy session with Dr. Bernard.' After that, she sat in silence, not knowing what to say. 'I'm not sure I want to do that; especially now. I'm sorry to say this, but I don't trust your father anymore.'

'Not sure if I do. So, don't worry.' They looked at each other as though the other would have a solution. 'Anyway, let's eat.'

Eva felt strangely relieved. It was as though a weight had been lifted off her shoulders. Steve hadn't reacted weirdly. He seemed to be on her side. It was a good feeling to know there were no longer any secrets between them.

Christine waited for Eva in a pub near the modelling agency. Eva finally talked her into joining her for a great new haircut. It was perfect; they both felt they deserved some cheering up and what better way to cheer up a girl than a new hairdo. Eva made the appointments at Armando's, *the best* hair salon in the city.

Luckily, she was able to book two appointments at the same time. She always referred the new models to Armando's for a fresh look. Now, it was time to call in a favour. Christine was nervous. She didn't have Eva's confidence. Eva could shave her head and still look feminine. Christine secretly loved her long, wavy hair and was horrified by the thought of someone cutting it all off.

Eva ran into the bar all flushed. 'I'm sorry I'm late. Some silly girl wouldn't stop talking about facial expressions. Don't they realize I'm not the best person to give advice on this? I told her to start practicing in front of the mirror. I'm seriously losing interest in my job. In the beginning, I thought it was very glamorous, but now I find it irritating. If I hear one more stick-insect complain about her thighs or belly, I'm going to hang myself.'

'Calm down. You're not late at all. We still have fifteen minutes, and the salon is just around the corner. Have something to drink and tell me about this salon. I'm petrified that some scissor-happy creature is going to cut off all my hair.'

'Don't be silly. They discuss the cut first. It's not some television make-over show where they start to cut or colour without your consent. Relax, they'll give you the greatest hair cut ever. They didn't become the best by making people unhappy.'

As they walked into the hair salon, Christine started feeling even more agitated. All the hairdressers, or stylist as they preferred to be called, were looking and acting like superstars. They checked-out the clientele in the mirrors but didn't bother to greet or even acknowledge anyone.

Christine and Eva took a seat on the black leather sofa. The receptionist, obviously a big fan of peroxide, was too busy on the phone to greet them. All of a sudden, a larger-than-life character walked over to them.

'Eva, my darling. How wonderful to see you.' He air-kissed Eva and clapped his hands together. 'I'm *so* looking forward to giving you the hair cut of a lifetime.' While he was talking, he worked his fingers through Eva's hair. 'You have great hair. I love it. And who is this beautiful woman?' He had spotted Christine, who felt dreadfully embarrassed by the over-the-top attention she was about to receive.

'Christine. I'm Eva's roommate.'

He grabbed the hand she had put out to introduce herself and kissed it. He started to play with her hair and spun her around as if she was a Barbie doll. 'I can see some colour for you, my dear.'

Christine realized he finished checking her and turned around to face him. He wore leather jeans and a white pirate shirt. His chest was covered with an array of necklaces; some made of silver, some of gold, and some he must have made in a community centre jewellery course. He had an enormous belt buckle and his red snake-leather cowboy boots made his feet look like fishing boats. Christine smiled shyly and hoped he didn't realize how uncomfortable she was feeling.

'I have the perfect stylist for you, my dear,' he said, while holding her hand. '*Antoine*,' he called out in a surprisingly authoritative voice. Christine realized that his outrageous manner was for show only, underneath the over-the-top exterior lay an astute businessman.

'Antoine, this lovely lady is Christine. She is an especially important lady, and this is her first time in our salon. I want you to give her some more depth in colour and maybe a few honey-coloured highlights. You can start by making her feel comfortable and give her a glass of champagne.'

He let go of Christine's hand. Antoine changed from an arrogant wannabe into a caring and concerned cutie. He walked her to his workstation and handed her a glass of bubbly. 'I suggest we don't take too much off the length, but I think that a bit of colour will lighten up your face.' Antoine was speaking in an animated way and with a slight French accent.

'Okay.' Christine felt more relaxed as she sipped her drink. She decided to fully enjoy this royal treatment.

'You must be Eva's sister,' Antoine said, making conversation.

'No. We're roommates. But we may as well be sisters. We have known each other all our lives.'

'That's wonder....' Antoine started to say.

'Christine! Is that you?' Christine looked up and, to her horror, she saw Marlene Patterson walking up to her. 'How *wonderful* to see you,' she said as she pushed Antoine out of the way to give Christine one of her trade air kisses. 'I'm organizing another get-together next week on Wednesday. You and Eva *must* come. I've invited some fantastic people. I would like you to meet them.'

'Thank you, Marlene. That is truly kind, but I'm not sure if we're free Wednesday.'

'Nonsense. I insist.'

'In that case… we'd love to come.'

'Must rush. I have an appointment. Please give my regards to Eva.' Marlene hurried out of the salon; no doubt she had an important meeting at a nail salon.

'You know Marlene Patterson?' Antoine asked with a wicked smile on his face.

'Unfortunately, I do,' Christine said and smiled back.

25

Another Party

When Christine and Eva left the salon, they were walking on air. They looked wonderful. Christine loved her new colour and highlights. Antoine styled her hair with large Hollywood-type curls that made her feel irresistible. Eva's dark hair was straightened and, what were her usual masses of curls, lay soft and shiny on her back, stretching to her waist.

'We should go out this evening. We look super.' Eva took Christine's arm.

'I'm sorry. I can't this evening. I already made other plans.' Christine felt awful but she wasn't ready to tell Christine she was seeing Eric.

'Pity. I'll just have to surprise Steve this evening.'

'Before I forget, did you see Marlene in the salon?'

'Marlene? She was there? Thankfully, I missed her. What did the old bat want?'

Christine giggled, 'She's having another soiree next week on Wednesday, and we are duly invited,' Christine said with a very posh accent.

'Joy of joys. Another wild evening at casa Patterson. I can't wait.'

***

Christine looked around the theatre lobby for Eric. She spotted him at the information desk buying a program. She tapped him on the shoulder and could see a flicker of approval in his eyes

'You've changed your hair. It looks wonderful.' Eric kissed her on her cheek

'Glad you noticed.'

'Do you want a drink before the show starts?' Eric asked. Christine nodded and asked for a glass of white wine. 'Take a seat at that little table in the corner. I'll get the drinks.'

Christine sat at the table and felt great. The looks she received when she walked into the theatre had not escaped her. She felt confident. She was wearing a lace halter neck with ladder stitching that draws the eye to the high mock neck. She wore a fitted waistline of an elegant lace sheath dress with whimsical, scalloped lace edges. Her stunning wavy hair hung on her bare back. Eric walked back to the table with two glasses of white wine.

'You were always beautiful, but this evening you are simply breath-taking.' Eric picked up his glass and toasted her. 'I'm glad we have some time before the show starts. I'm just going to talk, and I want you to listen...' Christine nodded. 'I've made a huge mistake breaking up with you and I am seriously regretting it. I want to be with you, Christine. You are the woman I love. This time I will not let you down and I'll give you all the attention you deserve.' He took her hand and looked her deeply in the eyes. 'Please, Christine, give me another chance. I know that I can make you happy.'

'Well, that was something,' Christine said. She didn't know how to respond.

'What do you think?'

'Eric, I'm not sure. So much has happened. You hurt me and I'm not sure if getting back together so soon is such a good idea.'

'But I told you, Chris, I'm a changed man. I'll *never* let

anything get in the way again.'

Christine thought for a moment. 'I think I'd love to give you another chance, Eric. But please don't hurt me again.'

Eric got up and took Christine in his arms and kissed her passionately. 'You just made me the happiest man in the world. Before I forget, I know it's a bit presumptuous, but I couldn't resist.' He took a small blue box with a white ribbon from his pocket.

Christine opened the little *Tiffany* box and inside were the sweetest pearl earrings surrounded by brilliant diamonds. 'These are beautiful, Eric. Thank you.' She got up and kissed him. Christine stared at the earrings. Never had Eric bought her something this beautiful.

'Now, I'll have to take you somewhere where you can show them off,' Eric said.

'I have the perfect occasion. Next week, Wednesday, I've been invited to a party by Marlene Patterson. These earrings are perfect for that event. I would appreciate it if you could come with me.'

'Gladly. I did tell you that this time everything will be different.'

The bell for the start of the show rang. Eric and Christine walked into the theatre hand in hand. Christine felt terrific. She could start thinking about her perfect house and perfect family again.

***

'You are the biggest fool I have ever met!' Eva said to Christine as they stood outside the Patterson's house.

'I knew you would be angry, but I am entitled to make my own decisions, even if it means getting hurt again.' Christine defended herself. 'Eric is going to be here this evening, and I'd appreciate it if you could act civilly towards him.'

'Christine, you're putting yourself in such a vulnerable position. Did you forget how much he hurt you? Because I sure haven't. You were in the hospital for goodness sake! Why do you want to expose yourself to that again?'

'People change. Eric told me he is truly sorry for what he did to me and I believe him. Isn't that what matters most, how I feel?'

Eva looked at Christine for a moment, thinking about what she just said. 'I suppose you're right. But make sure he doesn't hurt you again.'

'He won't. I'm certain of it.'

'Okay. If you say so. Come. Let's go inside. We have an evening of pure pleasure ahead of us and I don't want to miss a minute,' Eva said, sarcastically.

As usual, they were greeted by yet another hired maid and were ushered into the living room were the other guests had already gathered. To their surprise, there were some new faces in the crowd, even some young ones.

'Hello, girls. Welcome,' Marlene said in a rather bored voice. 'Please make yourselves comfortable and get a drink. Eva, please take it easy.' She tried to joke but, judging by her eyes, Eva knew she wasn't.

Eric walked across the room. 'Hi, Chris. I've been waiting for you. You look stunning.'

'Thanks. I'm wearing my new earrings. Look.' She showed off her earrings with pride.

Eva searched the room for Steve. She spotted him sitting in a corner with an amazingly beautiful woman. They were chatting amicably, and Eva felt a pang of jealousy. She was unsure what to do. Should she walk up to him and kiss him? Or should she give him space and wait for him to notice her? This was just the thing she hated about being in love; the insecurity and anxiety freaked her out.

'Eva, I brought you a Martini.' Marlene had sneaked up behind her and handed her a cocktail glass. She was wearing a yellow silk sleeveless dress. Eva had to admit she looked beautiful. Marlene looked tanned and her hair and make-up were exquisite. The high stiletto heels made her almost as tall as Eva.

'Marlene, you startled me,' Eva said, trying to act as normal as possible.

'Don't they look wonderful together?'

'What do you mean?'

'Steven and Annabel, obviously. Weren't you looking at them?'

'Uh-umm.'

'Annabel has just returned from travelling the world. She has only been back for six weeks and has already managed to be chosen for a position as a senior buyer at *Debonair's Fashion House*.' Marlene sipped her dry white wine. 'Not a surprise. Annabel is a natural when it comes to fashion, and she has amazing connections. Her family is one of the most prominent in the city.'

'She is stunning,' Eva mumbled. 'If you'll excuse me, I'll go over and say *hello* to Steve.'

'Better not,' Marlene said, with a cold glare in her eyes. She grabbed Eva by the wrist.

'Marlene, you're hurting me!' Eva exclaimed.

'What's going on?' Christine appeared behind Marlene and saw what was happening. 'Marlene, please let go of Eva. Can't you see you're hurting her?' Marlene let go of Eva's wrist and walked away. 'Did you see that look she gave me?'

'Did you see what she did to my wrist? That woman is deranged. I always knew she didn't like me, but this is pushing it.'

'Eva, what happened?' Steve asked. He had seen the commotion.

'Your mother didn't want Eva to come and greet you when you were talking to that woman. She nearly broke her wrist,' Christine said.

'Come with me to the bar and we'll put some ice on it,'
Steve said. Eva was happy to be pampered.

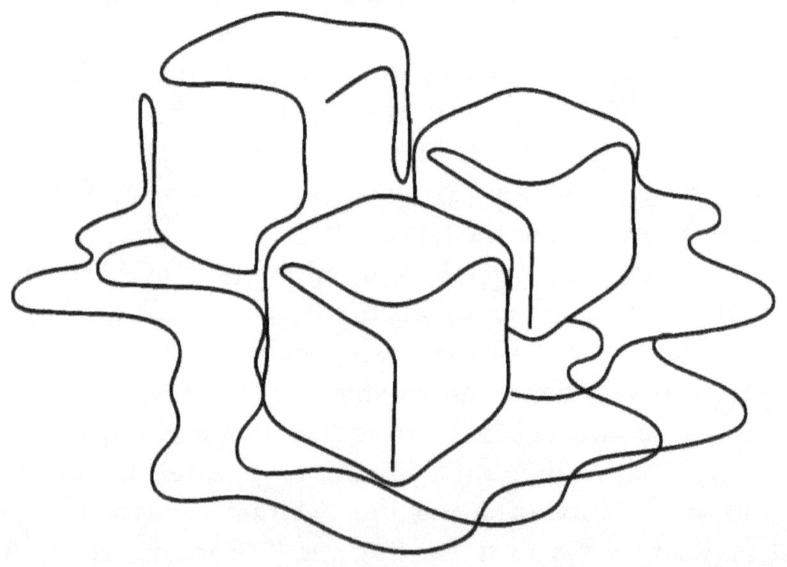

26

Defending Eva

Christine saw Marlene talking to Dr. Patterson and Dr. Abrahams in the corner. She decided to confront Marlene immediately.

'Christine, how wonderful to see you,' Dr. Patterson said as she walked up.

'You look more beautiful every time we see you,' Dr. Abrahams joined in. 'I hear you are dating my 'number two,' Eric Woodland. I'm genuinely pleased for both of you.'

'Thank you, Dr. Abrahams,' Christine said without even looking at him. She turned to Marlene. 'What were you thinking, Marlene? You nearly broke Eva's wrist,' she said, her eyes staring angrily at Marlene.

'Don't be silly, Christine. Do I look like a woman who could break someone's wrist? I have enough problems opening a bottle of water.'

'I can assure you that Marlene doesn't even have the strength to break the leg of a spider,' Dr. Patterson said, and chuckled at his joke. Christine knew it would be useless talking to them. They would pretend it never happened.

'Christine, how wonderful to see you.'

'Good evening, Dr. Alamilla. How are you?' Christine greeted Dr. Alamilla but was unable to bring a smile to her face. Christine saw Eric walk up to her and felt a wave of relief. 'Eric, I'm not feeling very well. Do you mind taking me home?'

'Christine, you're surrounded by doctors. I'm sure one of them can give you something to feel better.' Everyone laughed at Eric's joke.

'Eric, I would like to go home.'

'Give me five minutes to catch up with these gentlemen.'

Christine made her way to the bar to join Eva and Steve. 'I've asked Eric to take me home. I won't stay here for another minute. I'm sorry, Steve.'

'Where is he?' Steve asked her.

Christine turned and pointed in the direction where Eric had been. 'He's over there, talking to Dr. Abrahams and Dr. Alamilla. Jeez… he told me he only wanted to say *hello* to them.' Then she asked Eva, 'Are you sure you want to stay here? Can we ask Steve to drop both of us at home?'

'No. I won't let Marlene bully me.'

Christine ordered another drink. When she checked her watch, she saw that thirty minutes had passed. 'Where have you been? You said you'd be five minutes,' Christine was angry when Eric finally showed up.

'Christine, these people are my superiors. If they want to speak to me, they want to speak to me. What can I say? I'm deeply sorry, Chris. Let's go. I'll take you home.'

'We're leaving,' Christine said, and kissed Eva and Steve goodbye.

They'd been driving for about ten minutes when Eric brought up the subject, 'Dr. Patterson told me there was an episode between Mrs. Patterson and Eva.'

'Well, is that what he calls it? Marlene Patterson grabbed Eva's wrist so hard she nearly broke it.'

'Don't be so silly,' Eric said. 'Marlene Patterson is a tiny woman, and I can't see her breaking anything.'

'Well, she did.'

'Eva has always been a bit of a hothead. She likes to

exaggerate,' Eric said.

'That's not true. Why would you say something like that?'

'Marlene told me that Eva became terribly upset when she saw Steve talking to Annabel Malmesbury. She probably got jealous and made up some story to get Steve's attention. Eva's a nice girl but she does like to be the centre of everything.'

Christine felt herself getting angry. Who did Marlene think she was? She didn't think it was necessary to defend herself to Eric. 'Maybe Eva likes attention, but she certainly doesn't make up stories,' Christine said dryly.

'I'm sorry, Chris. I didn't mean to upset you. It's just that the whole story about Marlene nearly breaking Eva's arm is somewhat unlikely. I do, however, believe you. And if you say it happened – it happened.' He leaned over to the passenger seat and kissed her. 'How do you feel about spending the night at my place? I make a wonderful breakfast.'

'Sounds great,' Christine said and looked at Eric as he was driving. She was pleased they were back together. She was already picturing herself married this time next year.

***

Eva's wrist was still red and swollen but had stopped aching. 'Who was that woman you were talking to?'

'That was my mother's favourite daughter-in-law,' Steve said. 'Her name is Annabel Malmesbury. I told you about her, didn't I? My mother thinks we would make a lovely couple.' He put his arms around Eva and pulled her tight. 'You, my little princess, have nothing to worry about.'

'I wasn't worried,' Eva lied.

'Good.'

'Eva, you look particularly beautiful this evening.' Dr.

187

Abrahams checked her out from top to toe.

'I'm glad you approve.'

'May I have another Martini, please?' she asked one of the waiters. She needed some courage as she could see Dr. Alamilla approaching too.

'Good evening, Eva.'

'Dr. Alamilla, I recently found out that you all work together at Dr. Patterson's pharmaceutical company. I always assumed you were just fellow physicians. You must have known each other for a very long time.'

'We have indeed. Most of us go back over thirty years.'

From the corner of her eye, Eva could see Dr. Alamilla gesturing to Dr. Patterson. 'Where are you from originally, Dr. Alamilla? I'm sure I can hear a Spanish accent.'

'You heard correctly, Eva. Dr. Alamilla is from South America. Chile, to be precise,' Dr. Patterson stepped in.

'Dr. Patterson, good evening. Chile. That must be a wonderful and interesting country. Have you been there, Dr. Patterson?'

'Steven, I believe it best if you take Eva home. I think she's had a few too many Martini's.'

'I'm sure she's fine, father. Eva can hold her drink.'

Eva shot Dr. Patterson a glorious look. He couldn't put his son against her. She put her arm around Steve and rested her head on his shoulder. 'Did you know that Dr. Alamilla is from Chile? I've met people from Argentina and Brazil, but never Chile. Have you ever been to Chile, Steve?'

'Can't say I have. But my father has.' Dr. Patterson's face became stern with anger.

'I think maybe the two of you have had enough to drink. I insist that you take a taxi home. Maria,' he called one of the maids, 'please call two taxis for my son and Ms. Williams.'

'Maria, one taxi will do. Ms. Williams and I will be going home together.' Eva smiled.

Dr. Patterson stormed off, leaving his guests. He closed his study door and poured himself a large whiskey. After a few seconds, Marlene and Alan Abrahams joined him. 'Something needs to be done. We cannot take the risk of being exposed.' Dr. Patterson was red in the face and his nostrils moved in anger.

'What do you suggest we do?' Marlene asked her husband.

'I'll think of something to stop this once and for all. I have had more than enough of those girls. Even their nightmares don't interest me any longer.'

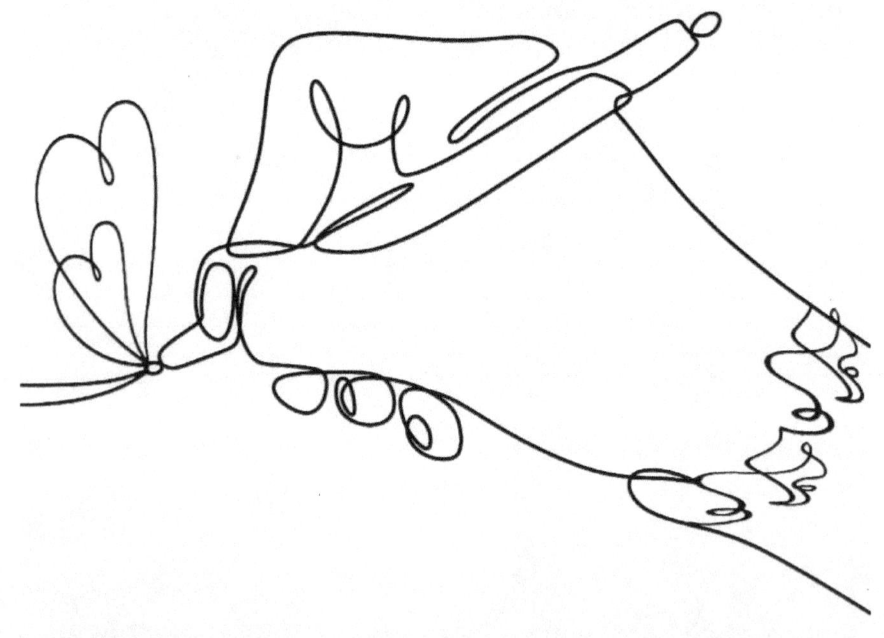

27

Mrs. Austin

'I spoke to Liz today and asked her about her patient in the nursing home who has the nightmares,' Eva said, holding the phone in one hand and doodling with the other.

'That must have surprised her; you asking about one of the old folkies.'

'Funny enough, she wasn't. Liz loves her people, as she calls them. She assumes everyone else feels the same way. She told me the nightmares are continuing, and that the nursing home doctor keeps increasing her medication. I asked Liz if we could visit her.'

'Now, that must have caused a raised eyebrow,' Christine smiled.

'I'm sure she was surprised, but she hid it well. She said that Mrs. Austin - that's her name, by the way - doesn't get visitors and that a visit just might cheer her up. We can visit her whenever we want to. The home doesn't have set visiting hours. So, what do you think? Should we go?'

'I feel a bit like an inheritance hunter, but I'm interested in meeting this woman. How about tomorrow after work? That way, I can build up some courage this evening.'

'Perfect. I'll phone Liz.' Eva picked up the phone and dialled Liz's number. 'I've spoken to Christine, and we would like to visit Mrs. Austin tomorrow after work if that's okay?'

'What's your interest in this woman? You've never really cared for the elderly. I'm not saying you shouldn't come. I'm just a bit surprised.'

'Not as surprised as I am, Liz. Maybe it's time I start showing a bit more interest in the old folkies. Heck, I hope to be one someday.'

***

The next day, both Christine and Eva were agitated all day. Eva made a gigantic mistake by sending wrong models for a *go-see*, which led to her boss screaming and shouting like a banshee. Christine did nothing but play endless solitaire on her computer. She kept watching the clock. She had a lunch date with Eric in a lovely little diner close to the library.

As she walked to the restaurant, she wondered if she should have cancelled. She knew she wouldn't be good company, but she felt it was too early to tell Eric about the nightmares. As she walked into the quaint little restaurant, she looked around and discovered that Eric had not arrived yet. She sat in one of the booths and looked over the menu.

'Miss, would you like to order?' a round-faced, middle-aged waitress asked her.

'I'm waiting for my boyfriend. I'll have tea with lemon for now.' As she sipped her second glass of tea, Eric walked into the diner. 'Eric, I've been waiting for over fifteen minutes. Really? You could have called to let me know you were going to be late.'

'Hi, babe. Have you ordered already?' he asked, ignoring her remark; nor did he apologize.

'No. I was waiting for you.'

'Okay. Well, let's order quickly. I have to be back in the office in thirty minutes.'

'Well, I'm so pleased you could find the time to grace me with your presence,' Christine snapped.

'I'm going for a bowl of soup. That should be nice and quick,' Eric said, and called the waitress. 'I'll have onion soup.' And, without looking up, he asked, 'Christine, what are you having?'

'I'll take the Caesar salad with chicken and a small serving of French fries please.'

'What sort of combination is that?' Eric asked.

'What's wrong with that combination? I like them both. So why not eat them together?'

'That's one of those things I love about you. You're so simple in your choices.'

'What's that supposed to mean – *I'm simple*?'

'It's a compliment, Christine. You don't mind putting on a few pounds or eating two things that don't go together at all. I think it's sweet.'

'I'm pleased you find me so endearing.' Christine could feel herself getting terribly angry. In one sentence, he called her dumb and someone who doesn't mind getting fat and ate like a child. 'Maybe you can send me to a finishing school where they can teach me all about your sophisticated world.'

'What's gotten into you? I make time for you in my busy schedule, and you act like a spoiled child.' Eric said, chewing on the bread served with his soup.

'You know something, Eric, this little spoiled, unsophisticated child has lost her appetite.' Christine got up but, before leaving, she quickly put a handful of fries in her mouth.

As she walked back to the library, her mobile phone rang. She saw Eric's name and let it ring. Maybe Eric wasn't the right man for her after all. She couldn't believe how condescending his remarks were. Did he see her like that? She switched her phone off when it continued to ring. She didn't want to talk to him. She would call him back this evening or tomorrow when she felt less annoyed.

***

Eva was already standing next to the rented car. 'Ready for this?' she asked when Christine walked up. 'Can't say that I am.'

'I'm not sure how I feel about this visit,' Christine said, while driving.

'I'm so nervous. If Liz is right, the woman is not even awake. So, why do I feel so scared? I think it's because we will be properly confronting our nightmares for the first time. Yes, we know it's freaky, not to mention abnormal, but we never once really talked or did anything about it. Not with each other and certainly not with other people.'

'Since when did you become so rational?'

'Christine, think about it. The reason why we're having such a difficult time is because we have to face some random stranger who suffers from the same weird dreams. Now, we no longer have an excuse to ignore it.'

'At least we have each other. I couldn't imagine doing this alone,' Christine said.

They drove up to the nursing home, which was just outside the city. It was an exquisite home with beautiful green surroundings. 'What a beautiful place. It must cost a pretty penny to stay here.'

'I'm sure it does. Whenever I become a needy old woman, make sure you bring me here,' Eva said.

They parked their rented car and walked into the hall where the reception was situated. The inside was decorated for luxury and comfort. The reception desk, staffed by an impeccably presented lady in her mid-forties, was enormous. There was a large vase of fresh flowers sitting on the far end. She smiled as Christine walked over to her. 'How may I help you?' she asked in a surprisingly low, raspy voice.

'We're here to see Mrs. Austin.'

'Mrs. Austin? Are you family?'

'No. We're not.'

'We're friends of Liz O'Connor. Could you call her for us please,' Eva interrupted.

Without responding, the receptionist put out a call for Liz. Christine and Eva stood motionless by the reception desk. 'Please take a seat. Liz should be here shortly,' the receptionist said.

They walked to the large sofa and sat like two statues; straight backs and clinging on to their handbags.

'Eva, Christine, how are you?' Liz said, walking toward them with a big smile on her face.

Liz was one of those people everyone liked instantly. She had a round face and was always smiling. Her dark red hair was pulled back in a ponytail. She was slightly overweight, but this didn't take away from her beauty. The truth was she probably looked best with a few pounds more. Her white pressed nurse's uniform was spotless. She wore a dark purple knit cardigan over her shoulders that was stunning with her hair colour.

'I'm so pleased that Mrs. Austin finally has visitors,' Liz said. 'In all the years she has been with us, you two are the first.'

'That's terribly sad,' Christine remarked. 'She has no living family?'

'Not that we know of. And, if she does after all these years, can you still call them family? Come, I'll show you to her room.' Liz walked down a long hall. 'Miranda, I'm taking these ladies to see Mrs. Austin,' Liz told the receptionist, who nodded and smiled as they passed her desk.

They walked through a wide corridor. The home had elegant lounges on every floor where residents could socialize together with family and smaller lounges for quiet, peaceful visits. All the doors to the rooms were closed. At the end of the hallway was a large window that looked out over the back garden. Liz stopped at one of the doors and knocked.

'I thought you said she was out-of- it?' Eva asked.

'Eva, you're so blunt. She's probably sleeping, but I feel it's polite to knock.' Liz opened the door and walked in. Both Christine and Eva froze. They looked at each other. Panic was written all over their faces. 'You can come in.' Liz peeked around the corner.

Christine went in first. She clutched her handbag to her chest. Eva was closely behind her and was peaking over Christine's shoulders. There she was. It almost seemed ridiculous to think they were nervous. The woman they saw lying in bed looked so vulnerable that it nearly broke their hearts. She was lying in a large, single hospital bed. Her brown, curly hair, with grey strands mixed in, was spread over the three pillows that supported her head. Her eyes were closed. As Christine and Eva stepped closer, they nearly fainted.

'I need to do my rounds,' Liz said. 'I'll be back in about twenty minutes.'

'Uh-Ummm,' Both Christine and Eva mumbled without giving a real response. Liz walked out of the room and closed the door behind her.

'It's her, Eva. It's her! It's the woman from the photo!' Eva was still unable to speak and nodded. 'Mrs. Austin. Mrs. Austin, can you hear me?' Christine whispered near Mrs. Austin's ear.

'I don't think she can hear you.'

'Of course, she can hear me. She is so drugged that she can't respond. Mrs. Austin,' Christine shook her shoulder softly. 'Wake up, Mrs. Austin.'

'It's no use, Christine. What are you talking about anyway? If she's drugged, she won't hear you. That's for sure.' Both girls sat next to Mrs. Austin's bed. They both just stared at the woman.

'Who is she?' Christine asked.

'I can ask Liz later. Maybe she knows something about

her. I mean she must have been brought here by somebody, and someone must be paying the bills?'

'Excellent point.' Christine's face lit up. For the remainder of the visit, both girls sat quietly, deep in their thoughts.

Liz returned after what seemed forever. 'I'm sorry girls, but I must run. We have an emergency I have to attend to,' Liz said, slightly out of breath. 'I have to say *goodbye* for now.' She quickly kissed the girls *goodbye* and ran out of the room.

'I suppose I'll have to call her tomorrow for the details,' Eva said.

'We'll come back,' Christine leaned over and whispered in Mrs. Austin's ear.

'I told you before, Chris. She can't hear you!'

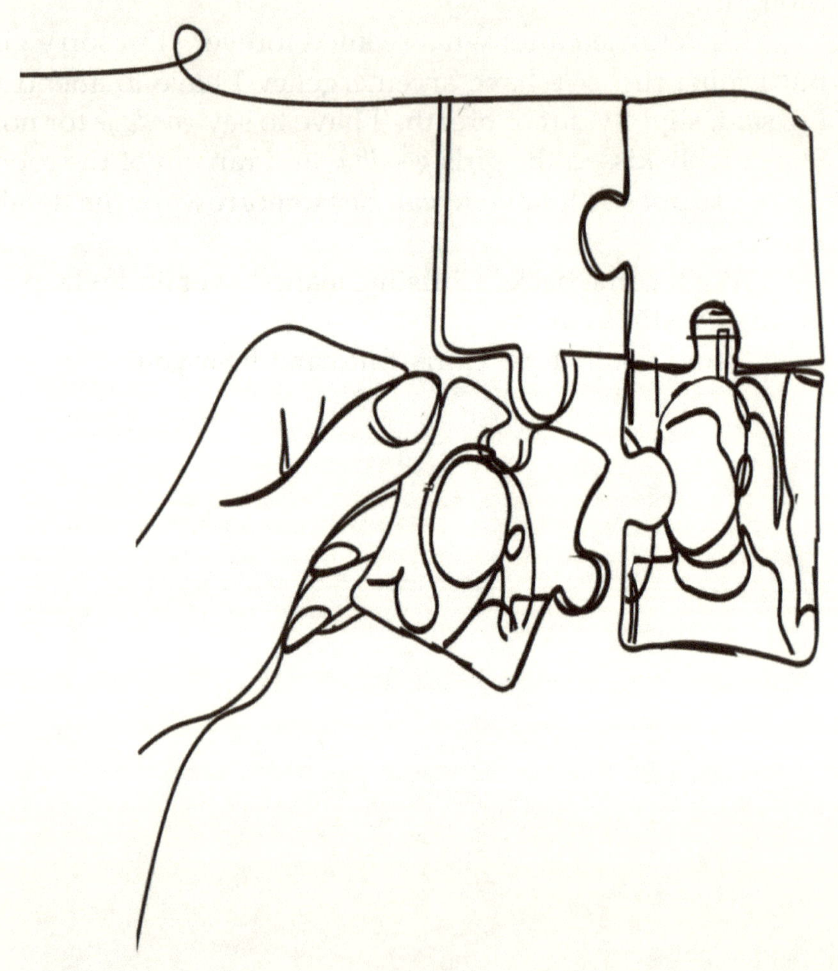

28

What Next?

'So, this is what we know so far,' Christine said. 'We know that one of the ladies in the photo is Mrs. Eastman, who died in a car accident while leaving Dr. Patterson's party. The other lady is Mrs. Austin, who is lying drugged to her eyebrows in a nursing home. Then, we have Dr. Bernard, Dr. Abrahams, and Dr. Alamilla, who all work at Dr. Patterson's pharmaceutical company now.'

'I'll contact that police detective who investigated the car accident. I never really did muster up the courage to phone him,' Eva said.

'And ask him what exactly?'

'He must have done a decent investigation. Maybe there were some serious suspects but, because of the lack of evidence, no one was charged. I mean, you hear about those kinds of things all the time.'

'Yeah. On *Law and Order* maybe,' Christine said.

'I'm so sorry. Do you have a better suggestion? The only thing all your purposes have in common is Dr. Patterson.'

'Eva, don't be ridiculous. Didn't Dr. Patterson save my life when he found me after the sleeping pills episode?'

'I know. But that was before we had the photo and, come to think of it, why did he visit us that day? We've lived here for the past seven years and that man has visited maybe three

199

times.'

'I think you're becoming a bit paranoid.'

'It's not paranoia. You're suspicious too. You're just too stubborn to admit it,' Eva said.

'I don't think I'm stubborn. I think you're overreacting.' Christine tried to stay calm.

'As I said, if you have a better idea, please tell me. I'm all ears,' Eva responded, annoyed.

'Okay. We'll do it your way. You phone that inspector and see what he has to say.'

'Do you mind doing it?' Eva asked in a small voice.

Christine looked at her and sighed. It was apparent she was the eldest. 'Do you remember his name?'

'Inspector Peter McMillan.'

Christine picked up the phone and dialled the local police station's number. She didn't want to think too long about phoning the inspector. Otherwise, she most certainly would change her mind. 'Good afternoon. I'm looking for an inspector named Peter McMillan. He worked for the city about twenty years ago.'

She kept looking at Eva while she spoke on the phone. 'Yes. I understand… But we really would like to speak with him regarding a case he worked on. Yes, indeed. It was a car accident involving a Dr. and Mrs. Eastman. Really….? Thank you.' Christine picked up a pen and jotted down a telephone number.

'What did they say?' Eva asked, with big eyes.

Christine ignored Eva's question and immediately dialled the number. 'Inspector Peter McMillan, please.' Eva jumped up excitedly, and walked over to Christine and grabbed her arm.

'Good afternoon. My name is Christine Rhodes. I would like to speak with Inspector McMillan regarding a case he worked on about twenty years ago. Is it possible to make an appointment? It was a suspicious car accident. Two people,

Dr. and Mrs. Eastman, died. Sure. Thank you for your help.'

'What did they say?' Eva asked, shaking Christine's arms.

'Calm down. I only spoke to a detective. He told me he would discuss it with Inspector McMillan. I have to phone back this afternoon.'

'What I don't understand is that most of the people in the photo are doctors or wives of doctors working with Dr. Patterson. What was Mrs. Austin doing there?' Eva asked.

'Let me get out my crystal ball and I'll tell you all about it. Stop asking me silly questions.'

'Wow! Why are you so ticked off?' Eva asked, somewhat taken aback.

'I'm sorry. I don't like what's happening. I like my life predictable, unlike you. You want another coffee?'

'No, thanks. I'm going to take a bath.' Eva left the room, leaving Christine with more questions than she could ever imagine.

29

How It All Began

Late 1980's Years before

Jennifer Earl travelled with two of Dr. Patterson's colleagues, Dr. Bernard and Dr. Abrahams, to the hospital in Chile. By the time they finally reached the hospital deep in the Chilean Andes, she was exhausted. The three flights they took were terrible; but nothing compared to the dreaded car ride over the rugged and unsteady road leading to the Barros Rosario hospital in Santa Tecla. They must have travelled for at least thirty hours. Jennifer felt shattered.

As they drove into the small town of Santa Tecla, Jennifer was pleasantly surprised. The houses were painted in lovely soft blue and pink colours. The streets were asphalted and clean. Several little shops sold food and general home care items. As they drove down the main street, some of the local people waved at the passing car as though a government official had arrived. Jennifer felt embarrassed, but waved back, nonetheless, at the happy smiley faces.

They pulled up outside the hospital. It was small, but charming; a whitewashed building with a red roof and large arched windows. There was a perfectly resurfaced road leading to the hospital. The hospital was surrounded by native evergreen coihue trees and, at the front, the myrtle bushes were in full bloom. The entire village was an oasis.

Jennifer was surprised tourists didn't flood the place. She was surprised even more so because she was well-travelled but had never heard of Santa Tecla. She stepped out of the Jeep and stretched her arms and legs. Her body ached from being tossed around by the never-ending rocky roads.

She turned around and saw snow-covered hilltops in the distance. Dr. Abrahams and Dr. Bernard walked ahead. Jennifer followed them quickly into the hospital.

Although she just spent the past thirty hours with them, she felt she knew nothing about them. During the trip, they read medical journals or slept. Neither made any attempt to talk to her, other than the fundamental questions.

When she wandered into the reception area, she felt she was back home. This didn't look like a Chilean country hospital. It resembled a four-star hotel. The wooden reception desk had five ceiling spotlights pointing down on the impressive local prints displayed on the back wall. A nurse in a pristine white uniform was behind the desk. Her nameplate read *Pilar Gonzales*. She smiled when Jennifer entered. 'Ms. Earl, we've been expecting you.'

Jennifer was surprised to hear her name. 'Thank you. That is so kind.'

'Our porter is bringing your luggage to your living quarters. If you'd like to follow me, I'll take you there.'

Although Pilar had a thick Spanish accent, her English was perfect. Jennifer followed her outside and they walked to the right side of the hospital to a small apartment complex that faced the street with views of the beautiful snow-capped mountains Jennifer had admired earlier.

'You'll be staying on the second floor,' Pilar said, and walked up the stairs. 'The doctors occupy the apartments on the first floor in case of emergencies.'

'Are you from the village?' Jennifer asked, trying to make conversation.

'No,' Pilar replied shortly; she wasn't interested in telling Jennifer where she was from. Jennifer thought it best not to ask any further questions.

Pilar opened the door and switched on the light. The apartment was delightful. It was furnished with local art and materials, which gave it a warm and inviting feel.

'Over here is the bedroom and bathroom. As you can see, there is a small kitchenette, but we all tend to eat at the hospital's restaurant.'

'There's a restaurant?' Jennifer asked, surprised.

'Yes. All the staff have a sit-down for lunch and dinner every day. Dinner is served at seven, so you have some time to unpack and rest.'

'Is Dr. Patterson here?'

'Yes. Dr. Patterson arrived three days ago. He'll meet you for dinner.'

'Will you be there this evening?' Jennifer asked.

'Of course. I told you all the hospital staff eats together.'

'Oh, yes, so you did.'

'I'll leave your keys on the kitchen counter. Goodbye, Ms. Earl.'

Jennifer sat on the surprisingly comfortable sofa. She looked around and was pleased with the small apartment. All the furniture was made of pinewood. The couch was covered with a wool material with a Native Indios design. A colourful, hand-loomed tapestry covered nearly one entire wall. Jennifer opened the black shutters and held her breath when she saw the beautiful view from her window.

She glanced at her watch and realized she had an hour before dinner with Dr. Patterson and the other staff of the hospital. She walked into the small, but functional, bathroom and took a shower. She felt much better. The hot water softened her stiff muscles.

Then, she walked downstairs in search of the restaurant. As she walked into the large dining room, she spotted Dr.

Patterson sitting with Dr. Bernard, Dr. Abrahams, Pilar, and another gentleman.

'Jennifer, I'm so pleased you're here.' Dr. Patterson jumped up when he saw her come in.

'Hello, Dr. Patterson. It's good to see you.'

'Did you have a pleasant trip? Let me rephrase that. Did you have a decent trip? I know the road from the airport to Santa Tecla is appalling.'

'Well, let's say it wasn't one of the better experiences of my life, although Santa Tecla is fantastic. It's like an unexpected oasis.'

'I'm pleased you like it. We've spent a great deal of money making the place look like this. It's worth it. We, the other doctors and I, spend more time here than back home.'

'Well, I think you've done a fantastic job,' Jennifer smiled.

'Jennifer, let me introduce you to Dr. Alamilla and his wife, Pilar, whom you met earlier.' Dr. Patterson took her arm. 'Are you hungry?'

'To tell you the truth, I'm starving.'

'Let me show you the buffet. We have an excellent chef who makes the most wonderful dishes.'

After enjoying a surprisingly good meal, Jennifer realized she was exhausted.

'Jennifer, if you'll excuse me,' Dr. Patterson said. 'I have a long day ahead tomorrow. I'd like to see you in the morning to discuss the procedure. No rush, any time after you wake up.'

'No problem. I'll come by your office tomorrow morning. Goodnight, Dr. Patterson.'

'Please, Jennifer, we're all friends here. Call me Matthew.'

'Well, in that case, goodnight... Matthew.' When Jennifer said *goodnight* to the other doctors, they barely acknowledged her. She made a quick stop in the kitchen to thank the chef and returned to her room.

She felt overcome by emotions. She loved her new surroundings and knew she would be happy in Santa Tecla. She had a smile on her face as she fell asleep in the large wooden bed. She just knew everything was going to work out wonderfully. She looked forward to helping other, less fortunate women and, the icing on the cake; Dr. Patterson would give her a lovely healthy baby.

***

Jennifer had been in Santa Tecla for eight months and had fallen in love with the quaint old village. She worked as an administrative assistant in the hospital, which involved nothing more than collecting information from patients; a job which could take days. In the rural areas, passport or identification documents were uncommon.

Jennifer threw herself into her new life. She studied Spanish whenever she could and made sure to speak to the patients and locals in the village in their native language whenever her vocabulary allowed it. Soon, she became a beloved person in the village. A stray cat had chosen Jennifer as her new owner. Jennifer enjoyed having the animal around. Whenever she came back from work, Lola, the name she gave the cat, was waiting for her, purring on the sofa. Jennifer always left a window open, so Lola could come and go as she pleased. She always wanted to have an animal, but with her busy job, she found it unfair to leave an animal by itself locked up in a flat in central London.

Every day, before starting her working day, Jennifer saw Dr. Patterson for a general health check and a simple blood test. 'Good morning, Jennifer. I have wonderful news. We're ready to proceed with the treatment,' he told her that morning. 'Please, take a seat and I'll explain the procedure in detail.' Jennifer took a seat. She had a huge smile on her face.

'You'll receive a powerful anaesthetic medication through a catheter we place in your vein. So, you'll be unconscious during the egg retrieval procedure. You won't feel any pain.' Dr. Patterson smiled at her and shared her enthusiasm. 'Recovery is usually straight forward with mild to moderate cramping for a few hours or so. Afterwards, eggs are held in the lab in a test tube (in-vitro). About four hours after we retrieve your eggs, sperm is injected individually into each egg. As I told you, our donors remain anonymous. However, I can tell you that your donor is a healthy white male with an I.Q. of 130.'

'Great. I'm not sure what to say to that, other than that we share the same I.Q.,' Jennifer said, and smiled again.

'The following morning, we examine the eggs for evidence of fertilization. The embryos are cultured in the laboratory for two to five more days before one or more is placed into your uterus by the embryo transfer procedure.' Dr. Patterson continued to explain, 'And then, fourteen days after the initial egg retrieval, we look for evidence of the good news we have all been hoping for. To do this, we test your blood for HCG (human chorionic gonadotropin - the pregnancy hormone.) If that's positive, you are pregnant.'

As Jennifer listened, she looked at Dr. Patterson with teary eyes. This was precisely the news she had hoped for.

The following day, Jennifer walked into the hospital. She over-slept a little due to all the excitement. She changed into a blue hospital gown and proceeded to the examination room. When she walked in, she was surprised to find that Dr. Abrahams, Dr. Alamilla, Dr. Bernard, and Dr. Eastman were also in the room assisting Dr. Patterson.

'Hello, Jennifer. I'll be supported by the other doctors today.'

'Good morning, all. I wasn't expecting an audience.'

Dr. Patterson gave her a warm smile and Jennifer laid on the examination table and placed her legs in the stirrups.

He administered the anaesthetic medication and waited for her to fall asleep. Dr. Patterson inserted a speculum and then inserted a catheter through her cervix. 'All done,' Dr. Patterson said. 'We have now taken some of your eggs. They will be inseminated and in two weeks will be placed back into your womb.'

'Already? I had no idea the procedure was so quick.'

'Well, we're not finished yet. The last and final step must be taken. After we fertilize the eggs and place them into your uterus, we wait to see if they nest in the wall of the uterus in the endometrial lining.' Jennifer felt she understood the process fairly well.

Two weeks later, Dr. Patterson told Jennifer the embryos were ready to be placed into her womb. And, a week later, Jennifer returned to Dr. Patterson. He told her that they found the pregnancy hormone in her blood. Jennifer was pregnant. 'Remember our talk, Jennifer. Being too concerned will affect implantation. It causes unnecessary stress at a time when you should be doing your best to relax. So, continue with your life and take a break whenever you feel tired,' he said, and then continued, 'Then, of course, are the usual no-no's; no alcohol and no smoking. I have the feeling, though, that this is going to be a great pregnancy.' With that, Dr. Patterson took off his surgical gloves and left them for one of the nurses to dispose of.

'Thank you, Dr. Patterson. Thank you, Dr. Abrahams, Dr. Alamilla, Dr. Bernard, and Dr. Eastman,' Jennifer managed to say as the doctors left the operating room. This time they each gave her a nod and a dry smile.

Jennifer changed and walked to her apartment. As she stood in front of the mirror in the bedroom, she gently stroked her belly. Lola rubbed against her legs, 'We're going have a baby, Lola.'

30

More Investigating

It was half-past two. Christine sat staring at the phone. It was time to phone Inspector McMillan again. She was so bold before, but now she felt dreadfully nervous. Suddenly, she picked up the phone but, before dialling the number, she quickly hung it up. She stared at the phone as though it was the enemy. She took a deep breath, picked up the phone again, and dialled the number very quickly.

'Good afternoon. My name is Christine Rhodes. I'm calling for Inspector McMillan.'

'Ah, yes. Ms. Rhodes. I've spoken to Inspector McMillan and he would like to speak with you.'

'Thank you very much.'

'Inspector McMillan.'

Christine was surprised to hear a man speaking sternly. 'Good afternoon, Inspector McMillan. My name is Christine Rhodes. I'm calling regarding a car accident that caused the deaths of Dr. and Mrs. Eastman many years ago,' Christine said very quickly.

'Are you a family member of the Eastman's?'

'No, no.'

'So then, what is your interest in this case?'

'It's an awfully long story, but we, my roommate Eva and I, read an article in the paper about the car accident. We wanted to ask you if there were any suspicious parties or circumstances involved.'

'Ms. Rhodes, even if there were any suspicious parties or circumstances, as you call them, I cannot share that information with you. Can I ask you what your interest is in this twenty-year-old case?'

'I'm not sure, Inspector … I'm sorry to have wasted your time.' She put the phone down quickly.

'What did he say?' Eva asked.

'Exactly what I expected. He thought I was an idiot and told me that he could not comment on the case.'

'Why not?'

'It's an old case and we're not family.'

'I suppose he does have a protocol to follow. Imagine the police discussing their cases with the general public.'

'I suppose you're right. Crap, what do we do now?'

'Not sure,' Eva mused. 'Maybe we should visit him?'

'Yeah… perfect! Then I'll be known at the police station as *Christine Rhodes, certified nutcase: to be avoided at all cost.*'

'Please get me all the information you can find on Christine Rhodes and her roommate, a certain Eva, I didn't get her last name. I want to know who they are, who they know, what they do, and with whom,' Inspector McMillan barked.

'Certainly, Inspector. I'll get on it ASAP.'

***

Eva and Christine drove to the nursing home again. Liz said she would join them today so they could ask her some questions regarding medication and insurance. They parked their car in the same spot. As they walked into the reception area, they saw that Miranda was tidying up her desk. She looked up when they entered. 'I didn't know you were visiting today?'

'Yes. We're here to visit Mrs. Austin again. Hopefully, she'll be slightly clearer today,' Eva answered in a confident tone.

'Sure. Shall I call Liz for you?'

'Yes. Thank you.'

Miranda put a call out for Liz and sat behind her desk again. She started filing some of the papers that were sitting in her in-tray.

'Hi, girls,' Liz greeted them as she made her way around the corner. She was wearing her nurse's uniform, only this time her knit cardigan was a deep pink colour.

'Hey, Liz,' Eva said.

'Shall we go straight to Mrs. Austin's room? Her medication is due in half an hour, so this should be her most lucid time of the day.'

'Great. Let's hope so.' Christine and Eva followed Liz down the corridor to Mrs. Austin's room.

'Mrs. Austin, look who have returned to see you. Christine and Eva.'

Christine and Eva sat next to Mrs. Austin's bed; each on opposite sides. Although Mrs. Austin was by no means a short and petite woman, she looked frail. Her skin was pale and covered with wrinkles. Her arms looked bony and her hands were dry with chipped fingernails.

Liz followed their stare and said, 'The medication does that. It dries out her skin. I try to moisturise her as much as I can, but I don't always have time.'

'She doesn't have visitors?' Eva asked.

'No. I've never seen anyone. Sad, isn't it?'

'Who pays her hospital bills? Surely a place like this doesn't come cheap.'

'There's an association; some charity that pays her bills. Strange, they pay for her stay and medication, but none of their members have ever come to visit,' Liz said and shrugged her shoulders.

Mrs. Austin murmured and Eva and Christine sat up straight in shock. 'Is she awake?' Christine asked.

'You can speak to her and find out. She won't bite you,' Liz replied.

'Mrs. Austin, can you hear me? My name is Christine Rhodes and I have some questions I would like to ask you regarding a photo we found of you. You're standing in front of a hospital in Chile, South America.'

Mrs. Austin moved and grabbed Christine's arm. Christine let out a startled yell.

'Christine, calm down. I told you she's conscious.'

'I'm so sorry. I wasn't expecting her to move.'

'My baby…'

'What about your baby, Mrs. Austin? We saw that you were pregnant in the photo.'

'My baby is dead.'

Christine looked towards Eva for support. Eva, however, remained quiet.

'How did your baby die?' Christine asked.

'Matthew.'

'Who's Matthew? Are you talking about Matthew Patterson?'

Mrs. Austin didn't answer. They could see tears running down her bony cheeks.

'What's going on here?' Dr. Daniel Johnson, the medical director of the facility, asked.

'Dr. Johnson…These are my friends, Christine Rhodes and Eva Williams. They are here to visit Mrs. Austin.'

'They're upsetting her. You should know better than to allow strangers to see our patients, Liz. I suggest you leave now before you upset Mrs. Austin any further,' he ordered Christine and Eva to leave.

'Could we ask her another question?' Eva asked. She put all her charm into the question.

'Did you not understand me? You are upsetting her. I

don't like my patients upset. It's not good for them.'

'Calm down. We're leaving,' Eva responded.

Dr. Johnson took out a syringe and injected Mrs. Austin in her arm. Judging from her face, she went into a deep sleep, as all the emotions they had witnessed, disappeared.

'Liz, thanks again,' Christine said to Liz outside Mrs. Austin's door.

'No problem.'

'Do you think we got you in trouble?' Eva asked, knowing now that Dr. Johnson was a cold creep.

'Na. Don't worry about it. However, you better leave now.'

Christine and Eva quickly walked to the rented car. 'Do you think she was talking about Dr. Patterson when she mentioned *Matthew*?'

'Who else?' Eva answered.

When they walked back to their car, the sun had gone down, and it was getting dark. Eva decided to drive and started the car. As they drove down the dark country lane, Christine searched for some good music on the radio. She stopped searching when she heard *The Reflex* by Duran Duran.' Both girls hummed to the music when, suddenly, out of nowhere, a car shot onto the road.

'What the …?'

'Eva… watch the road!'

'I'm trying. Hold on!'

'Watch out! *STOP*!!!' the car tires were squealing.

They swirled off the road into the woods. Eva was breaking frantically and tried desperately to keep the car under control. There were too many trees and the vehicle hit full on into a large tree.

'Eva…you okay?' Christine asked.

'Aaaah,' Eva was still hunched over the steering wheel. 'What in the world was that?' she mumbled.

'Not sure. Some idiot came out of nowhere and stopped

in the middle of the road.'

'Wow! He could have killed us!' Eva exclaimed.

'Let's have a look.' Christine opened the passenger door and slowly got out of the car.

They walked to the road and looked in the direction where they lost control of the car. There was no other car to be seen.

'The maniac drove off. Who does that? Drive their car in the middle of the road without headlights, cause an accident, and then drive off?' Christine was standing in the middle of the road, almost yelling.

'Goodness, Christine. Are you okay?'

'Yeah. I think so. I slammed my head against the windshield.'

'You're bleeding. Are you sure you're okay?'

'Yeah …Let's go back to the car and see if it'll start. We might have to walk back to the nursing home.'

'I'm not walking back all that way.'

'Maybe we won't have to. Let's try the car. We should phone the police. That guy is a real maniac.'

'And tell them *what* exactly? *Mr. Policeman, there was a car in the middle of the road without headlights and now they're gone.* Christine, we don't even know what type of car it was.'

'Eva, he could have killed us.' Christine was getting upset and put her arms around herself, and slowly rocked from side to side.

'Calm down…We're not dead. Let's see if we can get the car started. I don't feel like hanging around. Who knows, he might come back.'

31

After the Incident

Eva climbed back behind the wheel and turned the key. The car started immediately. They both let out a sigh of relief and Eva reversed the car onto the road as carefully as possible. When the car was back on the asphalt, Christine got out and inspected it.

'We'll have to drop it off at the car rental. Thank heavens we have full insurance.'

'Get in Christine. Let's go home. I want to get out of here as quickly as possible. We'll check the car properly tomorrow.' Christine got in and Eva drove off toward the motorway. A dark grey Chrysler was parked in the woods.

A man in a dark suit watched them drive off.

'Hello.'
'Did you get them?'
'No. They swirled off the road into a tree, but they weren't injured, and the car still drives.'
'Did they see you?'
'Absolutely not. That road is pitch black.'
'We'll have to try again.'
'Yes, And, by the way, I'm fine. Thanks for asking.'
'Don't be a baby.'
Click!

'I feel like I was in a boxing match with Mohammed Ali last night,' Eva said while lifting her shirt.

'Eva, you're black and blue! I can almost see the outline of the steering wheel.'

'I know! Even my bra hurts. You don't look much better yourself.'

Christine looked in the bathroom mirror and checked out her cuts and bruises. She opened the cabinet and took two painkillers.

'I'm sure it's nothing serious, but it hurts like heck. How am I supposed to cover this up? I can't go to work looking like this.'

'I haven't slept a wink. Everything hurts. Look at my eyes. I look like a serious drug addict,' Eva said. She took the bottle of painkillers from Christine and took two as well.

'I'm going to make some coffee; you want some?' Christine asked.

'Yes, please. Chris, are you staying at home today?'

'Yes. I think so. I don't want people to see me like this. You?'

'Yes. My chest hurts like heck. I hope I haven't broken anything.'

Christine walked into the kitchen and switched on the coffee machine. She was thinking about the car last night. *Who would stop on an isolated country road waiting for someone to pass by just to hurt them?* She thought, *crazy mad world we live in.* Christine snapped out of her thoughts and poured the coffee. Rather than sitting, Christine leaned against the kitchen counter and observed Eva. 'Are you also thinking about last night?'

'I keep thinking about it. Who leaves their car in the middle of the road without any headlights? They didn't break down because they drove off the moment we swirled off the road. Do you think they were local teenagers?' Eva asked.

'I thought about it. But wouldn't they have chosen a busier road?'

'So, you think it was purposely against us?'

'Of course not, don't be silly,' Christine said, not convinced.

'What about Mrs. Austin?' Eva said, 'We haven't talked about her at all.'

'She is the woman from the photo, which means that Dr. Patterson knows her.'

'Maybe we should go back again and find out what medication she takes and ask Liz if there's something the nursing home can do to keep her more lucid.'

'Good idea. I'm curious to find out what her relationship is to Dr. Patterson,' Christine answered.

'I'm scared. Lately, everything has been a bit weird; too many coincidences,' Eva said, staring at her coffee.

'I know exactly what you mean. I sometimes wished we'd never found that photo.'

***

'They went back to the nursing home.
They know a nurse who works there.'
'Talk about our luck. Tell Miranda to
call me immediately if they return.'
'Sure.'
'Needless to say, they are getting too
close. We need to do something drastic.
They must be stopped.'
'Leave it to me.'
Click

***

That evening, Eva decided to stay at Steve's place. She packed an overnight bag and said *goodnight* to Christine. She needed to get away from the apartment and from Christine. She needed to relax her mind and not think about Dr. Patterson or Mrs. Austin. She just wanted Steve's arms around her and to feel safe. The car accident left her more upset than she let on, but she didn't feel like upsetting Christine even more by talking about it.

As she opened the entrance door to Steve's apartment block, she shook her shoulders to literally get rid of any negative thoughts. She wanted to have a lovely, cosy evening with Steve.

'Hey, beautiful,' Steve said. He was wearing a pair of jeans, a white t-shirt, and was barefoot. He took her in his arms and kissed her passionately. 'Dinner's ready and the wine is open,' he said.

'Are you really real? You must be one of those perfect men I read about.'

'Well, I'm sure there are some people who would contradict you there. But thank you very much for the compliment.'

'Christine and I had a car accident the other night.'

'What happened? Why didn't you call me?'

'It was late, and we weren't hurt. I didn't want to upset you.'

'What do you mean, you didn't want to *upset* me?'

'I don't know.'

'The next time something happens, you *have to* call me, understand?'

'Yes, sir.'

'Was the other person injured?'

'Don't know. We swirled off the road and by the time we got back on the road, the other car had already left.'

'Creeps! Did you at least get a registration number?'

'Nothing. It was so dark we couldn't even make out

what type of car it was.'

'Did you go to the police?'

'With what?'

'I suppose you're right. But promise me you'll phone me next time.'

'Yes, boss… What's for dinner this evening?'

'Pasta with porcini mushrooms and a big, juicy steak to follow.'

'Steve Patterson, you are so perfect. I should marry you.'

'You know what Ms. Williams; I think that might not be such a bad idea.'

Eva felt her heart jump. Was that a proposal? Or had she proposed? She decided to laugh it off and quickly poured herself a glass of Chianti.

***

As Liz passed the reception area, Miranda stopped her. 'Dr. Johnson wants to see you in his office.'

Liz nodded and walked to the staff room to leave her coat and handbag. She took a coffee from the vending machine and walked to Dr. Johnson's office. She knocked and entered.

'Good morning, Liz. Please take a seat.'

'Good morning, Dr. Johnson. Did you work all night?'

'Yes. It has come to my attention that your friends have already visited Mrs. Austin once before. I also understand that they are no relation to her whatsoever.'

'That's true. I didn't see any harm in it. Mrs. Austin has not had any visitors ever since she arrived, and I thought that it might help her. Maybe she needs more human interaction.'

'You are one of the best nurses we have in this facility.'

'Thank you.'

'Don't thank me just yet. I want you to understand that you are just that, a nurse. Doctors make decisions on what

221

may or may not be beneficial to patients. I hope you understand the serious nature of this talk. This cannot happen again.'

'Of course not, Dr. Johnson. I'm sorry. I didn't think it would hurt Mrs. Austin to have some visitors.'

'Also, why did they want to visit Mrs. Austin? Surely we have other patients who might be more interesting to them.'

'They both feel that Mrs. Austin looks familiar. That's all. They're not after her money.'

'I don't appreciate your tone of voice, Liz. I must add this episode to your overall performance chart. You can leave now.'

'Thank you, Dr. Johnson.' Liz got up and slammed the door behind her. She walked straight to the reception desk. 'Miranda, I just wanted to let you know that my little chat with Dr. Johnson went well. I'm going to work now. If anything out of the ordinary happens, and since I'm just a nurse, I will make sure to run it past you. That way, you can inform Dr. Johnson immediately.'

'It's part of my job to keep the doctors informed about what is happening in the home.'

'Yes. I'm sure that a patient having a visitor is major news and, you as a receptionist are more than qualified to assess that.' Liz didn't wait for a response and walked down the hall to start her day.

***

Eva arrived at the office after spending the night at Steve's and phoned Christine. 'Steve has invited us to the country home,' Eva said.

'That's nice. I'm not sure if I want to leave Eric for the weekend.'

'Not just you, silly. Eric as well.'

'What about Marlene?'

'Steve told me he asked for her permission and she agreed. The woman is slowly growing a heart.'

'Fantastic. I could do with a couple of relaxing days with Eric. Thank Steve for me. I'll call Eric and see if he's up for it.'

Christine was excited. She loved her last stay at the country home and now it would be even more special. She would be there with Eric. They could take long, romantic walks or just lay in the sun enjoying the beautiful scenery. She picked up the phone immediately. 'Eric, it's me. Listen we've been invited by Steve and Eva to join them at the Patterson's country home this weekend. Are you up for it? You better say *yes* because it is the most amazing place ever.'

'Sure. I can do with a few days of rest.'

'Great. That's settled. Are you able to take tomorrow afternoon off? That way, we can leave around 2 o'clock?'

'An afternoon off...? That might be difficult. I have so many outstanding projects in the office. Can I pick you up around 4?'

'Perfect – see you then.'

32

The Explosion

Christine was more excited than she had been in weeks. She even went shopping to get some suitable, elegant clothes. She made an appointment for a leg wax at lunchtime and was ready for a weekend filled with romance. Eva left early with Steve to make sure the barbeque would be up and running by the time she and Eric arrived.

Christine was sitting in the living room waiting for Eric, who was running late as usual. When her doorbell finally rang, she ran out the door.

'I'm sorry, Chris. It was hectic in the office, and I couldn't get out of a meeting. I'll change my clothes when we get to the house.'

Christine took a seat in his black Porsche and leaned over to kiss Eric. 'No problem. However, maybe next time you can call me. Not a long call, just a call to let me know you're running late. It's five-thirty. I've been waiting for over an hour.'

'It's not easy to interrupt a meeting to make a phone call.'

'It's okay. It is. Forget about it.'

***

They arrived at the house around eight-thirty. Christine never knew Eric drove like a maniac. She suddenly realized that in all the time they'd been together, he'd never taken her out of town.

Eva walked over after they parked the car. 'You made good time. I'm sure you put your foot down in this baby.' Eva was checking out the Porsche.

'Hello, Eva.' Eric kissed her on the cheek. He was a sucker for compliments.

'Are you going to let me take that car for a drive this weekend?'

'We'll see.'

'Steve's putting the meat on the grill. We should be ready to eat in about fifteen minutes. Christine, you and Eric are in the same room you stayed in last time.'

'Thanks. We'll just freshen up and we'll be down in a minute.' Christine took Eric by the arm and walked him to their bedroom. 'Isn't this the most beautiful room,' she said when they entered. 'It's a shame it's dark. Tomorrow you'll see the amazing views. They are truly breath-taking.'

'One day I'll have a house like this.'

'I'd be happy with you in any house,' she walked up to him put her arms around his neck and kissed him.

'I'm sure you would. But I want a house like this.'

'Come, let's go. They're waiting for us.' They walked downstairs and joined Eva and Steve on the patio. 'Steve, how are you?' Christine gave Steve a quick kiss on the cheek.

'Hi, Chris. Good to see you.'

'This is Eric. I'm not sure if you two have ever met at your parents' parties.'

'I don't think we had the chance. Good to meet you, Eric. Can I get you a glass of red? We've opened a wonderful Chianti that my mother had delivered from Italy.'

'Excellent. Sounds great,' Eric said.

'I'm cooking the sausages now. After this, we'll have the

steaks. How do you like your steak, Eric?'

'Medium. But that will be all for me. I don't want any sausage, thank you.'

'No sausages? You don't know what you're missing.'

'Other than cholesterol, not much.'

'Eric, I have to agree with Steve. The sausages are delicious and lean,' Christine tried to convince him.

'No, thanks. I'll have the steak. While you eat your sausages, I'll have a quick look around, if that's okay, Steve?'

'Sure. No problem.' Steve looked at Eva, who was standing on the other side of the grill. She realized that Eric and Steve would never become best friends. She wondered if Eric had any friends at all.

'The weather should be great tomorrow. Maybe we can even go for a long walk,' Eva said, trying to ease the tension.

'Don't you have a boat here? I'd love to go out on the lake,' Eric asked. He was referring to the Llangorse Lake that was about an hour drive away.

'We do. Usually, it's in the boathouse, but my father asked Harry to give it a service and a good clean. We're in luck, and I think it's a perfect plan.'

'I didn't know you liked boats that much,' Eva commented.

'As long as they go fast,' Eric replied with a smile and winked at Christine.

'I think it's wonderful. Maybe we can bring a picnic,' Christine said, pleased they'd found something in common.

After dinner, everyone was exhausted. So, everyone went the bed early. Christine had bought a cute nighty and was waiting for Eric. When he got out of the bathroom, still fully dressed, Christine sat up. 'Aren't you coming to bed?'

'I'm not sure. I was so tired, but now I feel wide awake. Do you mind if I go for a brief walk? I'll be back in half an hour?'

'Do you want me to come with you?'

'No, you sleep. I'll be back soon.' He walked up to the bed and kissed her.

***

The following day, Christine got up early to make breakfast for Eric.

'Looking good, Christine,' Steve said.

'Good morning, Steve. I hope you don't mind my using the kitchen. I thought it would be nice to bring Eric breakfast in bed.'

'Of course not. Perhaps you can speak to Eva. I'd love breakfast in bed. I see you're ready for the trip. You're even wearing boat shoes.'

'Yeah. How predictable am I?'

When she walked into the bedroom with the breakfast, Eric was on the phone in the bathroom. 'I'll be right there, Chris. I have to take this call.'

When Eric came into the bedroom, she noticed he had already showered and shaved. He was wearing a pair of green plaid knee-length shorts and a polo shirt. 'You look very handsome this morning.'

'Uh-um.'

'You should switch off your mobile and enjoy your weekend.'

'I had to make an important call. I'll switch it off now.'

'Would you like some juice?'

'Yes, please. You were right, Chris. This view is fantastic.' Eric stood by the window overlooking the countryside.

'Told you. It's a crime the Patterson's don't use this house more often. I think that Marlene finds it challenging to leave the city. Somehow she's not a countryside woman.'

'I don't know. She has many social engagements. I only met her once and she seems a genuinely nice lady.'

'But you know Marlene, don't you?'

'No…. I never met her before the party.'

'That's not true. I saw you some months ago near your office. You were waiting at the corner. After a few minutes, Marlene Patterson arrived, and you took a taxi together. Unless you're in the habit of taking taxis with strange women, you must know her.'

'Have you been following me?' He turned toward her with his eyes squinted.

'No. It was purely coincidental. I just saw you on the street after I'd been shopping.'

'What are you talking about, Christine? When I tell you, I met Marlene Patterson for the first time at the party, then that is the truth. Maybe you thought you saw me, but I assure you it wasn't me.'

'No need to get worked up about it,' Christine said slightly taken aback by Eric's aggressive reaction.

'I just don't like being accused of something I didn't do.'

'I never accused you. It was just a question.'

'I think we should go for that boat trip,' Eric said abruptly, and walked out of the room.

Christine picked her sweater up and followed Eric downstairs to join the others. Eva and Steve were waiting by the car, eager to drive to the lake.

No one spoke much in the car. They listened to the radio. When they arrived at the lake, Steve drove to an allocated spot and could see the boat docked in front of him. The boat was an impressive looking cruiser. It was very spacious and could comfortably seat six people, with two additional spaces on the elevated swim platform.

'This is one good-looking boat, Steve.' Eric whistled.

'There's even a small kitchen and a lovely bathroom downstairs,' Eva excitedly whispered to Christine.

'I still can't believe it,' Christine said, taking Eva aside. 'You have to pinch me. I think I might be dreaming. You and

I, both with boyfriends, in this beautiful spot.'

'I know. Life is perfect right now.' The girls made their way back to the deck and took a seat on the built-in sun loungers.

'Come on, Steve. Let's see what this baby can do,' Eric said cheerfully.

'Are you girls ready for a white-knuckle ride?' Steve yelled to the back of the boat.

'Yeah. Let's go for it!' Eva yelled.

Steve pushed the boat to speed and, before they knew it, the boat was flying over the water. All four of them were shouting with excitement. As Steve lowered the speed, Christine and Eva both pulled their hair out of their faces.

'My! That was fantastic. It must be a real sight, seeing this in action,' Eric said.

'Well, we can always drop you off and speed past you if that would make you happy,' Steve joked.

'Could you? That would be great. I can take a short film.' Eric took a small camera from his pocket.

'Are you serious?'

'Absolutely. It'll be great.'

Steve turned the boat around and headed back to the pier. 'Are we going back already?' Christine asked.

'Eric wants to make a film of the boat from shore.' Steve looked at Eva and shrugged his shoulders.

'Are you mad? Why would you want to do that?' Eva asked.

'I love speed. And the way this boat flies over the water is just too good to miss.'

'Whatever makes you happy,' Eva said and shrugged her shoulders. Steve dropped Eric off on the pier.

'Maybe I should stay with you, Eric,' Christine said.

'No, Christine. Stay on board. I would love to get you in the film.'

Christine sat back down and looked at Eric as Steve

steered the boat back to the lake. She waved at him, but he didn't wave back. 'Maybe he can't see me,' Christine said.

'Are you kidding me? He's looking right at you.'

'Oh well. Maybe it's the sun.'

'You ready girls?' Steve asked.

'Ready as we'll ever be,' Christine mumbled to herself.

Steve revved the engine as if he was entering a speeding contest. He turned around with a great big grin on his face. Steve was having fun, that was for sure. He let the boat go and, before they knew it, they were speeding over the water again. 'Eric better take a good film of this.'

'I'll be happy when it's all over,' Christine yelled and held on to her seat, keeping her eyes closed.

'What's that smell?' Eva shouted to Steve.

'What…?'

'The smell…'

Eva looked at Christine and they both panicked. 'Steve! Stop the boat!' Christine shouted.

'What? I can't hear you,' Steve yelled back, pointing at his ears.

'Stop this boat right now!' Eva yelled as loud as she could. They saw smoke coming from the cabin. The boat was going too fast for the girls to move toward Steve. 'Steve… stop the boat!'

Steve turned around and saw both girls in a panic. Flames were coming from the cabin and he could smell gas. Without even a second thought, he pulled the keys from the ignition and ran to the girls. 'Jump!' he yelled. 'Eva… Christine, jump!!!'

The girls looked at each other in terror. Tears were streaming down Christine's face. Eva was hunched over and held her head. 'Jump! We have to get off the boat now!!!' Steve grabbed both girls and dragged them with him to the side of the boat. He pushed them overboard and jumped after them.

'Swim! Swim as fast as you can!' Steve pulled both girls

with him. The water was freezing cold and Christine was gasping for air. She went under several times and swallowed water. When she came back up, she coughed uncontrollably. Eva was overcome with shock and was shivering.

'Swim! For goodness sake, Eva, swim!'

Steve grabbed Eva by her hair to prevent her from going under water. It was evident from her breathing that she was hyperventilating. The three of them huddled together and tried to swim to the shore. Suddenly, there was an enormous *bang!* behind them, burning debris was flying all around them.

'Christine, dive underwater!' Steve yelled as he pulled Eva underwater to avoid getting burned. Christine gasped for air when she came back up. There was a ball of fire behind them; the remnant of what had been the boat. The three of them were still huddled together. Eva was slowly calming down.

'Are you okay, Christine?' Steve asked.

'I think so. I'm… not sure.' She was still coughing heavily.

'Can you try to swim to the shore while I take Eva?' Without answering, Christine started swimming as well as she could. Eva was hanging onto Steve's arm as he tried to swim with the other. They were a long way from the shore. Christine kept swimming in robot-like fashion in front of him.

'You hang in there, baby. Try and swim with me,' Steve said to Eva. Just then, Steve heard the sound of a motor and saw a small, bright yellow dingy speeding their way. He started waving and shouting for help.

'Steven, what happened?'

'Harry, Thank God!'

33

Tempers Flaring

Harry switched off the small engine and leaned over the side to pull Christine out of the water. Steve helped as Harry pulled Eva into the dingy and finally climbed into the small boat himself. Both Christine and Eva where shivering terribly. They were as white as ghosts and were unable to speak.

'We've to get them back as soon as possible. Otherwise, they'll go into shock,' Harry said. By now, Steve was also severely cold and tired, but was unable to respond. He just nodded.

Harry started to the small engine and steered them back to the house. When they reached the shore, Harry ran to the car and brought back towels. 'You poor girls. Here, put this around you.'

'Thank you, Harry,' Steve said, taking one of the towels. 'We *must* get them warm. The boathouse has a shower.'

'Make the water as hot as possible to get their blood flowing,' Harry yelled after Steve, who was walking as fast as he could with both girls.

As Steve put the girls under the shower, Eric came in. 'What the heck happened?' he said, out of breath.

'We...we...had an accident,' Christine muttered. She was unable to stop shivering.

'We need to get back to the house and keep the car very

warm,' Eric said.

When they arrived at the house, Steve took both girls to their rooms and turned on the shower again. 'You okay, Christine? Call me if you need anything.' Christine nodded and started to undress. Steve walked back to the room he shared with Eva. She had already taken off her clothes and was wearing a bathrobe.

'I would have died without you,' she said to him in a serious voice.

'Don't be silly. You wouldn't even have been on that silly boat if it wasn't for me.'

'What are you saying, Steve? Stop it! You saved my life.' Steve walked to the bed and laid next to her. He took her in his arms, held her close, and rocked her like a baby. 'I think we better go and get a warm drink,' Eva said, lifting herself on her elbows.

They walked out of their room and Eva knocked on Christine's door to check up on her.

'Chris, are you okay?'

Eric opened the door. Eva saw that his clothes didn't even have a wet patch. 'She's fine. She just finished her shower.'

'Are you coming down for a warm drink?' Eva yelled into the room over Eric's shoulder.

Christine walked out of the bathroom. 'Sure. Oh, I see you're going down in your bathrobe. I'll do the same.'

'I think it'd better if you get dressed first,' Eric said.

'Don't be silly, Eric. After what we've been through just now, dressing appropriately is the last thing on anyone's mind. Come, Chris. Let's go and get that hot whiskey drink.'

'Are you coming, Eric?' Christine asked.

'I'll be there in a minute,' He answered, without looking up.

***

Harry had prepared a wonderful fire and put four chairs around it. Four glasses with steaming hot drinks were waiting for them on the small table.

'Wow! What's in here?' Eva asked when she took a sip.

'Drink up. It's good for you,' Steve said, smiling.

'I don't get it. Your father asked Harry to check the boat yesterday,' Eva said with a frown on her forehead. The three of them sat in front of the fire, carefully sipping their drinks. All were deep in thought when Eric entered the room.

'Ahhh, an excellent drink,' Eric said.

'Thank you, Eric. We're doing fine. We nearly died but we're perfectly fine now. Thanks for asking. You enjoy your drink,' Eva said. 'By the way, I hope you managed to take your precious film. Did you get the bit where the boat exploded? Not to mention a nice scene of us in the ice-cold water. That must have been a wonderful cinematic moment.'

'Eva, please calm down,' Steve said.

'No. I won't calm down. You are a real jerk, Eric Woodland. And you don't deserve to be with Christine. Just where were you when we were in the cold water, nearly drowning? Were you checking the best angle?'

Christine got up abruptly and walked upstairs. There were tears in her eyes. Everyone could hear the bedroom door slam shut.

'Great. Thanks, Eva. Not only did she have a traumatic experience, but now you also managed to upset Chris. You and your big mouth,' Eric said, and walked out of the house into the garden.

'What was that all about?' Steve asked.

'He's the biggest jerk. That's what he is. He is an arrogant, mean, and selfish schmuck. Why Christine took him back is beyond me.'

'It's Christine's choice, not yours. And it's not his fault the boat exploded. It could have happened when he was on board.'

'Ohhh, really wonderful! You're taking his side?'

'Calm down, woman. I'm not taking his side. All I'm saying is that this might not be the best time to let the world know how you feel about Eric Woodland. Trust me, I don't like him all that much either. But he's with Christine and only Christine can decide if he's good for her or not.' Steve stroked Eva's arm.

'That's where you're wrong. She thinks she's in love, but she's in love with love itself. All she wants to do is get married and have children.'

'I'm sure you're right. But this is not the time.'

Eva sank back into her chair, took several little sips from the glass, and was quiet for several minutes. 'You're right. I have to go up and apologize.'

'Give her some time. We all had a terrible experience. Leave it till this evening or even tomorrow.'

'Don't you think it's strange that Eric didn't come to rescue us?' Eva re-filled her glass. 'He said he was going to film the boat so he must have seen the whole thing happen. Film the boat – what crap. The rubber boat was tied up by the pier when we left.'

'Eva, what are you saying?'

'Harry,' Eva called to the kitchen, 'when you ran to the pier, was Eric there?'

'No. We thought Mr. Eric was with you.'

'Thanks, Harry. Told you so. Making a film about a speeding boat, what a load of crap.'

That evening, Eva knocked on Christine's bedroom door. 'Chris, can I talk to you?'

'What do you want, Eva? You want to share more pearls of wisdom with me?'

'I am so sorry for what I said, Chris. I had no right to say those things and I wish I could take it all back. I don't know what got into me. I couldn't control myself.'

'Sure. That's always the case with you. Nothing is ever

your fault and, whenever something goes wrong, you didn't mean it; something just takes over.'

'That's not fair.'

'Isn't it? You always speak before you think and, afterwards, you expect to be forgiven because you didn't mean it. Eric and I will leave first thing tomorrow morning. We're going back to the city.'

'Don't, Christine. Please stay.'

'Eric is very offended, and he doesn't want to stay. We would have left this evening, but I feel far too shook up to drive back.' Christine sat up. 'I understand you don't like Eric, but he's my boyfriend. You don't like him, fine that is your prerogative. But you can at least be civil to him, if only out of respect for me.'

'You're right. I'm so sorry and I'll apologize to Eric. Are you sure you want to leave tomorrow?'

'I think it's for the best. A few days apart will do us good. You've not only upset him, but you also hurt me.'

'I'm so sorry. You're right. Will you at least come down for dinner?'

'No. Can you ask Sarah to bring something upstairs?'

'Okay. I'll see you back in the city.'

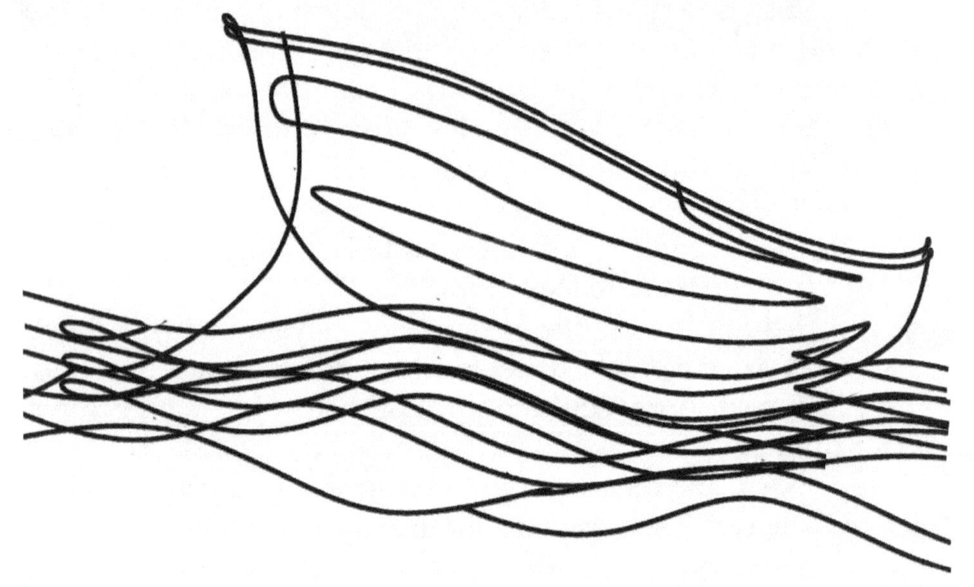

34

Staying With Liz

Eva walked into a dark apartment.

'Chris, are you home?' Eva turned on the lights and found a note on the kitchen door. *Staying at Eric's. Will be back Monday night.*

She opened the fridge and poured herself a glass of orange juice. She looked through the post but, other than bills, there was nothing exciting. When the phone rang, she quickly walked over to the living room.

'Eva, hi. It's Liz. How are you? I've been trying to reach you for days.'

'I was with Steve at the lake.'

'How romantic. You're so lucky.'

'Lucky's not the word I would use right now.'

'Everything okay?'

'Yeah. Sorry, just me and my big mouth again.'

'Listen, there's something I wanted to talk to you about. It's about Mrs. Austin.'

'Why don't you come here? Christine's staying at Eric's, so I'm all by my lonely self. We can order a pizza and have a girly night.'

'Perfect plan. I'll be there in about an hour.'

Eva picked up the overnight bag she had taken to the country house and walked into her bedroom to unpack. Then, she decided to leave it for another day. She changed clothes and sat in the living room, thinking about all the things that had been happening lately. When she heard the doorbell, she rushed to the door. 'Hi, Liz. Come in,' Eva said when she opened the door.

'You look lovely and comfortable. I wish you'd have let me know. I would have worn my sweats too.'

'Can I get you a drink?'

'Have you got any wine open…?'

'No. But, I'll open a bottle now. I can do with a glass myself. Go into the living room. I'll be there in a minute. By the way, the pizza menu is on the coffee table.'

'Yummy. Pizza.'

Eva walked into the living room with a bottle of red and two glasses. 'What about Mrs. Austin? Is she okay?' Eva asked.

'Yes. Nothing is wrong with her,' Liz said. 'Well, in other words, she's the same.'

'Then what?'

'After you and Christine came to visit, Dr. Johnson called me into his office and reprimanded me severely. The lovely Miranda keeps him informed about everything that goes on in the home. She told him that you came to visit before.'

'What a hag. What's it to her?' Eva asked.

'He got stroppy with me because you're not family and wanted to know why you wanted to visit Mrs. Austin. I have never seen that man interested in any of the patients and now, all of the sudden, he needs to know the ins and outs,' Liz said, and took a large gulp of wine.

'Did you tell him?'

'Tell him what…? I told him that Mrs. Austin looks familiar to you and Christine. That's all. He asked me where you had seen her before. I told him I didn't know.'

'Thanks.'

'He told me that you and Christine are not allowed to visit her anymore and if he finds out you have; I'll probably get the sack.'

'What a creep. Can he do that?'

'I wouldn't be surprised. I told him that it might be good for Mrs. Austin to have some visitors and that she might even snap out of her depression. I don't believe she suffers from depression, though, and that remark will be included in my performance review. I'm so angry I could strangle him.'

Eva could see Liz was getting upset just thinking about the episode. 'Let's order this pizza. I'm always calmer with food in my stomach.'

'I'll have the capriccioso and garlic bread as well,' Liz said.

Eva smiled. She walked over to the phone and placed the order. 'I had to order the cheesecake, too. It's delicious. It should be here in twenty minutes.' Eva sat back down next to Liz.

'Anyway, remember you know how you asked me who pays for Mrs. Austin's medical care? I did investigate that. The charity that pays for Mrs. Austin is very odd. First of all, they do not have a website and, secondly, I couldn't find a listing for them anywhere. Pretty odd for a charity that exists on donations only. I contacted the charity register to get information. It turns out that the chairman is a lady named Marlene Patterson.'

'Marlene Patterson?' Eva asked, stunned.

'Yes… and you know who Marlene Patterson is?' Liz continued without paying attention to Eva's reaction. 'She's the wife of Dr. Matthew Patterson; the doctor who admitted Mrs. Austin and who is also in charge of prescribing her medication.'

'Dr. Patterson is responsible for admitting Mrs. Austin?' Eva could feel her heart racing.

'What's the matter? You look all pale,' Liz asked.

'What's the story anyway with Mrs. Austin? Why are you so interested in her?'

Without responding, Eva got up, walked over to the small wooden dresser underneath the window, and opened a drawer. She took out a large white and red envelope and walked back to the sofa. She took out the photo and showed it to Liz.

'Here's Mrs. Austin; and this is Dr. Patterson. The other men at the back are doctors that work for Dr. Patterson at a pharmaceutical company called PharmaTech.' Eva pointed at each face when she spoke.

'Where did you find this photo?' Liz studied the photo closely.

'Dr. Patterson is also our physician. He's been looking after Christine and me ever since we were babies.' Eva stopped there. She didn't want to tell Liz where she found the photo and hoped Liz wouldn't ask again.

'Mrs. Austin looks so happy and so young in this photo.'

Eva nodded. She started to feel restless. She desperately wanted to speak to Christine. It couldn't be a coincidence that Dr. Patterson was looking after Mrs. Austin and them at the same time. There had to be something else, some connection.

The doorbell rang. Eva stood up and took her change-purse from her handbag. 'Do you mind paying for the pizzas?' Eva asked. 'I'll fetch plates from the kitchen,' and handed her purse to Liz. As Eva walked into the kitchen, she picked up her phone and called Eric's house. 'Eric, it's Eva. Can I speak to Christine?'

'No. She's taking a bath at the moment,' he snapped at her.

'Can you ask her to call me when she's done?'

'Okay.' Eric was not in the mood to speak with her and he put the phone down without saying anything further.

Eva stared at the phone, surprised, and shook her head. What did Christine see in this guy? He was rude and obnoxious. She collected the plates from the cupboard, opened the drawer to get knives and forks, put a roll of kitchen towels under her arm, and walked back to the living room.

She smelled the pizza and suddenly felt very hungry. She opened the box with the garlic bread and placed two big pieces on her plate. Without using her knife, she tore off a piece and stuck it in her mouth.

'Yummy. This is delicious. I was so hungry,' Eva said with her mouth full.

'You don't have to tell me. I'm starving too. You better eat quickly, before I finish it all.'

Eva smiled. She loved Liz. She was such easy company. Eva felt comfortable with her. She liked that she could tell her anything and everything without being judged.

'You know what I am going to do?' Liz had already moved on from the pizza. 'I'm going to decrease Mrs. Austin's medication slowly. I'm the one who gives it to her every day. What if I give her a drop less a day and maybe half a tablet less every other day?' she said while sticking a large piece of pizza in her mouth. 'That way, she should not have any nasty side effects. Hopefully, she'll become slightly more lucid and we can find out what her relationship with Dr. Patterson is and why he put her there in, what could not be described other than, a coma.'

'You can't do that, Liz. First of all, we don't know how badly she needs her medication and, secondly, you could lose your job. I appreciate that you want to help, but I'm not sure that this is the way to go. Heck, you could end up in jail for malpractice.' Eva picked up a slice of pizza.

'What do you suggest we do? I can tell you for sure that Mrs. Austin's brain will be boiled in about two years. The amount of medication she takes is insane. I always had a suspicion there was something not right. Mrs. Austin is not suicidal or insane for that matter.'

'But are you willing to take the responsibility?' Eva asked. 'You could be wrong, and Mrs. Austin may be crazy or whatever. And what about when she becomes more lucid? I'm sure she gets regular visits from the resident doctor or even Dr. Patterson?'

'Dr. Patterson hasn't been to the nursing home for about a year now,' Liz said and paused. 'You know what? I have never met him. He only visits in the evening when no regular staff is on site.' She thought about it for a moment and shook her head. 'I can give Mrs. Austin her medication before Dr. Johnson does his rounds once a week. That way, she'll be asleep.'

'I'm not sure,' Eva said. She was, however, getting excited by the idea that she might be able to talk to Mrs. Austin.

'I've made up my mind. I'm not just doing this for you. I'm also doing this for Mrs. Austin,' Liz said firmly. 'She deserves a better life than the one she has now. I'm a fully qualified nurse and I can do this. If I start decreasing her medication slowly from tomorrow on, she should be able to have a reasonable conversation in about two weeks.'

'But what do we do then? Miranda is watching over the nursing home like a prison guard and she and Dr. Johnson have made it very clear Christine and I are not to visit anymore.'

'You can come in the evening, when the reception is closed.'

Eva opened her cheesecake and dug in. She was nervous. She knew that what they were about to do was extremely dangerous. She thought about Dr. Patterson. She had known him all her life but was only now finding out what a powerful man he was; and what a *dangerous* man he was. Did they want to mess with him? The phone rang and Eva nearly jumped out of her seat.

'Hi, it's me. What do you want?'

Eva was surprised Eric had given Christine the message. 'Are you coming home tonight? Liz is here and she has news about Mrs. Austin.' She heard a click on the phone.

'I'm staying over at Eric's this evening. I left you a note on the fridge. What news does she have? Something about the photo?'

Eva suddenly freaked about the click on the phone line. 'Nothing really. I'll tell you another time. You have a lovely evening, and I'll see you tomorrow.' Eva put the phone down and stared at the receiver. She knew she heard the click on the phone, but that could have been a technical problem.

Eva walked back to the living room and, all the sudden, felt scared. She tried to shake it off but was unable to get rid of the feeling. 'Christine's not coming home this evening. She's sleeping at Eric's. Do you fancy sleeping over here? We can open another bottle of wine and get hammered?' Eva hoped she didn't sound too desperate.

'I have to go home. I have to work tomorrow morning.'

'Do you mind if I sleepover at your place? I don't want to be alone this evening. Steve had to go out of town for a meeting, so I can't go there. I know I'm being silly, but I would appreciate it.'

'Of course, you can stay. Let's go to my house and open a bottle there. What do you say?'

Eva jumped up and scurried to her bedroom to get her overnight bag, which she left for unpacking later after coming back from the country home. She emptied the bag into the washing bin, put in some fresh underwear, and decided that jeans and a shirt with her overnight make-up bag were enough to take for one night. She looked around and caught a glimpse of herself in the mirror. She stared at herself for a moment. Something was going to happen; she could feel it.

35

Burgled

The next morning, Eva took a taxi to her office. She had slept well and, although she had a slight headache, she felt good. She decided that taking public transport was out of the question. Liz didn't live centrally or near any convenient bus route or underground station, and it would take her hours to reach the office. She walked into the modelling agency at ten to nine and switched her computer on.

'What's your day like today?' Zaria asked.

'Zaria, I'm sorry I didn't know you were already in.'

'Your diary?'

'I'm pretty booked today. I have several *go-sees* to prepare and have meetings with a few girls to discuss their performances.'

'Make sure you see me in my office around ten. I need to talk to you about some of the girls' diets.'

Skinny seventeen-year-old girls on diets. What is the world coming to? Eva thought as her boss walked back to her office. Zaria had an authoritative manner about her. She had been a model herself, and somehow could not get a grip on the fact that she was not able to model any longer due to her age. She took her frustration about this out on her staff. She could be especially hard on Eva, who was not a size zero and had curves that men loved. Eva never understood this habit of being so skinny. Especially when many in the world were starving. Young girls were playing with their lives and health, and no one thought anything about it.

Eva was becoming more and more aware that she needed to start looking for another job. She admired and envied Liz. She had such passion for her work and was dedicated to her patients. Eva knew she would never work as a nurse or caregiver though. However, there must be something in between. Around eleven she picked up the phone to call Christine but got her *out of office* message.

'Hi. It's me. Are you free for lunch today? I have some news about Mrs. Austin. Call me.' Around noon Eva still hadn't heard from her and decided to phone again. Christine's *out of office* message was still on. Eva put the phone down without leaving a message. She'd speak to Christine this evening at home.

At five on the dot, she switched her computer off and packed her bag. 'Eva, are you working part-time today?'

'Hilarious, Mark. But, unlike you, I do have a life outside this office.' She gave him a raspberry and walked out.

She walked out of the building, promising herself to pick up a paper and start looking for another job. When she arrived at the bus stop, it was already busy. Eva knew she would have to work hard to get on. When she saw the bus coming in the distance, everyone started to move to get to the front of the queue, including Eva. 'Hey, lady. Watch where you're going!' A lady with many shopping bags said to her.

'I'm so sorry. Please forgive me,' Eva said with a big smile. She was an expert at this. She slowly, but persistently, worked her way forward. She excused herself to everyone she touched as though it was her prerogative to skip the queue. She parked her back against the back end of the bus and started reading the paper. When she finally reached her stop, she jumped out and let out a sigh of relief. She loved living in London but hated the commute.

It was a beautiful day, and Eva started walking briskly uphill. Even though she hated it, at least she could burn off some of last night's calories.

***

Eva opened the door to the apartment and let out a scream. 'What...what happened here?' She walked into the kitchen. The drawers had been emptied and all the pots and pans were laying on the floor. All the rooms in the house were disrupted as well.

Eva looked around and saw that their TV, DVD, and laptop were missing. Their CD collection was spread on the floor. Many of them were broken, as someone had stepped on them. She picked up a cushion, put it on the chair, and sat down, looking around in disbelief. They had been burgled.

'Why burgle this house? We have nothing!' Eva said out loud to herself. She heard the key in the door and ran into the hall. Before Christine could say anything, Eva was shouting. 'We've been burgled.'

'What...?'

'Look around. They've turned the whole place upside down. They took the TV, DVD, and laptop, but left the CD player.'

Christine walked through the flat without saying a word. She walked from room to room, shaking her head and finally said, 'Why ...? Did you phone the police?'

Eva shook her head but started looking for the telephone under the papers. She dialled the number and reported the break-in. 'They'll be here shortly,' she said.

Christine also picked up a cushion and sat on the sofa. 'I suppose we have to leave everything as it is. Maybe they want to take fingerprints.' They sat next to each other without speaking.

'Sir, you wanted me to gather all the information we could on Ms. Rhodes and Ms. Williams. The response team has just received a call from Ms. Williams. Apparently, their apartment has been burgled. Here are their files.'

Inspector McMillan looked up. He opened the files and glanced through them. 'Please tell the response team I'll be joining them.'

Inspector McMillan got up, took his coat, and walked out of his office. He got into his Range Rover that was in his parking space outside the police station and drove off. As he approached the girls' apartment, he saw that the response team had already arrived. He parked his car in front of the entrance and walked into the building. The door to the apartment was open.

'Good afternoon, Inspector. We've gone through the apartment, but we can't find signs of forced entry.'

'Where are Ms. Williams and Ms. Rhodes?'

'They're in the living room. The first door on the left.'

McMillan made his way to the living room where he found the girls sitting on the sofa, being interviewed by a police officer he had never seen before. The officer looked up from her writing pad and told McMillan to wait in the hall.

'My name is Inspector McMillan. I'll take it from here.' He waved the young cop out of the room. He hated smug rookies. He had seen too many over his long career, and few of them become skilled inspectors. He seemed to feel that they were usually power-crazed, insecure little people that needed a uniform to feel superior to others.

Eva and Christine smiled when they saw him. Something about this tall, big man was very re-assuring. 'Aren't you a bit too important to take on a small break-in?' Christine asked.

Inspector McMillan closed the living room door and

took a seat on one of the rattan chairs. 'They left a nice mess here,' he said as he looked around. 'Did they take anything?'

'Just the TV, DVD, and laptop. We don't have jewellery or any other things of value,' Christine replied.

'Anything else they might have taken? Something that is important to you, but does not necessarily have any cash value?'

Christine looked at Eva and shrugged her shoulders. 'I can't think of anything.'

Suddenly, Eva jumped up and started to rummage around in the mess on the floor.

'What are you doing?' Christine asked, surprised

'The photo... Christine, the photo. Help me look for it. It's in the large white and red envelope.'

Christine dove on the floor and frantically started to search for the photo with Eva. After five minutes of anxiously searching, Eva sat still on the floor. 'It's gone... they've taken it, Christine. They've taken the photo. Both copies were in the envelope.' Eva was shaking.

'What are you talking about? What photos? And why are they so important?' McMillan asked.

'It's an awfully long story and it probably means nothing,' Christine said as she got up from the floor. She felt exhausted.

'Let me be the judge of its importance. By the way, I have plenty of time on my hands,' McMillan said. He called out to one of the police officers, asking them to bring a glass of water in for Eva.

'No worries. I'll get it myself.' She came back into the living room with a bottle of wine under her arm and three glasses in her hands. 'I think a glass of wine might be in order.'

'I'm on the job. You girls have a glass. Calm down and tell me about these photos.'

Christine told the story about how they had taken the

photo from the country home. She hesitated for a moment but decided to tell Inspector McMillan the entire story.

'You girls know Dr. Patterson well?' Inspector McMillan asked. He didn't look up from his writing pad.

'He's been our physician since we were babies. Eva and I were brought up at the Mercy Home Orphanage. We were told by one of the caregivers that Dr. Patterson had offered his services after he read in the paper that we were left on the steps,' Christine said.

She felt odd talking about her past. Whenever someone asked her about it, she would say she was an orphan, but never told anyone she was left on the steps. Now that she was speaking to a total stranger, she suddenly realized she was embarrassed by the fact her parents didn't want her.

'You should know that I'm dating Steven Patterson. He's Dr. Patterson's son,' Eva interrupted.

Christine realized that Eva was a nervous wreck. The shock of being robbed was one thing, talking about their past was another.

'Why are you asking us about Dr. Patterson?' Christine asked. 'You haven't asked us anything else about the break-in. Surely you're here because we were robbed.'

Inspector McMillan put his notebook down and wiped his face with his hands. For a moment, he looked as if he was deep in thought; as though he wasn't sure if he should speak or not. 'You phoned my office to ask me about the Eastman accident and any suspects. My prime suspect in that case was Dr. Patterson.'

McMillan looked uncomfortably at the girls. 'The accident was caused by a damaged break line, which we discovered during the investigation. We did find break oil in front of his house but, because the oil was not found on his actual property, there was nothing I could do.'

Christine laid her hand on Eva's and nodded for Inspector McMillan to continue. 'You should also know that

Mrs. Eastman contacted the police department several weeks before the accident. I didn't speak to her because her accusations and fears were based on nothing specific and, quite frankly, we wrote her off as a dramatic and paranoid housewife. Dr. Patterson was a well-established and influential doctor. When Mrs. Eastman contacted us, accusing Dr. Patterson of being a murderer, the police department, unfortunately, paid no attention.'

Inspector McMillan got up and walked to the window. As he was looking the outside over, he said, 'Dr. and Mrs. Eastman were found dead ten days later in their tampered car. We moved in on Dr. Patterson immediately but, as I said, we couldn't find any concrete evidence against him. We were forced to call it an unfortunate accident.'

Suddenly, he called out to one of the rookies to bring him a glass of water. He didn't speak until he finished drinking the entire glass of water. 'I've never forgiven myself. If only I had paid attention, Dr. and Mrs. Eastman would still be alive,' he said, and sighed deeply. 'In my job, it's not always easy to guess who is sincere or just plain crazy. When the two of you called my office, I was intrigued; two young women interested in this old case. I'm sorry to say that I have read everything there is on file about the two of you and I came across Dr. Patterson. Over the years, I've gathered all the information possible on him. However, he is very well protected. He appears to be no saint but, whenever I dig deeper, I run into a brick wall of people protecting him. There's nothing tangible I can tell you, however, what I do know is that this photo is of great importance to your Dr. Patterson.'

'How…?' Christine asked

'It's evident from the burglary that it was staged. They took your TV, DVD, and laptop, which are probably worth nothing on the black market. They came here for something else.' Inspector McMillan reached into his coat pocket. He took out two business cards and handed them to Christine and Eva. 'All my numbers are here. If you remember anything, no matter how small, please call me immediately, no matter what time,' he said, and walked out of the room; leaving Christine and Eva stunned.

Eva was the first to get up. She started picking up papers from the floor and, without looking, put them back in the dresser. She left the room and came back with a brush to brush up the broken glass that was lying around.

Christine stared at her as she brushed up the glass and, without saying anything, walked into the kitchen where she started to tidy up. They worked for about two hours before they had the apartment in tolerable order.

'You want a cup of tea?' Christine asked Eva, who had taken a seat at the kitchen table. Before she could respond, Eva burst into tears. She was crying as she had never cried before. She gasped for air; sobs shook her entire body. She was unable to stop. Years of pain and grief came to the surface. Christine walked her to a chair and rocked her like a baby.

36

Planning Another Visit

Liz walked into Mrs. Austin's room to give her, her medication. Dr. Johnson was doing his rounds that evening and Liz needed to make sure Mrs. Austin was asleep by the time he visited her room. While Liz stood next to the bed, preparing a syringe, suddenly, Mrs. Austin grabbed her wrist. Liz jumped back and let out a scream. 'No more medication,' Mrs. Austin whispered.

Liz sat on the side of the bed and put her hand on Mrs. Austin's arm. 'Mrs. Austin, listen carefully,' Liz whispered. 'I have to give you this medication. Dr. Johnson is doing his rounds. If he finds out I've been cutting down, I will be fired, and you will probably be prescribed even heavier medication. Mrs. Austin, you have to trust me. Can you understand me?'

'Huuummm.'

'Please, Mrs. Austin. If you understand, squeeze my hand.' Liz put her hand inside Mrs. Austin's and was relieved when she felt a squeeze. 'The medication I'm giving you will wear off quickly. I'll come by first thing tomorrow morning.' Liz heard steps in the hall, coming closer. She injected Mrs. Austin quickly.

'Liz, what are you doing here?' Dr. Johnson asked.

'I just wanted to make sure Mrs. Austin was comfortable and properly tucked in for the night,' Liz said.

255

And, without waiting for a response, she walked out of the room. She quickly made her way to the nurse's station to get her purse. She was finished with her shift and wanted to leave the care house as soon as possible. She passed the reception desk and wished Miranda a pleasant evening. When she got into her car, she took the syringe out of her uniform pocket and placed in on the passenger seat. Mrs. Austin's reaction to the decreased medication was remarkable. She looked at her wrist and smiled. The old girl sure did have some strength left in her.

Liz decided to drive to Eva and Christine's to give them the news. She turned the radio on and hummed along to a song she had never heard before. She drove onto their street and parked her car in front of the apartment building.

'Liz, what a pleasant surprise,' Christine said when she saw Liz outside the door. 'Come in. We're in the living room.'

Eva jumped up when she saw her friend coming through the door. 'Liz, how are you? I can't tell you how happy I am I slept over at your place last night. We were burgled. They turned the entire apartment upside down,' she said.

'That's horrible. Did you call the police?' Liz asked.

'We did. But they couldn't do much other than advising us on new locks for the door and the windows.'

Eva decided not to tell Liz about the missing photos and their conversation with Inspector McMillan.

'Thankfully, both of you were out. Being burgled is one thing; being in the house when it happens must be terrifying.'

'Take a seat. Make yourself at home,' Christine offered.

Liz took her coat off and got herself comfortable in the beige Napoleon III-inspired chair. 'I just came to tell you about Mrs. Austin. This evening she was quite lucid. I had to give her an injection because Dr. Johnson always makes his rounds on Tuesday evening. She grabbed my wrist and told me not to give her more medication.'

'That's wonderful,' Christine said. 'When do you think we can speak to her?'

'Probably in about a week or so. We must organize it carefully. We must make sure that Miranda and Dr. Johnson are not in the building.'

'Of course… You let us know when you think it's a good day and a good time,' Christine said.

The girls talked more about the burglary and Mrs. Austin and what, if anything, she could tell them about the photo. After an hour, Liz said, 'I have the early shift tomorrow morning. I'd better go. I need my beauty sleep.'

'Sure. Thanks again, Liz. You're the best,' Christine said, and hugged her.

Christine put lasagna in the oven. The delicious smell of meat, tomato sauce, and cheese filled the apartment. Christine kept hoping the timer would move faster. She was starving. She had already put the plates on the table and was ready to eat. She took a chair and sat in front of the oven. Although she was waiting for it when the timer rang, she nearly jumped. She put the frog-green oven mitts on and took out the steaming hot lasagna.

'Eva, dinner's ready,' she yelled.

Immediately, Eva ran into the kitchen; like a lion was chasing her. 'I'm starving. Make sure you give me a big piece.'

Christine divided the lasagna into two pieces and dished it up. Neither spoke during dinner. After she finished, Eva sat back and stroked her stomach. 'Eating is good. I always feel so warm afterwards,' she said and took off her jumper.

Christine smiled and, after she finished, Eva took the plates and put them in the old dishwasher. 'Can't believe this old baby is still going.'

'Don't jinx it. I'm expecting it to break any day now,' Christine said and walked to the fridge to get two beers. She handed one to Eva and they both drank from the bottle.

Christine walked back to the table.

'Be careful not to trip over the cracked linoleum,' Eva joked.

'This place is falling apart. We need to look where we walk, the locks don't work, and there are single windows,' Christine said and took a seat next to Eva.

'So, next week is D-day. On the one hand, I do want to talk to her. On the other hand, I'm also anxious about what she has to say. What if we have it all wrong and she's not even the woman from the photo. Or worse, she's an excellent friend of Dr. Patterson.'

'We'll soon find out,' Eva said. Her demeanour was blasé, but she was as nervous as Christine. She had had enough excitement to last her a lifetime. 'I'm going to phone Steve,' she said.

***

Christine sat in the old kitchen and looked around. Everything appeared so tired. She never really cared much for the apartment. For her, it had always been temporary, although they had been living there for over seven years now. She had focused on getting married most of the time. As she looked around, she realized she had been kidding herself. *This* was her life now. She wasn't sure if this realization made her feel relieved or sad. She thought about phoning Eric but decided against it.

'What are you doing?' Eva asked when she walked back into the kitchen.

'Nothing...'

'Well, it looks like you're doing something.' She stood behind Christine, peeked over her shoulder, and saw Christine was making the famous *pro and con* list for Eric. 'Do you need my input?' Eva asked with a cheeky smile.

'Get out of here. Give me some privacy.' The pros were

coming very quickly. He was handsome, had a good job, and had excellent taste. On the cons side of the list, she wrote: *He doesn't love me the way I want to be loved.*

She stared at the piece of paper and continued writing: *I don't love him.* She put her pen down and knew that her relationship with Eric was over!

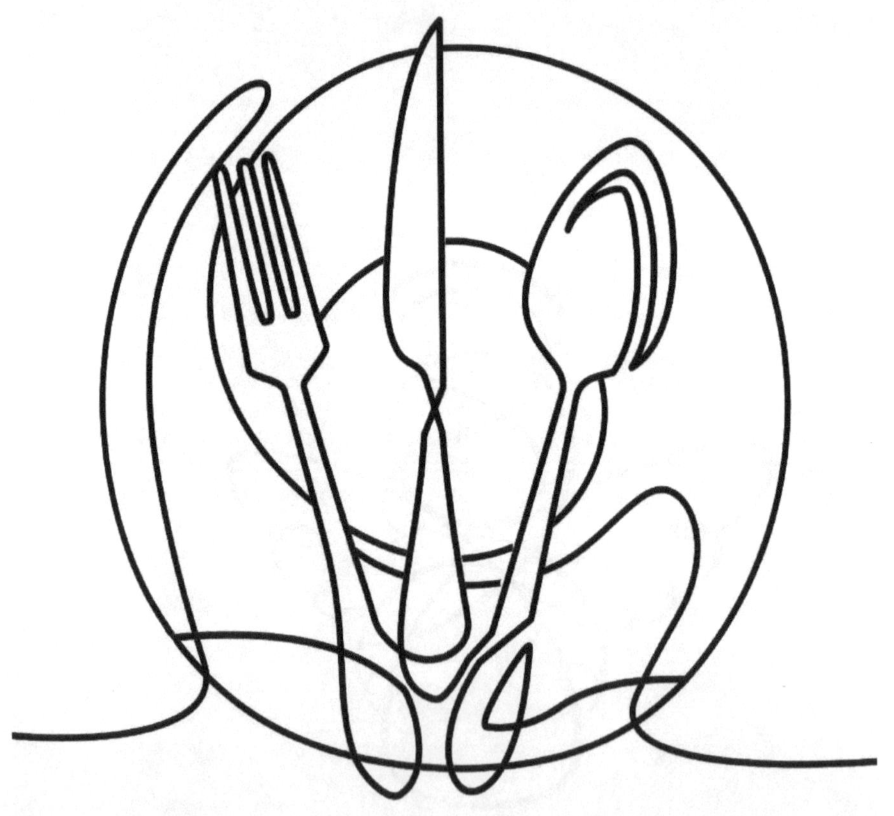

37

Café des Arts

'My mother invited us for dinner,' Steve said, almost laughing. He already knew what Eva's reaction would be.

'Fantastic. Just what I need.'

'This time it will not be at the house. She has booked a table at *Café des Arts*.'

'*Café des Arts*. Isn't that the pretentious French place in town?'

'It sure is.'

'Jeez, Steve, I don't know. I have nothing to wear and I'm sure that I'll make a total fool of myself.'

'Wear whatever you want. You always look amazing.'

'Yeah, sure.'

'There's more bad news. Daulton and Annabel Malmesbury have also been invited.'

'Steve, no! Can't you make up some excuse for me? I'm sure your mother only invited me to embarrass me.'

'Eva, don't be so silly. You'll do just fine. It's important to me you come. We have to show my mother we're a couple. If you don't show up, she'll see it as an invitation to meddle even more in my life.'

Eva sighed deeply, 'You're right. Let's do it.'

'Great. I'll pick you up around 7 o'clock.'

Eva looked through her wardrobe for a suitable dress.

261

She sighed heavily. Most of her dresses were already on the bed. She finally decided on a simple knee-length black dress. 'Chris, can I borrow the black shoes you bought?' Eva yelled from her bedroom.

'As long as you look after them.'

Eva spent hours in the bathroom, putting on face masks, shaving her legs, tweezing her eyebrows, and applying make-up. As always, Steve arrived on the dot. She opened the door and saw the approval on his face. 'You look stunning.'

'Thanks,' she said and kissed him. 'Let's hope all goes well. By the way, what about the menu? Do they have regular food or is it only frog legs and snails?'

'Eva, I'm sure they'll make a burger and French fries if you ask them,' Steve said, squeezing her waist.

They parked the car nearby and walked to the restaurant. Eva felt her heart racing. She hated the effect Marlene had on her. That woman knew how to make her feel hopeless and simple. Whenever she was around Marlene, she felt like a ten-year-old.

They were greeted at the door by an elegant hostess. 'Follow me, Mr. Patterson,' she said with a heavy French accent. The restaurant was very sophisticated. All the waiters were dressed in classic black and white and the tables were presented perfectly. As they walked to their table, Eva saw the others had already arrived.

'Steven, how wonderful to see you,' Marlene said and got up to hug her son.

'Eva, good to see you,' Daulton said. He seemed genuinely happy to see her.

Eva greeted Annabel Malmesbury, who was dressed in a full-length dark blue halter neck dress. Annabel nodded and gave her a top to bottom look. Eva felt her nerves racing. She was absolutely out of her element and everyone knew it.

'I hope you don't mind, but we have already started

with the wine.' Marlene spoke only to Steve. When she finished stroking Steve's arm and inquired about his work and general health, she turned her attention to Eva. 'Eva, I'll get you a menu. I'm afraid the menu is only available in French. But I can fix that.' She gestured one of the passing waiters to bring her an English menu.

Eva felt desperately unhappy. Not only did she not speak French, but she also had no idea what would be appropriate to order in a restaurant like this. Eva smiled at the waiter who handed her the menu. He didn't acknowledge her friendly gesture. *Great, even the waiter thinks I'm a loser*, she thought.

'Did you know that Annabel has spent considerable time in Paris and St. Tropez?' Marlene said. Then, she turned all her attention back to Steve once again. 'I've already asked her to order for me.'

'Marlene, please. You're too kind, but stop embarrassing me,' Annabel said, with a fake smile.

Eva tried to decipher the menu. She couldn't make out the appetizers and entrées and had absolutely no idea if she should order from both sections. She decided she would order something from the *les specialtés* list and hope for the best. The *English* menu never materialized.

'Do you need some help with this silly menu?' Daulton, who was sitting next to her, whispered.

Eva was shocked. She looked over and, for the first time, saw him with a cheeky smile on his face. 'I'd like something with chicken. Nothing fancy; just something I can eat without embarrassing myself. I'm not sure about the starters. Why don't you choose something for me?'

'Leave it to me. I'll make sure you'll eat something good. I can't promise it will be large portions, considering this is a fancy French restaurant.' Eva laughed out loud and instantly realized this was not acceptable.

'Why are the two of you being so loud?' Marlene

turned her attention to Daulton when she heard Eva's laugh.

'Nothing important, mother,' Daulton answered.

Steve put his hand on Eva's leg, leaned close, and kissed her cheek. 'Have you managed to find something to order?' he asked and gave her the same cheeky smile Daulton had given her. Eva suddenly realized they weren't as different as she had initially thought.

'Daulton has offered to order for me.'

'Good man,' Steve said and winked at his brother.

The evening passed without any further awkward moments for Eva. Daulton had ordered her a perfect starter of chicken liver mousse, followed by honey-roasted chicken. Marlene spent the evening desperately trying to find a theme Steve and Annabel had in common. Dr. Patterson didn't speak. He occasionally commented on the food.

'Please excuse my husband. He's working too much lately. He is exasperated,' Marlene spoke solely to Annabel.

'I understand,' Annabel replied politely. 'Being such a celebrated doctor must be strenuous.'

'Steven told me your apartment was burglarized last week,' Dr. Patterson asked Eva, out of nowhere.

'Yes. Fortunately, both Christine and I were out.'

'Did they take anything?'

'Other than our TV, DVD player, and laptop, nothing at all.' Eva looked at Dr. Patterson, searching his face for any emotion. Instead, his face remained blank.

They finished the evening with coffee and a delicious dessert wine. In the car, on their way home, Eva felt she could finally relax. 'I was surprised by Daulton this evening. I never really expected him to have a sense of humour.'

'Daulton has always suffered my mother's demands more than I have. I think he's scared of her, or maybe he doesn't want to disappoint her. Her influence has made him extremely reserved.'

Steve and Eva kissed passionately for over ten minutes

in the car in front of the apartment. Even though they kissed many times, Steve's kisses still drove her crazy. 'Should I come in for a moment to make sure the apartment is safe?'

'Don't worry. Chris is home. Surely the burglars must know that we have nothing of value to steal.' Eva jumped out of the car and waved to Steve before she opened the front door.

***

Eva went to her bedroom and took off her dress. She walked into the bathroom to take off her make-up and, while she was brushing her teeth, she suddenly stopped. She heard a noise in the kitchen. She stared at herself in the mirror. She was waiting for her reflection to tell her what to do. She slowly opened the bathroom door. *Maybe it was Christine who had woken up and wanted something to drink*, she told herself. Eva tiptoed to the kitchen and turned on the light. There was nobody. The windows were closed, and nothing appeared out of place. She turned the lights off and walked back to her bedroom.

As she passed Christine's door, she stopped and softly opened it. She could see Christine fast asleep in bed. The room was freezing. This was a matter of difference between them since they lived in the orphanage. Christine loved to sleep in a cold room. Eva, on the other hand, liked her bedroom nice and warm. She slowly closed the door and walked into her bedroom. She turned off her bedside lamp and went to sleep.

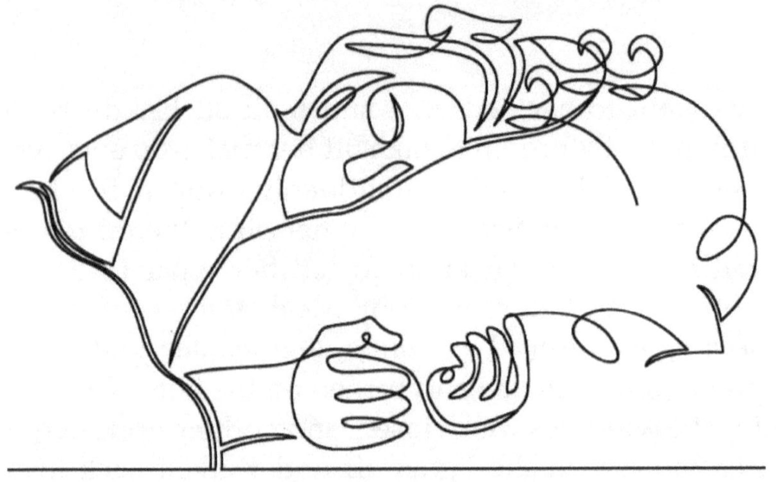

38

The Gas

Someone was shaking her. Why didn't they leave her alone? She was feeling tired and didn't want to wake up. The shaking, however, didn't stop. Eva tried to turn around again to get away from the disturbance. Something cold was being thrown in her face. She must have drunk too much last night. She had a headache. She felt the cold water dripping all over her and wanted to cover herself with her duvet.

Eva could feel herself slipping away into a deep sleep. She was vaguely aware of being dragged out of her bed. She felt nauseous, and someone was slapping her face. 'Eva. Eva, can you hear me? Eva, wake up!'

She wanted to speak, but realized she had something over her mouth. She slowly opened her eyes and realized she was not in her bed. As she looked around, she saw a man in a green shirt sitting next to her. 'Eva…? Don't worry. You'll be fine. We're driving you to the hospital,' the man in the green shirt said.

What was this man talking about? Who was he? She was starting to panic, but she was unable to move. She felt sick, closed her eyes, and felt herself slipping into a deep sleep.

When she woke, it took her some time to realize she was in a hospital bed. She desperately looked for a call button.

When she finally found it, she pressed it continuously and nervously waited for someone to come and see her.

'Why am I here? What happened?' she asked the pretty blond nurse who walked into the room.

'You were brought in last night due to gas inhalation.'

'Where's Christine? What happened to Christine?'

The nurse walked over to her bed. 'Christine? Is she your roommate?' Eva nodded. 'She's fine. She woke up during the night and was able to get you out of the apartment. She's downstairs in the restaurant. I'll ask her to come and see you.'

'Thank you.'

Soon, Christine came running through the door. 'Thankfully, you're okay,' she said and hugged Eva. 'How are you feeling?'

'I feel like I've been partying for two weeks non-stop. My head hurts and I feel nauseous. What happened last night?'

Christine got a white plastic, uncomfortable seat and moved it close to the bed. 'I woke up in the night with a headache. It was pretty bad. I decided to take an aspirin. When I opened my bedroom door, I could smell gas. I went back into my bedroom to get a shirt to hold in front of my nose and mouth. I tried to wake you, but you were so far gone that even cold water in your face didn't help. I dragged you out of the apartment and phoned for an ambulance.'

'So, being a freak and sleeping with the windows open even when it's freezing outside does have a purpose,' Eva said with a tired smile. Christine smiled and stroked Eva's hair.

'Good morning, ladies.' Daulton Patterson walked through the door. 'How are you feeling?' he asked Eva, while checking her pulse. 'You gave us quite a scare. Thankfully, Christine was able to get you out of the apartment in time.' He smiled at Christine while he kept checking Eva. Christine felt herself blush and walked back to the sink to get some water for Eva. She felt ridiculous. She wasn't a teenager.

'When can I go home?'

'I would like you to stay overnight and, if everything goes well, you can go home tomorrow morning,' he said, while making notes on Eva's patient chart. 'Did you have someone come over to check the gas leak?' Daulton asked Christine.

'Not yet. I'm staying at Eric's now. I'll try to organize an engineer to come to the apartment today.'

'You girls have not been fortunate in that apartment recently,' Daulton commented, his arms crossed.

'Maybe it's time we move.' Christine looked at Eva, who nodded in agreement.

'Did a doctor give you a check-up?' he asked Christine and, without hesitation, grabbed her wrist and started taking her pulse. Christine was red behind her ears and could feel her heart race.

'Yes. I'm fine. They also took some blood samples.' She pulled her arm back.

'Good. I'll come and check up on you later, Eva,' Daulton said and left the room. 'Good to see you, Christine.'

'Did I just see you blush over Daulton?'

'No. I didn't. I'm drained and agitated.'

'If you say so,' Eva responded in a child-like voice.

'Eva, why do you always have to be so in-my-face? Stop picking on me.'

'Sorry. Come and sit with me….'

The next morning, Christine took a taxi to the hospital to pick up Eva. She had stayed over Eric's. She didn't want to spend any time alone in the apartment - first, the burglary and now, the gas leak. Daulton was right. It was time to find another apartment and leave the bad memories behind.

When Christine's taxi drove up to the entrance of the hospital, Eva was waiting by the door. 'How are you feeling?'

Christine asked, as she helped Eva into the car.

'Fine. I'm happy to get out of this wheelchair.'

It was apparent to Christine she was not ready to talk about the recent events. When they arrived at the apartment, there was an engineer from the gas company working on-site. Christine helped Eva into the apartment and walked back outside. 'Did you find the leak?' she asked the engineer.

'It's not out here. All the pipes leading to your home are in perfect order. I still have to check inside the apartment,' he said. Christine let him in. The engineer walked into the kitchen and moved the cooker from the wall. 'Did you clean behind here recently?' he asked.

'No,' Christine said, almost embarrassed. They never cleaned behind the cooker.

'Well, the pressure-relief valve is completely broken. This is a big leak, and it would have killed you within hours if you hadn't woken up.' The engineer shook his head. 'Are you sure you didn't clean behind here? Maybe your roommate did. These valves don't come off that easily.'

'I told you, neither of us cleaned behind the cooker.' Christine walked out of the room, not sure why she felt so angry. 'We have to move immediately,' Christine said as she walked into Eva's bedroom and started to pack her clothes. 'The engineer is convinced we cleaned behind the cooker and we broke the valve off.'

'It could have just broken off by itself.'

'The engineer told me that it is almost impossible for the valve to have broken by itself. Eva, please. I don't feel safe here anymore.' Christine sat on Eva's bed. 'I can't take this anymore. Last night at Eric's, I had another nightmare.' Christine's shoulders were shaking while she cried quietly.

'You're right, Christine. I've been trying to ignore it, but I'm also starting to feel scared here. At first, I thought it was silly paranoia, but now I'm not so sure. I'll call Steve. We'll stay with him until we find another apartment. Go and pack some things. I'll finish packing in here. We'll leave straight away.'

***

Christine and Eva had been at Steve's for about a week and were enjoying themselves. Eva was thrilled that Christine liked Steve so much. She felt absurdly proud.

Steve was working late Monday night when Eva received a call from Liz. 'Dr. Johnson and Miranda are both out this evening and Mrs. Austin is doing very well. If you still want to talk to her, I think you should come over this evening.'

'Should we come over around 8?'

'Yes, that's fine. But make sure you park your car behind the hospital. You have Steve's car, don't you?'

Eva asked Christine to drive. She couldn't stop her hands from perspiring. Christine agreed, but only because she had no other choice. They were both agitated in the car. As they drove to the nursing home, the tension was unbearable. Christine parked the car behind the building like Liz told her to and remained seated.

'We don't have to do this, you know. We can pretend it never happened. We never found the photo. We look for another doctor and never see Dr. Patterson again,' Christine muttered.

'Let's go Chris. The sooner we do this, the sooner it'll be over,' Eva ordered, and walked briskly towards the entrance.

Christine locked the car door and ran after Eva. Liz was standing in the reception area and opened the sliding doors. 'Hi, Liz. Thanks for doing this for us,' Eva said and hugged her.

Liz started walking through the hall toward Mrs. Austin's room. Eva took Christine's hand and pressed it gently. The walk through the corridor seemed like the longest

271

walk they had ever made. Christine could feel her heart racing and her breathing was shallow. She was light-headed and stopped in the corridor to rest against the wall.

'Chris, it'll be alright....' Christine could see the same anxiety she was feeling on Eva's face. It was apparent that Eva was pretending to be brave. 'I can go in alone.'

'No. You're right. Let's do this,' Christine said.

Liz opened the door, switched the light on, and walked to Mrs. Austin's bed. She was sleeping. 'Mrs. Austin. Can you wake up? You have visitors.' Liz gently shook Mrs. Austin's shoulder.

'Mrs. Austin. We want you to wake up. This is important.' Liz shook her a bit harder this time.

Mrs. Austin opened her eyes and looked at Liz. 'What time is it?' she asked in a whispering voice.

'It's 8 p.m., Mrs. Austin. You have visitors. These are my friends, Eva and Christine.'

'Who are you?' Mrs. Austin asked.

Christine stepped forward and stood next to Liz. 'You don't know us, Mrs. Austin. But we both have a feeling we know you.' Mrs. Austin didn't answer. 'Mrs. Austin, we found a photo of you.'

Mrs. Austin didn't respond. Instead, she kept looking from Christine to Eva. 'Mrs. Austin, the photo was taken in South America and you are there with Dr. Matthew Patterson,' Eva continued.

'Get them away from me! Get them out of here!' Mrs. Austin shouted. 'Why did you bring them here?' She looked at Liz in shock and disgust.

Liz tried to calm Mrs. Austin down. She gestured for Eva and Christine to leave the room immediately. Both girls couldn't get out of the room quickly enough. In the corridor, they stared at each other. They both looked scared. They remained standing in the hallway for about five minutes until Liz stepped out of Mrs. Austin's room.

'I'm sorry. Something you said must have set her off. I've talked to her and convinced her you are good friends. She has calmed down and has agreed to see you. She doesn't want you to come close to her, so keep your distance.'

Christine and Eva walked back into the room, subdued. They were scared Mrs. Austin would get upset again, so they stayed close to the wall, as far from the bed as possible.

'Mrs. Austin. I'm sorry we upset you. We were hoping you could answer some questions. We found the photo at Dr. Patterson's country home,' Christine said.

'What photo are you talking about?'

'It's a group photo. There is you, Dr. Matthew Patterson, Mrs. Eastman, Dr. Ronald Bernard, Dr. William Abrahams and...'

'Dr. Carlo Alamilla,' Mrs. Austin finished Christine's sentence.

'That's right. And there are also some local women in the photo.'

'And...' Mrs. Austin began to ask, 'why are you so interested in me or any of the people in that photo?'

'Mrs. Austin, this may seem very strange, but Liz told us you suffer from dreadful nightmares.'

'Do you discuss all your patients with your friends?' Mrs. Austin asked Liz, irritated. Liz ignored Mrs. Austin's remark and nodded at Christine to continue.

'We, Eva and I… we have the same nightmare.'

Mrs. Austin looked at them. Her eyes were almost mocking them. 'A nightmare? And what nightmare might that be?'

'There is some earthquake and a lot of confusion. Then, when everything seems to be quieting down, there is a blue light at the horizon. The blue light travels fast until it overtakes everything.' Eva leaned against the wall. She realized that when she was recounting the story, it didn't seem scary. She did, however, feel terrified just talking about it. Christine stood next to her and put her arm around her. When they looked over at Mrs. Austin, they could see tears running down her face.

'Mrs. Austin, please, what does it mean?' Christine asked. 'This nightmare has been haunting us ever since we were fifteen years old.'

'It's a long story. First, you have to tell me what your relationship is with Matthew Patterson.'

'Dr. Patterson is our physician. He has been our physician ever since we were babies. We have known him all our lives.'

'Come here.' Mrs. Austin called them close. 'Whatever you do, do not trust that man. Do not trust his wife. Do not trust his colleagues.'

'But what is your relation to Dr. Patterson and the others?' Eva asked.

'Dr. Patterson gave me a baby. He performed in-vitro fertilization. In those days this was not a procedure available like it is today. Other doctors would never offer it to a single woman.' Mrs. Austin took a deep breath. 'Dr. Patterson told me he would help me. So, I worked with him in Chile. I got pregnant as you know from the photo… but my baby died.'

It was apparent Mrs. Austin was exhausted. Suddenly, they heard a noise in the corridor. All three girls stared at each other at once.

'I'll take a look. Stay here,' Liz whispered and walked to the door. She softly opened it and glanced around the corner. She jumped back and turned off the lights.

'It's Dr. Johnson with another man I've never seen before. You have to get out of here.' She pushed Christine and Eva towards the window. Liz had problems opening the window; she couldn't budge the handle. They could hear the steps in the corridor coming closer.

'What is happening?' Mrs. Austin asked.

'Mrs. Austin, pretend to be asleep. Dr. Johnson is

coming this way and he cannot see you awake,' Liz whispered in a panicked voice. She pulled the window handle hard and finally managed to move it. 'Jump!' she hurriedly whispered to Christine and Eva.

'What about you?' Christine asked.

'I'll be fine. Get out of here.' Liz pushed them. Eva lost a shoe when she fell into the flowerbed beneath the window. She cut her arm on the rose bushes. Before she could move out of the way, Christine fell on top of her.

Eva tried not to yell, but Christine's fall injured her ankle severely. While they crawled away, Liz closed the window and pulled the curtain. She dove underneath Mrs. Austin's bed and tried to get her breathing under control when the door opened.

39

Mrs. Austin in Danger

The light came on and Liz rolled herself as small as possible. She could see two pairs of black shoes walking up to the bed. A voice she didn't recognize spoke, 'Jennifer. Jennifer. Why did you have to go and listen to Diane Eastman? Everything would have turned out just fine had you stayed quiet. That stupid woman thought it necessary to grow a conscience after her child drowned in their swimming pool. You and Diane nearly ruined everything for us. The thing is, I always liked you but, as always, Marlene was right. We shouldn't have kept you.'

'What do you want to do?' Liz recognized Dr. Johnson's voice.

'How much is she taking now?'

'We've been using a mixture of light anaesthetics. She's been out completely; unable to communicate or move by herself.'

'Maybe you can start increasing the dosage. Then, in about three weeks, add curariform. That should do it.'

'But, that's euthanasia,' Dr. Johnson replied.

'Don't be so innocent, Daniel. You have been giving this woman unnecessary medication for years and never had any problems with that.'

'Yes. But euthanasia.'

'Daniel. Don't forget who pays your extremely generous salary. I own this home. I'm your boss and you will do as I say.' The man left the room and Dr. Johnson followed closely. Liz let out of sigh of relief. She crawled out from underneath the bed and took Mrs. Austin's hand.

'Mrs. Austin, are you okay?'

'That was Matthew Patterson. He has finally decided to get rid of me for good,' Mrs. Austin said with a bitter voice. 'I knew this day would come. It was only a matter of time.'

'I'll get you out of here. I promise, Mrs. Austin. Don't worry,' Liz whispered.

'Those two girls that were here, I need to talk to them again.'

'Sure. I'll organize it. I must go now, Mrs. Austin. If they see my car, I will surely receive the same treatment as they intend to give you.' Liz slowly opened the door and quickly ran to the nurse's station to leave via the backdoor….

***

Christine and Eva sat in Steve's car behind the nursing home. They were too scared to start the car and drive off in case Dr. Johnson might see or hear them. After ten minutes, Christine opened the car door and got out.

'What are you doing? Get back in the car, now. They might see you,' Eva whispered.

'I want to see if Dr. Johnson's car is still parked in front of the hospital. Do you want to sit here all night and wait for the lovely Miranda to find us?'

Eva followed Christine. 'I lost a shoe,' Eva said. Her foot was sore. She stepped into the rose bush, which left her foot bleeding. They passed the kitchen and the several out-buildings housing wheelchairs, crutches, and boxes of cleaning products for the facility. They crossed a paved area, which connected further out-buildings with the main nursing home when an intruder light came on. Christine and Eva dove on the ground.

'Ahhhh!' Christine said silently and crouched, holding her hand. She had put her hand into a nail that stuck out of a wood frame. Blood was streaming down her hand and arm. She took the scarf from her neck and started to wrap it around the wound. They moved slowly and could hear one of the doors open. Christine and Eva hunched together. Eva realized she had stopped breathing, and thought she was going to faint. As they sat close together, they saw Liz sneaking out of the door.

'Liz,' Eva whispered.

Liz stopped and looked back. Christine and Eva got up and crawled on their hands and knees towards her. She was standing with her back pressed against the wall. 'What are two you still doing here?' she asked.

'We couldn't drive off. They would hear the car,' Eva whispered heatedly.

'There's a back entrance!'

'I'm so sorry. I didn't study the map more carefully before coming here,' Eva responded. 'Where the heck is this back entrance?'

Liz signalled them to follow her. They made their way through the dense prickly bushes behind the nursing home. Christine heard her clothes rip. When they finally made it, they stood still for a moment, all of them catching their breath.

'Your car is over there. Mine is just behind that garbage bin. I suggest you do not turn on your car lights until I do so,' Liz said and, without waiting for a response, she ran to her car. Christine and Eva ran to Steve's car. Christine started the engine and followed Liz.

They drove over a small, unpaved country lane. Liz was driving slowly and finally, after five minutes, switched her headlights on. Christine followed Liz's red Honda Accord until she pulled over. Christine parked behind her and got out.

'Sorry I snapped at you back there. I was so scared. For a moment, I thought I was going to wet myself,' Liz said. Eva got out of the car and limped towards Christine and Liz. 'What happened to you?' Liz asked, and could not help smiling when she saw Eva hobble towards them.

'I lost my shoe!'

'What happened in there?' Christine asked.

Liz told them about the visit Dr. Johnson and Dr. Patterson paid to Mrs. Austin. 'I was lying under the bed. I have never been so scared in my entire life.' Liz held one hand on her neck and was stroking it so hard her entire neck turned red. Eva could still see the fear in her eyes as she was speaking. 'We have a bigger problem,' Liz continued. 'They're planning to kill her in about three weeks.'

'What!' Christine exclaimed.

'They want to increase her present medication, and, in three weeks, they want to add another anaesthetic which will result in death. It is the same cocktail they use for euthanasia. I'm not sure how, but we have to get Mrs. Austin out of there.' Liz had tears in her eyes and looked at Christine and Eva for answers.

'Don't worry Liz. We'll think of something,' Christine said.

'Did he say anything else?' Eva asked

'Dr. Patterson talked about a *Diane Eastman*. I got the impression that she was one of the main reasons he put Mrs. Austin in the hospital to begin with.'

Christine looked at Eva. *Why, after so many years? Why did he want to kill her now? And not earlier?* Christine wondered. Also, she had no idea how to get Mrs. Austin out of the nursing home or where to take her. 'We have to go home. Can you drive?' Christine asked.

'Yes. I'll be fine,' Liz said. 'Eva, you better give me your shoe. You might have lost it in Mrs. Austin's room. If someone finds it, at least I can say they're mine.'

Eva stared at Liz, amazed. No matter how upset she was, Liz was still thinking straight. Eva took her shoe off and gave it to her. Without saying anything else, Liz got into her car. Before driving off, she opened the window. 'You can follow me to the intersection. That will take you back into the city.'

The following day, Eva's entire body ached. Christine's falling on top of her bruised her severely. She threw back the sheets and looked at her swollen ankle. The rest of her legs were covered in scratches. She got up and hopped to the kitchen to get some ice. She poured herself a cup of coffee as Christine walked in.

'Good morning.'

'Morning, Chris. Did you get some sleep?'

'As good as can be expected. What did Steve say?'

'He was already asleep when we got in and, this morning, he left very early… What are we going to do about Mrs. Austin?'

Christine thought for a moment and ran to get her cell phone. 'I have a plan on how to get Mrs. Austin out of that nursing home.'

***

Steve's doorbell rang. Eva answered the intercom. 'Christine! It's Eric for you,' she yelled

Christine walked into the living room. She had a large, bulky bandage over her hand, and her legs didn't look any better than Eva's. She opened the door for Eric and greeted him with a kiss. Eric stared at her.

'What happened to you?' he asked.

'Eva and I went hiking yesterday. We slipped and fell into a thorn bush,' Christine said. She was having second thoughts about their relationship and thought that letting him into her life now wouldn't be a good idea.

'That must have been some bush. Where did you go?'

'We went into the mountains towards the country home,' Eva said quickly, after seeing Christine's hesitation.

Eric looked at Christine, who blushed slightly. It was apparent he didn't believe them but didn't know how to approach the problem. 'You have to take me there, Christine,' he said.

'Christine has sworn off hiking. If anything, she was even worse than I was. You want anything to drink?' Eva tried to change the subject. She could see the irritation on his face.

Christine walked to the sofa and sat down. She was aware Eric was staring at her. 'Eva, do you think you can give us a minute.'

Eva looked at Christine with a suspicious face but had no other option than to oblige. Christine waited for Eva to leave the room and turned towards Eric. 'Eric, I'm sorry, but this isn't working for me. We've both tried, but it's obvious we want different things from life.'

Eric leaned back into the large plush sofa and sighed heavily. 'Christine, I love you. I don't want to lose you, not again. Maybe we want different things now, but in the long run, we want the same things.' He put his hand on her leg. 'I want to settle down and have a family with you.'

Christine didn't respond. She felt horrible. She searched his face but couldn't pinpoint what he was thinking. As if by cue, his eyes turned sad and desperate. He took her hands in his.

'Christine, please give me one more chance. I want to make you happy. I want to build a life with you. Never in my entire life had I expected to meet someone like you. I want you to be the mother of my children.'

He looked at her with big puppy-dog eyes. Christine felt awful. He must love her. But why didn't she ever feel it? Her mind was racing. She didn't want to hurt him.

'Maybe we can take a break?' She felt like a cliché. She stared at her hand in Eric's. The truth was she wanted him to leave and stop making her feel badly. As she looked up, she was stunned to see tears running down his face.
'Don't leave me, Christine. I can't live without you.' It was a desperate cry and Christine couldn't take it any longer. She kissed him. 'Christine, don't ever scare me like that again.' He took her into his arms and kissed her.

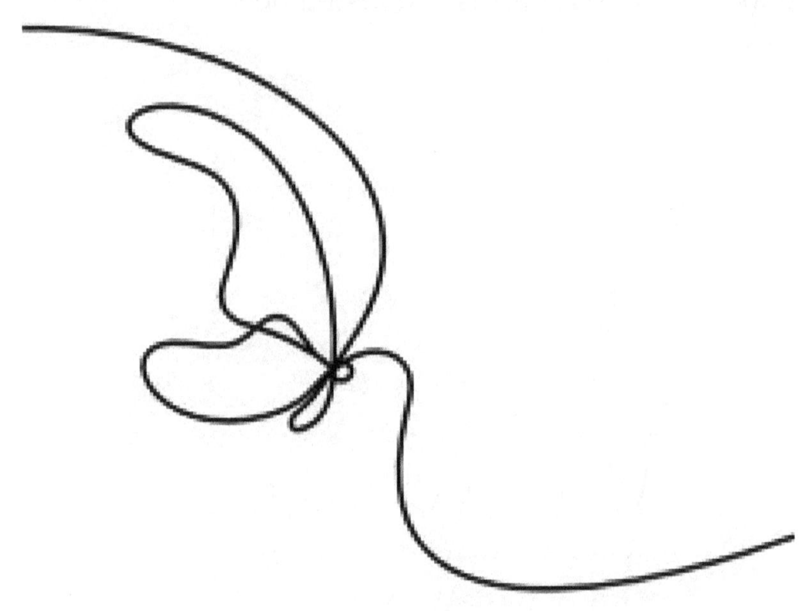

40

Saving Mrs. Austin

Liz made her rounds in the home. She stopped to chat with some of the patients. The next thing she did when she arrived that morning was search for Eva's shoe in Mrs. Austin's room and underneath the window outside. When she didn't find it, she assumed Eva must have lost it while walking to her car. She walked back to the nursing station for a coffee. One of her colleagues stopped her and told her that Miranda was looking for her. Liz sighed heavily. As she approached the reception desk, Miranda held up the shoe she was so desperately looking for.

'One of the cleaners found this in Mrs. Austin's room.'

'Good for him… Jane told me you wanted to see me,' Liz said calmly.

'Don't you think it's odd that someone found *one* shoe in Mrs. Austin's room? It's not exactly her style.'

'Please, Miranda. I have a busy day. Did you have something to discuss, or did you want to talk to me about a shoe?'

'There's one other thing. When I came in this morning, I noticed the security system had been switched off. I never forget to switch it on.'

'Well, maybe your memory isn't what it used to be. If there's nothing else…?' Liz turned and walked away. She prayed Miranda bought her bluff.

Liz finished her mid-morning coffee break and looked nervously at her watch. At precisely eleven, she stood up and went to Mrs. Austin's room. She took a bag from the wardrobe and started packing the few belongings Mrs. Austin owned. She woke Mrs. Austin and gave her a dark-blue, micro-fleece dressing gown to wear.

'What do you think you're doing?' Dr. Johnson walked into the room.

'We received a letter at the nursing station from Dr. Patterson saying he wanted us to prepare Mrs. Austin to be transferred to Hampstead Hospital.'

'Hampstead?!' Dr. Johnson walked out of the room and went to the nursing station. He found a letter signed by Dr. Patterson stating that Mrs. Austin was to be transferred and should be ready to be moved at half-past eleven. Dr. Johnson picked up the phone at the nursing station and dialled Dr. Patterson's practice.

'I'm sorry, Dr. Johnson, Dr. Patterson is in a meeting, and is under no circumstance to be disturbed.'

'Rebecca, this is particularly important.'

'I'm sorry. I can't help you. You'll have to call back later this afternoon.'

Dr. Johnson put the phone down and called Miranda. 'When did the letter from Dr. Patterson arrive?'

'It was hand-delivered this morning at around nine o'clock.'

'I tried to contact Dr. Patterson, but he's not reachable. You keep trying every five minutes,' Dr. Johnson barked at Miranda.

He walked into his office and slammed the door behind him. What was the matter with that old fool? Only last night, he gave him the order to euthanize Mrs. Austin, and now he was having her transferred.

He watched an ambulance pull up outside the entrance

hall. Two paramedics dressed in green uniforms walked into the reception area and informed Miranda that they were there to collect Mrs. Austin.

Dr. Johnson walked out of his office and saw Liz pushing Mrs. Austin in a wheelchair. Liz's heart was racing uncontrollably. She wanted to run down the corridor and get out of there. As Liz reached the reception area, Dr. Johnson joined Miranda behind the reception desk. She could see him frantically dialling a number on the phone. 'I need to speak with Dr. Patterson now!' he shouted.

Liz decided not to stop and continued pushing Mrs. Austin out of the building to the ambulance. The ramp to wheel the chair into the ambulance was not yet prepared. Liz stopped the wheelchair as close to the ambulance as possible.

'Mrs. Austin, I need you to be strong for me. I'm going to lift you, and I need you to work with me as much as you can.'

Liz grabbed Mrs. Austin under her arms to lift her. She was a lot heavier than Liz expected. Liz lifted her with all the strength she could muster and almost dragged Mrs. Austin into that ambulance.

'I'm sorry about this, Mrs. Austin. Everything is going to be okay. Christine and Eva will be waiting for you at the hospital.'

'Thank you, Liz,' Mrs. Austin said softly. Liz could see she was totally exhausted by the look on her face and her limp body.

Liz jumped out of the ambulance and walked back into the nursing home. Dr. Johnson was still trying to reach Dr. Patterson without success. He slammed the phone down and handed the ambulance driver the necessary release paperwork. As Liz walked by, he grabbed her firmly by her arm.

'I know you have something to do with this. Don't you dare think you'll get away with it!' As he said the last word, he pushed her away. Liz nearly fell to the floor. She walked to the nurse's station and collected her belongings.

'Jane, I'm not feeling well at all. I'm going home,' Liz said to one of her colleagues.

Liz ran out the door to her car. She sat several minutes, resting her head on the steering wheel. They had done it. Mrs. Austin was safe.

41

A New Apartment

'Mrs. Austin…' Christine ran up when Mrs. Austin appeared from the ambulance. 'Did everything go okay?'

'Everything is fine,' she answered, still fatigued. She was having difficulty sitting up straight in the wheelchair.

'Can you take this lady up to the fourth floor immediately,' Daulton asked one of the nearby nurses.

Christine walked up to Daulton. 'Thank you, Daulton. I can't tell you how much I appreciate what you have done.'

'I've done nothing. I'm admitting a lady you told me is not well. That's my job,' he said and gave her a warm smile. 'I'll go up and start running some tests.'

'Can you let us know when we can visit her?' Christine called after Daulton, who was already in front of the lift.

'I'll drop by Steve's apartment this evening.'

'Eva, it's Liz. Did she arrive okay?'

'She's fine. They're running some tests at the moment. Hopefully, we can visit her tomorrow.'

'I had to leave the nursing home. Dr. Johnson is suspicious and angry,' Liz said. She spoke amazingly fast. 'Also, they found your shoe in Mrs. Austin's room. Eva, I'm scared. Can I stay at your place this evening?'

'Liz, we're staying at Steve's. Let me see what I can do. I'll call you back in about an hour. Is that okay?'

'Sure.'

Eva put the phone down and walked back into the hospital. 'Christine, we need to find an apartment. Liz was forced to leave the nursing home and is terrified. She has nowhere to stay now.'

Christine walked outside and signalled for Eva to come with her. They took the nearest underground and got off at the stop where one of the largest Estate Agents had their office. When they arrived, they looked at the offers displayed in the window.

'Look at this one. It's on Harvist Road in Queen's Park.'

'Perfect. Let's go in,' Christine said. 'Excuse me. The fully furnished apartment with the two bedrooms, is it still available?' Christine asked the young realtor, who couldn't be older than nineteen-years-old.

'Let's have a look,' he said, trying to sound confident.

'Also, it needs to be available immediately,' Christine said quickly.

'Here it is. Yes. It's still on the market.'

'Great. We'll take it.'

'I'm sorry. Don't you want to see it first?'

'No. We'll take it.'

Without asking further questions, he asked them for their documents and took out a rental and tenancy agreement. 'I'll prepare the rental and tenancy agreement. I also need to complete an application screening. This is my first rental apartment,' he said, and laughed sheepishly.

'Why don't we come back in about an hour,' Eva said.

The boy looked up, relieved. Christine and Eva walked the streets until they passed a small diner. They walked in, sat at a table furthest from the door, and ordered lunch. 'We'll still be close to *Paradise by way of Kensal Green*, our favourite pub.'

'Liz, hi. It's Eva. We found a new apartment and you can stay with us.'

'What a relief,' Liz replied. 'How on earth did you manage to find an apartment that quickly?'

'It's amazing what you can achieve when you put your mind to it.' Eva gave Liz their new address and asked her to meet them there in about three hours.

'Thanks, Eva. See you later.'

'I'd better phone Steve as well to tell him we found a new apartment,' Eva said.

'Why don't you eat first and calm down. Before we get over-excited, let's wait until we've signed the contract and have the keys in our hands.'

'Superstitious? I never knew that about you.'

They sat in the little diner, waiting for the time to pass. They both ordered bangers and mash but were unable to eat much, no matter how good it looked. They kept staring at the clock. After one hour, Eva got up.

'It can't take him more than an hour to draw up the papers and do a credit check.' She walked over to the till and paid for lunch.

Christine got up. She was relieved. As they walked into the Estate Agent's office, the young man looked up and smiled. 'Everything is in order. I need both of you to sign on the dotted line,' he said, giggling at his silly rhyme.

Christine and Eva smiled back politely and signed the one-year rental agreement. With keys in hand, they walked out of the office.

'Isn't it amazing? We would have spent weeks searching for an apartment in any other circumstance,' Christine said.

***

Eva decided to take Steve's car and drive to the new apartment.

'Whoa. This looks great. I like the garden in the front. Look, they even have some benches,' Eva said

'It's a nice building. Where are we again?' Christine asked.

'Ground floor.'

They stood in front of their new front door for a moment. Then, they smiled for the first time in days when they walked into their new home. 'This is lovely,' Eva said.

The apartment had a large open-plan living room with a lovely dining area and open-plan kitchen. There was a beautiful bay window overlooking the garden and two double bedrooms and a modern bathroom.

The furniture was slightly dated. There was one dark beige sofa and a matching chair. The dining room table was made of dark wood with a glass insert and four matching chairs with wicker seating. Christine threw the keys on the oval glass dining table.

'I'll pick out my bedroom now.'

'Not if I pick mine first.' Eva playfully ran towards Christine.

'Well, they're pretty much the same,' Christine said.

The bathroom must have recently been renovated because it was very luxurious with a three-piece suite. They walked back to the living room and sat on, what was their, brand new sofa. There was an abundance of light in the room which was a lovely change from their dark and dingy living room in Kensal Green.

'Excuse me, miss. Can I phone my boyfriend now?'

Christine laughed. The doorbell rang and Christine answered the intercom. 'Liz, Come in. Welcome to our new abode.'

'Woah, Christine! This is amazing.' Liz was standing near the door next to a side window that gave the apartment a bright appeal.

'Isn't it? Let me give you the grand tour. Eva's on the phone with Steve.'

'This is a lovely apartment. Is it expensive?'

'Only about double the price of our old one. But I think it's money well spent.' Liz nodded and followed Christine into the living room.

'Jeez, Liz. I just realized we have nothing in the house, I can't even offer you a soda.' Christine picked up her bag. 'I'll go to the supermarket and buy some stuff for this evening.'

'Do you want me to come with you?' Liz asked.

'No, thanks. Stay here with Eva.' Christine could do with some alone time to digest the events of the day.

That evening, Eva went to collect Steve at Queens Park Tube Station in his car. He was coming over to check out the new apartment.

'This is a nice place. I'm pleased for both of you.' He looked around. 'Although, to be honest, I was enjoying your company at my place. I suppose I'll have to start cleaning up behind myself again.' Eva pretended to hit him on the head.

Christine was in the open-plan kitchen with Liz. 'Hi Steve. I'm happy you like the place,' Christine said. 'I've prepared some snacks for this evening.'

'Great.'

'Do you want a beer?' Eva asked.

'Just what the doctor ordered,' Steve said and took a seat on the sofa next to her.

The doorbell rang again, and three girls jumped. Nobody but the people in the room knew where they lived. 'I'm so sorry. That must be Daulton,' Steve said. 'He told me he was planning to meet you at my place this evening, so I gave him your new address.'

Eva got up and walked to the intercom to buzz him in.

Daulton walked into the living room with a bottle of red wine under his arm. 'Well, I see someone has already been shopping,' he said, as he put the bottle next to the others Christine bought earlier. 'This is a very nice apartment. How did you manage to find this so quickly?' he asked, predominantly to Christine.

'We just decided to take the first two-bedroomed furnished apartment that was available immediately. We were also surprised we managed to find it this quickly.'

'Very nice, indeed. What are you going to do with your other furniture?'

'We'll leave it all behind for the next tenant,' Eva said. 'Neither Christine nor I want to be reminded about our time there.'

'Daulton, I don't think you've met our friend, Liz,' Christine said, wanting Liz to feel comfortable and at home.

Daulton said *hello* to Liz, took a seat on one of the dining room chairs, and opened a beer.

'I didn't take you for a beer drinker,' Christine said.

'There's a lot about me you don't know,' Daulton responded with a wink.

Christine blushed and walked back to the kitchen. She finished putting the pies, garlic bread, and salad on the table and told everyone to help themselves.

'By the way, you both need to come back to the hospital,' Daulton said to Christine and Eva. 'Your blood samples got mixed up. Somehow one blood sample was tested twice.'

'Okay. No problem. Blood tests are my favourite,' Eva said cynically.

'How is Mrs. Austin doing?' Liz asked, concerned.

'She's doing surprisingly well. With the number of drugs that woman has in her body, it's a miracle she's still alive. You should be able to visit her tomorrow. She has been asking for you. I never knew you had an aunt, Christine?'

Christine felt terrible lying to Daulton after all he had done for them. She quickly glanced at Steve and hoped he hadn't heard anything. Without Daulton, Mrs. Austin would still be in the nursing home. She just smiled at Daulton and avoided the question.

Daulton was unaware of the uncomfortable silence and continued drinking his beer as though nothing had happened.

The evening turned out to be a success. After all the horrible experiences and the injuries they incurred the past weeks, Christine and Eva managed to forget their problems for a while.

'It's been a wonderful evening, but I'm afraid I have to leave,' Daulton said. 'I have an early start tomorrow.'

'It's already midnight. I better leave as well,' Steve said and got up. Eva walked to the door and let Daulton and Steve out.

'So, where am I sleeping this evening?' Liz asked.

'First, I thought with me. But then, we saw that the sofa is a pull-out bed,' Eva said. 'I hope it's comfortable.'

'I'm sure it's perfect. I'm exhausted. I'll sleep anywhere.'

'You're not alone. We'll clean up in the morning.'

'Goodnight, Liz.' Christine and Eva walked to their new bedrooms.

Liz crawled into the sofa bed and fell asleep the moment her head hit the pillow. Suddenly, she was woken up by dreadful screams coming from the bedrooms.

'What in the world…??!!' Liz was frantic. She didn't know what to do; turn on the light, escape through the window, what? Finally, she decided to open the living room door ever so quietly.

'Christine…? Eva…? Are you okay?' Liz asked in a small voice from the hall.

'We're fine. We are… we just had a nightmare.'

Christine walked into Eva's bedroom. 'Jeez, Chris. They're getting worse and worse,' Eva said, still out of breath.

'I know.'

'You want to sleep with me this evening?'

'Why do you think I'm here? Move over.' Liz was standing in the doorway, holding a sheet tightly around her. 'It's okay, Liz. This is the nightmare we were talking about with Mrs. Austin. You can take my bedroom tonight,' Christine said. 'This was by far the worst nightmare I've ever had,' she said, as she laid next to Eva.

'I just have a question for you both. What is this *Chaser Blazer* game?'

Christine and Eva laughed. 'It works like this. We take a stack of magazines and within fifteen minutes we have to find to best advertisement and, afterwards, we explain why.'

'Seems like an odd game for two fifteen-year-olds,' Liz commented.

'Maybe. But we loved and still love playing it.'

***

'What in the world are you talking about?' Dr. Johnson's face was red with embarrassment and dread. He finally managed to speak with Dr. Patterson around four that afternoon when he had made his way to the nursing home. 'Why would I *ever* write a letter like that?' Dr. Patterson screamed and smacked the letter back on the desk.

Matthew Patterson paced in front of the reception desk. Miranda was looking at both men and decided to keep herself as far away as possible from either man. Matthew Patterson picked up the phone receiver but, after a second, smacked the receiver on the phone-base several times. '*Where* did they take her?' he asked Miranda.

'Hampstead,' Miranda whispered.

Matthew Patterson walked over to Daniel Johnson and stopped an inch from his face. 'Someone will pay for this disaster!' Matthew Patterson stormed out of the nursing home, got in his Mercedes, and sped off.

Dr. Daniel Johnson stood frozen; his feet felt nailed to the ground. He knew he was in serious trouble. He was well aware of what Dr. Patterson and his partners were capable of. 'Miranda, I'll be out for the rest of the day.'

'Enjoy your day, Dr. Johnson,' she said, not knowing what else to say.

296

He decided to drive straight home, pack a suitcase, and leave the country as soon as he emptied his bank account.

42

Sisters

Christine and Eva arrived at Hampstead straight after their visit to Inspector McMillan. They walked to the information desk and asked for Daulton. They were in the gift shop buying chocolates and flowers for Mrs. Austin when Daulton arrived. He looked very sophisticated in his doctor's coat. His thick black hair was longer than Steve's, and beautifully contrasted with his white doctor's coat.

'Ready for some blood tests?' he asked.

'Sure,' Christine replied.

He walked them over to the lab. 'This is Nurse Jones. She is the best blood-drawer in the hospital.'

'Yoo-hoo,' Eva replied.

'I'll label the samples myself,' Daulton said to the nurse.

Christine's test was next. She looked away when the nurse inserted the needle. 'Can we see Mrs. Austin today?' she asked.

'As soon as we're done here, I'll take you there.' He didn't speak to them while in the lift and Christine and Eva felt slightly uncomfortable. Both of them were relieved when the door opened. As they walked out, Daulton's pager went off. 'My father's in my office. I'd better see what he wants. Mrs. Austin is in room 415.'

'Daulton,' Christine touched Daulton's arm as he

walked back into the lift. 'Please, can I ask you a favour without asking me any questions?' Christine was holding the lift door. 'Can you please try and stall your father for as long as you can. If he wants to see Mrs. Austin, please don't let him near her,' Christine begged.

'I'll see what I can do,' Daulton responded without asking any further questions.

Christine and Eva found themselves standing in front of room 415. This was the moment of truth. Both girls were shaking. 'Here goes nothing,' Christine said anxiously.

Mrs. Austin was sleeping when they entered the room. She was lying in a mountain of pillows and she looked frail. The room was typical of a hospital, impersonal and sterile. They were happy they brought some flowers to cheer up the room. Mrs. Austin had a needle attached to a drip inserted into her hand.

Eva looked at her and realized that, for the first time since they met her, Mrs. Austin looked peaceful. They each picked up a white folding chair and sat on either side of the bed. Without waking her up, they looked at her for several minutes. Mrs. Austin slowly started to move and opened her eyes. She smiled when she saw the girls sitting next to her bed.

'How are you feeling, Mrs. Austin?' Eva asked as she moved closer to the bed. Mrs. Austin nodded and picked up the glass of water sitting next to her bed. She sipped the water through a straw until the glass was empty. The three of them sat in silence for a few moments just staring at each other, not sure how to start the conversation.

'I'm pleased you're back. I need to talk to you about your nightmares. I know it's hard, but can you tell me again what it's about.' Christine looked at Eva and gave her a short nod.

Eva mechanically started to describe the nightmare. When she finished, she walked over to the water dispenser to pour herself a glass of water. When she returned, Mrs. Austin placed her hand over hers.

'I'm not sure how you can have this nightmare. This nightmare is mine. It is an experience I had in Chile.'

Eva looked at Christine. This was the moment. It was now or never.

'We need to know what it means,' Christine spoke decisively. 'Otherwise, we'll never be able to recover from the nightmares.'

Mrs. Austin sat up and Christine quickly fluffed the pillows and replaced them behind Mrs. Austin's back.

'I'll tell you the whole story from start to finish….' Mrs. Austin took a deep breath and started to tell them about how she had desperately wanted a child and about meeting Dr. Patterson and Marlene. She told about her consequent stay in Santa Tecla.

'As you can imagine, I was thrilled when I found out I was pregnant. The insemination worked immediately. I was one of those lucky women who suffered little nausea and who blossomed during pregnancy.' Mrs. Austin smiled as she remembered.

'Other women, including Diane Eastman and Carmen Aguilar, were also pregnant and we all had a wonderful time together. During that time, I'd grown remarkably close to these women. We shared our experiences and could feel our babies kicking. We would join each other whenever we had an ultrasound of our babies. I remember I saw my baby move and heard her heartbeat.'

Mrs. Austin stopped and looked at the girls. 'We were three women, each pregnant with our first child. All the doctors in the hospital treated us like royalty, especially Carmen, a local woman, and me. Towards the ninth month, the tension in the entire hospital was running high. This was going to be a fantastic experience. During that period, I was told my baby was in the wrong birth position and, according to Dr. Patterson, it would be safer to have the baby born by

Caesarean-section.'

Mrs. Austin's expression changed. 'Carmen, who was also having problems, and I were scheduled for the operation at the same time.'

Christine could see that she was struggling. Mrs. Austin's lips were shaking, and her eyes were moist. She looked so incredibly vulnerable. All Christine wanted to do was hug her. 'We can take a break, and maybe continue another time.'

Mrs. Austin looked at Christine and stroked her cheek. 'I want to continue. I remember being prepared for the operation. Pilar was the head nurse and Dr. Patterson and Dr. Alamilla operated on me. Dr. Bernard and Dr. Abrahams operated on Carmen.'

Mrs. Austin paused again and asked for water. Christine got up and re-filled the cup. Mrs. Austin continued, 'I remember wishing Carmen good luck. She told me *Buena suerte, hasta luego* when they rolled her into the operating room. I never saw her again after that. She died during the operation.'

She paused and then continued, 'Dr. Patterson told me everything was going to be fantastic and put an anaesthesia mask over my face. I started to feel drowsy. That's when it happened. I was barely conscious, but I could feel the operating table move and knew things all around me were beginning to fall. I was starting to panic but, due to the anaesthesia, I was unable to move. The last thing I remember was a blue, almost ultraviolet light that was placed over my eyes. I couldn't look into the light; it was too bright. I closed my eyes but could still see the blue light penetrating everything around me.'

'Mrs. Austin, I think we should take a break,' Eva said.

'I agree. This is far too emotional for you right now.' Christine got up from her seat.

'No. Let me finish, please.'

'Are you sure, Mrs. Austin?' Christine sat back down.

'That was the last thing I remember. When I woke up, the place was in shambles. There was horrible confusion. People were crying and looking for family members. I was wheeled out of the operating room and was placed in an ambulance. Dr. Patterson sat next to me as we drove off. I woke up again in a different hospital in Iquique, a large city in Northern Chile. Dr. Patterson visited me that afternoon. He told me there had been an earthquake while they were operating on me and that my baby and Carmen and her baby did not survive.'

Mrs. Austin closed her eyes and tears ran down her cheek. When she breathed in, her body gasped. 'I haven't told this story in years, but it still hurts,' she said, sobbing.

Eva looked at Christine. She had tears in her eyes. Christine got up and hugged Mrs. Austin. She held on to her tightly and the two of them remained like this for several minutes. Mrs. Austin finally released Christine and laid back into her pillows. She closed her eyes and breathed deeply.

'We'll come back later, Mrs. Austin. You should rest now,' Eva said quietly. Eva got up from her seat, but Mrs. Austin grabbed her wrist.

'There is more you should know.' Mrs. Austin looked exhausted and Eva felt sorry for her. She sat back down and let her continue.

'After I got my strength back, I flew back home and picked up my everyday life. I was married to a truly kind man who, unfortunately, died young. One day, I received a telephone call from Diane Eastman. She told me she had to talk to me about Chile. I didn't want to be reminded of that time and declined. She continued calling and, one day, she was outside of the office where I worked. She begged me for five minutes. She told me she had some information that she wanted to share with me. I reluctantly agreed. She told me that she was sure my baby hadn't died.'

Mrs. Austin looked tired and drained. A nurse walked into the room and told them visiting hours were over.

'We'll be back this afternoon,' Christine said to Mrs. Austin.

***

They stood in the corridor, not knowing what to make of the story. 'I don't understand. What does this have to do with us?' Eva asked.

'Absolutely no idea. Maybe it's just a coincidence.'

'Christine, please. A coincidence? Three women having the same nightmare.'

Daulton came out of the lift and walked up to them. 'Are you going to tell me what this is all about,' he asked Christine.

Christine took her coffee from the machine and stirred slowly, trying to buy herself some time. 'Do you trust me, Daulton?'

'I do. But that doesn't help me understand why my father is nearly ripping my head off because he wants to see Mrs. Austin. Plus, it doesn't explain why you are so desperate to keep him away.'

'Daulton, I need you to trust me... us...' she looked at Eva. 'I'll tell you exactly what's going on as soon as we know. All we know is that your father does not have Mrs. Austin's best interest at heart.'

Daulton stared at Christine for a moment and nodded. 'You have until tomorrow. After that, I cannot come up with reasonable excuses to keep my father away.' He paused for a moment. 'I need you and Eva to come to my office. There's something about your blood tests I need to talk to you about.' Daulton walked away abruptly, not waiting for them.

Christine and Eva looked at each other in despair. 'Chris, I can't take anything else now. What if something's wrong?'

'I know... Let's hear what Daulton has to say.'

As they reached the fifth floor, they saw Daulton walk into his office. The girls slowed down a bit and walked in a few seconds later. 'You sure walk fast. You must be the fittest doctor in the hospital,' Eva said.

Daulton ignored her remark and picked up a file. 'As you know, I was the one who labelled your bloodwork, so no mistakes this time.' He looked at them for a second before he continued, 'Still, the results are the same as before.'

Eva was getting annoyed by the delay. She had no time for build-ups. She was stressed enough already. 'And are you going to give us the results or are you going to sit there and make us guess?' Eva asked impatiently.

Daulton smiled at Eva's outspoken character. 'I'm sorry, but this might come as a big shock. The blood tests show you two are related.' Daulton paused for a moment to let his news sink in with the girls. Christine and Eva looked at him with skeptical expressions. 'It not only shows you're related, but you are also twins. Your bloodwork is so similar you are virtually identical.'

Daulton stared at them, waiting for a reaction.

'That's ridiculous. Surely if this were true, your father would have found this out years ago...' Christine said. 'Your father...' she whispered a few seconds later.

In the meantime, Eva was sitting in her chair with a puzzled look on her face. She was unable to process what Daulton had said. 'We cannot be identical. Christine is about a week older than I am,' Eva was speaking to no one in particular.

'And who told us that?' Christine asked.

'Are you absolutely, positively sure about this?'

'No doubt about it,' he answered.

Eva got up and walked over to Christine. She hugged her firmly. Tears ran down her face. 'Hello, sister!'

Christine, overcome by the news, started to cry too. 'I

knew it. We have always known there was a deep bond
between us. I love you, my sister, Eva.'

***

Eva and Christine sat in the hospital cafeteria. They
decided to wait in the hospital rather than go home. They
wanted to see Mrs. Austin again and were waiting for the
afternoon visiting hours to start.

'What do you make of all this?' Christine asked.

'I'm not sure,' she said, shrugging her shoulders. 'Don't
get me wrong, I'm thrilled we're sisters. I have always felt a
powerful connection. There are just too many things going on.
I feel confused and wish someone could explain everything. I
want to feel happy. I want to jump around. But, with
everything that's happening, I feel my emotions have reached
a peak.'

'I feel scared too. And I feel that if I let go, I'll lose it
completely,' Christine said, while holding Eva's hand.

'Hurry, duck!' Eva dove under the table.

'What are you doing?'

'It's Dr. Patterson. He's in the entrance lobby,' Eva
whispered.

Christine turned around and lowered her body the
moment she saw him walking towards the lift. 'Where is he
going? He can't be going to Mrs. Austin' room. Christine, we
have to do something,' Eva said.

'Maybe he's going to see Daulton on the fifth floor,'
Christine said, and pulled Eva by the hand.

They hid behind a rack of cards and waited for Dr.
Patterson to enter the lift. The moment the lift doors closed,
they ran over and started to press the call buttons for the
adjoining two lifts. It seemed an eternity before one of the lift
doors opened. They jumped out on the fourth floor and ran
towards Mrs. Austin's room. When they opened the door,

they let out a sigh of relief when they saw her sleeping peacefully.

'The visiting hours have not started yet,' a passing nurse said.

'Sorry. We're leaving,' Christine answered. Christine turned around and squatted against the wall. 'Thank goodness he hasn't found her.'

'Let's go back to the cafeteria.'

They made their way back and sat down again at the same table they were at earlier. The hospital was quiet, the visiting hours were over, and the patient's families and friends had all gone home. Patients in dressing gowns walked around; some of them even went outside to smoke cigarettes. Christine spotted Eric walking into the hospital. She stood up and walked towards him.

'Eric, hey. What are you doing here?'

'I spoke with Steve and he told me you were in the hospital; something about an aunt of yours. I didn't even know you had an aunt. You never told me about her,' Eric said, and gave her a hug.

'I'm with Eva in the cafeteria. Do you want to join us?' Eric nodded and followed Christine. As he took a seat, he received a telephone call on his cell. He answered and, immediately, stood and walked toward the sliding door and went outside.

'The office...' he said when he returned. Christine gave him a little nod, as though she understood what he meant. 'Why don't we go up and see Daulton?' Eric asked.

'I didn't know you knew Daulton that well?' Eva asked.

'I met him at the party, and we got on very well.'

'Okay. I don't see why not. Maybe you should give him a call first, he might be doing his rounds,' Christine said quickly.

The fact that Eva and Eric didn't get on well always made her nervous. But she knew she'd rather do something than sit in the cafeteria with the two of them.

'I'm sure he has time for us,' Eric said and stood up.

'I don't feel like it. I'll stay here,' Eva said stubbornly.

'Eva, please. Come with us. What are you going to do here all by yourself?'

Eva was surprised. Eric was trying to persuade her to come along. Christine looked at Eric and slowly turned to Eva. Even she was surprised. She was convinced Eric didn't want Eva around. 'I'll be fine, Eric. Thanks anyway.'

'I'll be back in about ten minutes. I'm sure Daulton and Eric can catch up in that amount of time,' Christine said.

***

Eva decided to give Steve a call. She wanted to hear his voice. She walked over the payphones.

'Steve, it's me. How are you?'

'I'm doing great. I miss you.'

'Eric just arrived. He and Christine went up to say *hello* to Daulton.'

'What does Eric want with Daulton?' Steve asked, puzzled.

'Eric said they met at the party at your mum's and that they hit it off.'

'Daulton doesn't like Eric at all.'

'What do you mean?'

'Daulton even asked me who *the creep* was during the party.'

'I have to go now.' Without waiting for a response. She put the phone down and ran to the lift. She pressed the button feverishly. '*Come on, Come on.*'

She ran to Daulton's office. His door was locked. She looked around and didn't know what to do next. She started frantically banging on his door.

'What do you think you're doing?' A nurse hurried

towards her.

'I *must* see Dr. Patterson!' she shouted without stopping.

'Dr. Patterson is doing his rounds. This is why his office is locked. Please calm down and go back to the reception area. The general public is not allowed on this floor. Please, don't make me call security.' The nurse took her arm firmly and pulled her away from the door.

Eva pulled herself free and ran towards the stairs. She nearly fell when she tripped over her own feet running down the stairs to the fourth floor. Her heart was beating like a scared deer. As she ran towards Mrs. Austin's room, she could see the door was open. She stopped at the door and realized that Mrs. Austin's bed was empty.

'Where did they take her?' she shouted hysterically.

'Some doctor and his assistant took her to another ward,' one of the nurses answered. 'I'm sure there was a perfectly good reason for moving Mrs. Austin. Please calm down.'

'What about my sister? Was she with them?'

'She wasn't here. Only the doctor and the other man. Why don't you take a seat and calm down,' the nurse told her.

'I need to use a telephone. Please, it's important.'

'You can use the one in the room. But only for a quick call.'

Eva thanked the nurse, ran to the telephone, and dialled. 'Mrs. Austin is not in her room and Christine is missing.'

'Where are you?' Inspector McMillan asked her calmly.

'At Hampstead hospital.'

'I'm on my way.'

***

Eva stood still. Her head was racing. *Where would Dr. Patterson take Mrs. Austin? And where was Christine?* She ran back into the corridor. Not having the patience to wait for the lift, Eva started running down the stairs, taking several steps at a time. She missed one and fell on the landing. Her knee started bleeding badly, and she had difficulties getting up. The ankle she strained at the nursing home started to pound, so she had difficulty walking. She tried not to think of the pain as she pulled herself up and continued making her way down the stairs. When she made it to the ground floor, she ran toward the reception desk.

'Please… Can you page Dr. Daulton Patterson?' she panted.

The receptionist, an aloof-looking woman in her fifties, just looked at her. 'Do you need medical assistance?'

'*Just get me, Daulton Patterson!*' Eva slammed her fist on the reception desk.

Just then, a young security officer walked over to the desk. 'Any problems here?' he asked.

Eva ignored him and turned to the receptionist. 'I need to speak to Dr. Daulton Patterson. I *must* speak to him, *now.*' She was leaning over the desk. The security man pulled her back by the shoulders.

'That's close enough. Why don't you go and sit down, and a member of the medical staff will attend to your injuries shortly.'

Eva turned around angrily. 'Don't you touch me!' she shouted. 'I *must* see Dr. Daulton Patterson.' Eva heard the security officer talking into his radio. As she turned to the receptionist, she saw that the woman had made no attempt to page Daulton nor was she going to. Eva shouted to the receptionist with tears running down her face. 'I asked you to page Dr. Daulton Patterson! Did you hear me?!! What is the matter with you? *I need to see Dr. Daulton Patterson NOW!*'

By this time, she was crying and in hysterics. When she turned around, she was surrounded by five security officers. One of them pulled her roughly by the shoulders. Eva felt hopeless and didn't fight back when she felt her wrists being cuffed.

'That is enough, gentlemen. We'll take it from here.' As Eva looked up, she saw the trusted face of Inspector McMillan; accompanied by two inspectors. He walked over to her and removed the handcuffs. 'What happened?' he asked, looking at her injured knee and the blood on her trousers.

'He has taken Mrs. Austin and Christine is missing!' Eva cried on his shoulder. 'I need to speak to Daulton Patterson. Maybe he knows where he has taken them.'

'You heard the young lady. Page Dr. Daulton Patterson, *now*,' McMillan said. The receptionist jumped out of her seat and dialled a number. Within ten seconds, the telephone rang, and Daulton answered.

'Dr. Patterson. I'm so sorry to disturb you,' the receptionist said.

Eva leaned over and snatched the telephone receiver from her hands. 'Daulton? It's Eva. Your father has taken Mrs. Austin and Christine is missing. I don't know where they are.'

'Stay where you are. I'll be there in a minute.'

'He's on his way,' Eva said to Inspector McMillan and threw the telephone receiver towards the receptionist, meanly hoping it would hit her in the face.

Daulton came running into the lobby. He looked at Eva's knee, but didn't comment. He turned to McMillan and quickly introduced himself. 'When did he take her?' Daulton asked Eva.

'I'm not sure. I think about fifteen minutes ago,' she said. 'Eric showed up. He told us he was a good friend of yours and took Christine to see you.'

'A good friend of mine?'

'When your office was locked, I went to Mrs. Austin's room and one of the nurses told me that a doctor and another man took her to another ward. Christine wasn't with them.'

Daulton thought for a moment. 'The only place I can

think they would take her is to my father's house. Taking Mrs. Austin and Christine anywhere else would attract too much attention. What's going on? What does my father want with Mrs. Austin and Christine?'

'Let's go,' Inspector McMillan ordered his two inspectors, ignoring Daulton's questions. He knew they couldn't lose a minute if they were to save Mrs. Austin and Christine.

'We're coming too.' Daulton took Eva by the hand and ran after them.

43

How it All Worked Out

'I never expected to see you again, Jennifer. Or should I say, Mrs. Austin,' Marlene Patterson said and walked towards Jennifer Austin. She leaned over and her nose almost touched Jennifer's. 'You haven't aged all that well. Must have been all that South American sunshine. You should have used sunblock.' Marlene walked around Jennifer as if she was a horse for sale.

Jennifer Austin was too tired to respond. Her eyes, however, were full of hate. At the hospital, Eric injected Christine with a sedative and walked her out the back entrance, put her in his car, and placed tape over her mouth. Christine kept her eyes on Eric who, until now, avoided any eye contact with her.

'Eric,' Marlene said, while pouring a drink. 'Why don't you remove the tape from your ex-fiancée's mouth?'

Eric walked over to Christine and brutally removed the sticky tape from her mouth. Christine screamed and could taste copper. The tape removed a small piece of the skin of her lip and it was bleeding heavily.

Christine, still groggy from the sedative, asked, 'Eric… *why?*'

'Sweet, innocent Christine. Did you think I would ever choose a woman like you?' he replied. 'I was only around,

pretending to care about you, to keep an eye on you and Eva.'
He stroked her cheek while he was talking.

With every word he spoke, Christine felt more and more
nauseous. She stared into his cold eyes and realized that he
didn't just dislike her, he despised her.

'You were so easy to trick. All I had to do was make a
sad face and you came running back, like a battered dog. Do
you have any idea how boring you are?'

'A boring pain in the neck,' Marlene said, laughing.

'Marlene and I refer to the two of you as the rabbits.
Every time we thought we had you killed, you quickly
hopped away.'

'The blue rabbits. Those ridiculous nightmares. *Oh, Dr.
Patterson, there is a scary blue light.*' Marlene was ridiculing her.
'Our two little blue rabbits boo-hoo-hoo.'

Christine felt her eyes filling up. She fought the tears.
She didn't want to give them the satisfaction. 'So, it was you
who tampered with the boat at the country home?' Christine
asked Eric, trying not to show emotion.

'The boat, the gas leak, and, let's not forget, the car
accident,' Eric said proudly. 'Now, I can finally get rid of you
once and for all and I can start dating some real women.'

Christine felt humiliated to her very core. This was the
man she thought she was going to spend the rest of her life
with. After several minutes, the door opened, and Dr.
Patterson made his way into the living room. He had several
syringes in one hand and was pushing a drip stand with his
other.

'Hello, ladies,' he said. He had a great big smile on his
face.

Christine looked at him and, for the first time, she saw
him for what he was, a positively insane human being.

'Marlene, be a darling and fix me a drink,' he said, while
pushing the drip stand toward Mrs. Austin. 'Jennifer, how are
you feeling?' he asked her, teasingly, as he passed her.

'Stay away from me, you evil son-of-a-%$#@%!' Jennifer jumped when Dr. Patterson tried to touch her.

'Now, now. No reason to insult my mother.' Dr. Patterson laughed at his pathetic joke.

He walked to the sofa and sat next to Marlene and Eric. The three of them sipped their drinks as if they were at a party.

'Eric, did you tell Christine the engagement is off?' Dr. Patterson asked.

'I did. It was ever so painful,' Eric said, mocking Christine. 'I will have to start looking for another fiancée; maybe Annabel Malmesbury. What do you think, Marlene?'

'Superb choice, Eric. Annabel is an outstanding catch. If only my sons had your impeccable taste. But instead, one of them is dating the other freak.'

'Are you going to tell me what you did to my child?' Jennifer Austin asked. Her voice was steady but detached.

'Jennifer. Let me explain a few things to you.' Dr. Patterson picked up a dining room chair and placed it in front of her. 'Jennifer, you were picked, or should I say, chosen. Marlene did her job very well when she investigated you. The moment you walked into the practice, Marlene and I knew we had found our perfect patient.' He turned around and smiled at Marlene. 'You were so very desperate for a child. You had no living relatives and last, but by no means least, you were so serious about doing good in the world. We needed you to come to Santa Tecla, and we knew that if we told you that you could help the local people, you would jump to the occasion. After we completed the blood tests, we decided that you would be perfect for our experiment.'

'What do you mean, *experiment*?'

Dr. Patterson ignored her question. 'If only that stupid Diane Eastman would have kept her mouth shut, none of this would be necessary. You could have lived happily ever after. But you had to listen to that ridiculous cry baby and look where it got you.' He picked up his drink and took a sip. 'Thinking about it now, we should have taken care of you there and then. But the thing is Jennifer, I like you. I genuinely like you.'

'You killed Diane Eastman?'

'Not me. You can thank Eric for that.'

'But that was years ago.'

'Yes. Eric has been with us for years. His father worked for us as a gardener. After his tragic accident, we decided to keep Eric. Eric didn't live with us, but we looked after him like a son. Eric has always been the child we never had. He is a fast learner and has always understood the priorities of this family.' Marlene nodded in agreement. 'At the tender age of ten, Eric personally cut the breaks of the Eastman's car.' He raised his glass and said, 'Here's to you, son.' Eric smiled, and raised his glass.

'You're all mad. You should be put away,' Jennifer Austin said in disgust.

Christine couldn't believe her ears. She had known these people all her life and she had been remarkably close with Eric on so many occasions. Not once had she noticed their insanity. Here was the doctor who had cured her colds and flues and who she considered a surrogate father and the man she thought was going to be the father of her children. Her entire life had been a lie. She wanted to scream. She wanted to slap Eric in the face. How could they do this to her?

'So, what about my baby? What did you do with my baby? Before you kill me, you can at least tell me what you did to her.' Jennifer sat still, waiting for an answer. She was surprisingly calm.

'*My baby, my baby,*' Dr. Patterson mimicked her in a childish voice. 'The day you gave birth, we had to act quickly. The babies that were born that day were perfectly healthy. That was all we needed. We had some success in the past with the local women, but the babies always had some defect from the day they were born. It was usually breathing issues, so they were of no use to us. The babies that day, however, were perfect. It was always Marlene's idea to use a healthy western woman and, as always, she was right.'

'Matthew, please,' Marlene started to say, 'you're embarrassing me.' She stroked her skirt to remove the invisible creases.

'We had to cover our tracks. Dr. Alamilla had a cousin who could help us with explosions. The moment we knew the babies where healthy, we had him blow up the hospital.'

'But the earthquake?' Christine asked.

'There never was an earthquake,' Dr. Patterson said proudly. 'Eric placed a little section with a photo on the internet, out of precaution. Eric has always been perfect at damage control.'

'What about the light? What was the blue light?'

'Oh, yes. The famous blue light. That was an accident. After the birth, we wheeled Carmen back into the room to recover with Jennifer. When the explosion happened, the ultraviolet light we used to kill infections fell on top of you. Dr. Alamilla's cousin detonated the bangs a bit too early. I am, however, very disappointed.' He turned towards Christine. 'I would have loved to study you and Eva a bit further. It's interesting how you both have the same nightmares from that one experience.'

Christine shifted back a little. Dr. Patterson's expression had become fearsome. He turned his attention back to Mrs. Austin. 'We took the babies back home and told you that Carmen and both your babies died,' Dr. Patterson said with his hands waving in the air as though he had just performed a magic trick. 'Well, Carmen *is* dead. We didn't have much use for her.'

'So, where is my baby now? Did you kill her too?'

'Not yet. But we will shortly. By the way, Jennifer it's babies, not baby.'

'What do you mean? I had twins? That never showed on the scan?' Jennifer was puzzled.

Dr. Patterson started laughing and turned to Marlene. 'Isn't she something? She still has no idea.' Marlene shook her head in disbelief. 'We cloned you. *You silly woman*! We undertook somatic cell nuclear transfer (SCNT). This type of cloning takes the DNA of an adult specimen and reproduces it so that an embryo with that same DNA is created. One embryo was placed in you, the other in Carmen. That's why one of your children is slightly darker than the other. She also picked up a bit of the Latin characteristics; far too loud that one.' Dr. Patterson spoke as if he was talking about a litter of kittens.

'What are you talking about, you mad psycho?' Jennifer Austin sat straight up.

'WOW, Jennifer! You are slow. Christine, meet your mother. Jennifer, meet your daughter,' Dr. Patterson said quickly, his hands moving from one to the other, like he was selling two different types of onions. I think we can say this, can't we? I'm not sure how one should address clones.' Matthew Patterson turned to Marlene; his face filled with amusement.

***

Mrs. Austin and Christine sat and stared at Matthew Patterson in disbelief.

'Now, we need to find that other child of yours. Then, we can put all of this behind us. Do you know that no other children have lived as long as yours?' he said to Jennifer. 'They are healthy, like fish. Do you remember that ridiculous sheep, Dolly, they cloned in England? That clone only lived for six years. Instead, your babies are perfectly healthy and are still going strong.'

'So why kill them?' Jennifer asked.

'We wouldn't have had to, but they became suspicious. When they stole the photo from my office at the country home, I got nervous. Then, when they found you in the nursing home, I knew we had to take action. Do you remember the country home, Jennifer? We had such a wonderful time there. *Delightful times. Delightful times.'*

As he spoke, he tilted his head back and a smile appeared on his face. 'Good times, good times.' He snapped out of his little daydream. 'I'm as disappointed as you are. Really, I am. I wanted to study them more. I found the nightmares so fascinating. You should have trusted me more, Christine. You should have agreed to undergo hypnotherapy. As a test subject, I would have kept you alive for years. The hypnotherapy surely may have brought back some memories, but memories of what? After all, the nightmare was your mother's. No, I was looking forward to opening the skulls of the three of you. That way, I could become the leading expert in cloning.'

Christine was in shock. She couldn't believe what she just heard. She looked at Mrs. Austin and, suddenly, she saw the resemblance between them and Eva.

Mrs. Austin felt her stare and looked her straight in the eyes and gave her the warmest, saddest smile she had ever seen. 'It has been a gift from God that I finally meet you. Something inside me always knew you were alive.'

'Same here,' Christine whispered. She was unable to say anything else.

'Matthew, please. Can you finish the job? They're becoming all soppy now. I can't wait to finally be relieved of them and get on with my life,' Marlene said hurriedly. She stood and refilled he glass.

'You're right, my love.' Dr. Patterson started to open the syringes.

Christine started to cry and pled with Dr. Patterson to stop. He just looked at her with a disturbing grin on his face.

Christine took one final look at Eric, who was looking at the scene in front of him as if he was at the cinema. To her horror, Christine realized that he was enjoying himself. She let her head hang down; she knew she was going to die.

***

'*Step aside!*' The living room door opened, and Inspector McMillan stepped in with his gun drawn.

Marlene Patterson tried to run past him but was stopped at the door by Daulton. 'Going somewhere, mother?'

'Daulton. You must help me. Please. I'm your mother.' Marlene was giving the best acting performance of her life. 'It has always been your father's idea. Really, Daulton. You cannot believe I would be a part of this.'

'I heard everything you said. As of this day, you are no longer my mother. You also put Steve's life in danger,' Daulton said, and threw his mother back onto the chair.

Dr. Patterson stood and looked at Inspector McMillan. He looked at Jennifer and Christine with arrogance in his eyes. 'Dr. Patterson, I hereby place you under arrest...' McMillan started to say. But, before he could continue, Dr. Patterson injected himself with the deadly cocktail intended for Christine and Jennifer. He fell to the floor, unconscious. Two minutes later, he was dead.

'Mrs. Patterson, Mr. Eric Woodland, I hereby place you under arrest.'

The door opened further, and Eva walked in. She walked to Christine and Mrs. Austin very slowly and released them. 'We're all safe now,' she said softly.

The three women sat together, holding hands. None of them spoke.

320

EPILOGUE

It was a beautiful October day. Christine and Eva walked together quietly, enjoying the last afternoon rays of sun. The branches of the cypress trees reached out as if to create a comforting roof over them. The cherry and persimmon trees had both dropped the majority of their leaves, which left a beautiful red and orange carpet on the ground beneath them. The wind was picking up and it was starting to get cold. It was peaceful. The only sound was that of the birds singing their last songs before they would settle for the night.

'James, please stay off the grass. Walk on the path,' Christine called out suddenly. The young boy turned around and looked at his mother, disappointed. He was a typical eight-year-old. He loved getting dirty and going places he was not allowed. He was a handsome boy. His honey-blonde, curly hair waved in the air. His nose, covered in a handful of freckles, made him look both endearing and naughty.

Christine was pushing her three-year-old son, Anthony, in a bright blue coloured three-wheeled pram. Anthony was the spitting image of his older brother, without the freckles. Eva watched at him and smiled. She loved and adored her nephews. She spoiled them rotten whenever she got the chance. Christine pretended to dislike Eva's indulgences, but secretly she loved the strong bond between her sons and their aunt.

Eva stroked her tummy. She was five months pregnant and had felt the baby's first kick a week ago. 'Did she kick again?' Christine asked when she saw Eva holding her tummy.

'No. I was just comforting her.'

'Why can't we have children without all the sickness and an increasingly round belly?' Eva said. Christine smiled and kept walking. 'No, really. We have drawn the shorter straw; the morning sickness which lasts all day, the weight gain, and, not to mention, the swollen feet and the gas.'

'Nothing you can do about it. So, stop complaining.'

Eva caught up with Christine. 'These hormones. I swear they drive me mad. I have become the woman I always loathed. Every time I see a pram, I dive into it and start making ridiculous baby noises.'

'It's your instinct. You're going to be a fantastic mum.'

Eva watched James playing and couldn't wait for her baby to be born. The doctor told her she was going to have a baby girl and Eva couldn't wait to hold her.

'How's Steve?' Christine asked.

'He's doing well. He's even more pathetic than I am. I'm sure that after the baby is born, he'll not even notice me anymore. This baby is going to be daddy's little princess. I'm sure he'll spend most of his time working from home,' Eva said.

She married Steve six years ago. Three years ago, Eva finally left her job at the modelling agency and took a year off to decide what she wanted to do with the rest of her life. With Steve's help, she opened a small boutique in the city centre. She sold the clothes of *up-and-coming designers* who were in desperate need of a break. Although the shop would never make her a millionaire, Eva loved it. She loved helping the young designers and loved it when a satisfied customer left her shop with one of the exclusive designs.

'What about Daulton?' Christine asked.

'He's doing very well. You know Daulton, ambitious as ever. He's opened his own clinic and is fast becoming the number one doctor in the city. By the way, he's getting married soon. I'm sure you'll receive the invitation shortly.'

'Good. I'm thrilled for him.'

'How's Andrew and life in the sticks?'

'Working too hard as usual. I wish he would slow down a bit, but he loves his practice and loves his patients.'

Christine said. 'Sometimes I go an entire day without seeing him, and we have the practice at our home.'

Christine married Andrew nine years ago. She met him in the library. He was a family doctor who visited the library once to research some papers.

After he met Christine, he kept coming back and checked out a book every day. He didn't stop until Christine agreed to go on a date with him. It took Christine several weeks to be persuaded.

The pain of the betrayal had paralyzed her. Not only because she had dated Eric, but also because she had always defended and trusted Dr. Patterson. Slowly, but surely, Andrew got through to her and she didn't hesitate when he asked her to marry him. They welcomed James eleven months later.

Andrew opened a general practice in a small village in the countryside and enjoyed his close contact with the local community. Christine loved being a stay-at-home mum and enjoyed working in their lovely, English-style garden. She loved her life of looking after her husband and children. She had all she'd ever wanted out in life.

'James! Come here!' she shouted to her son, who had fallen behind again; no doubt looking for trouble.

Eva waited for the boy to reach her and took him by the hand and followed Christine and Anthony. They made a left onto a smaller path and stopped by the third headstone:

Here lies Jennifer Austin,
Our beloved mother and grandmother.

Christine and Eva stood staring at the headstone. Jennifer Austin died two years ago of a stroke.

'Hello, mum,' Christine said, and placed a bunch of lilies on the headstone.

The past ten years had been a magical time. The three of them had grown very close. They shared a lovely house in town together and, for the first time ever, they experienced real family life. None of them ever spoke about the cloning. They were a family; that was all that mattered. The day they were reunited as a family, their nightmares stopped.

Eva put her arms around Christine. She smiled at Eva and the two of them stood, still staring at the headstone. Christine freed herself from Eva's embrace.

'James. Say goodbye to your grandmother.'

The boy walked up to the stone and blew a kiss. 'Bye-bye, Grandma Jennifer.' Christine took him by the hand and kissed his head.

Eva felt her baby kick and smiled. 'Even the baby says *bye-bye.*'

Christine took Eva's hand. As the two women looked at each other, they felt true happiness.

I.V. Everts

I.V. Everts is the lovely Ingrid . She is a talented and up-and-coming author. Ingrid was born in the Netherlands, but spent more of her life in the UK, France, and South Africa. Currently, she lives in Rome, Italy with her husband and her Golden Retriever, Texel.

She created this suspenseful thriller and hopes all readers enjoy her story as much as she enjoyed creating it.

Ingrid also wrote, "Golden Tales: Havoc in Rome" about her experiences with her beloved Golden Retriever, Texel. This is a collection of hilarious and heartwarming stories about days she and Texel had excitement in Rome. The book also includes many of the famous and must-see attractions in the Eternal City.

There is much more to come from Ingrid, so we all look forward to her next creative literary works!